THE SEARCH FOR
HEINRICH SCHLÖGEL

Sep 2014

Published by Tin House Books, Portland, Oregon,
and Brooklyn, New York

Distributed to the trade by Publishers Group West, 1700 Fourth St.,
Berkeley, CA 94710, www.pgw.com

Library of Congress Cataloging-in-Publication Data

Baillie, Martha, 1960- author.
  The Search for Heinrich Schlögel : a novel / Martha Baillie.
    pages cm
  ISBN 978-1-935639-90-9 (paperback)
  I. Title.
  PR9199.3.B342S43 2014
  813'.6—dc23

                              2014011907

First U.S. edition 2014
Printed in the USA
Interior design by Jakob Vala

www.tinhouse.com

For Jonno

"Cameras, in short, were clocks for seeing."

—Roland Barthes

Erratic: "A piece of rock that differs in composition, shape, etc., from the rock surrounding it, having been transported from its place of origin, esp. by glacial action."

—*Collins English Dictionary*

Archivist's Note

Of course, Heinrich Schlögel is often mistaken for some-one else. In airports and cafés, men and women approach, tell him how deeply familiar they find his face. They as-sure him he is a schoolteacher or TV host, that they've worked together on a civic action committee or been in-troduced while sailing or folk dancing. Heinrich stares at these people and tries to imagine where he might have seen them before but can find no clue, not in their chins, eyes, or mouths. He does not like accusing them of being in the wrong but is forced to conclude that the error is theirs. With mild regret, he notes how gratifying it feels to be enthusiastically recognized, even as someone he isn't.

PART ONE

Tettnang

1

The Naked Eye

Like all living creatures, I had a mother and father;
but I never knew them. I know that they met each
other last summer; for several days they flew side
by side and together sipped from the same flowers. Then for several hours they united. During this
union my father pressed the tip of his belly against
my mother; it is in this way he was able to slip tiny
grains into her body, grains so small no person could
see them with his naked eye.

—Animals and Their Families: The Butterfly

The sentences that Heinrich loved best were hard as rock
candy and lasted. As a child, he did not read with ease but

listened and remembered—what was read to him he savored. His favorite books were those that depicted the lives of animals. The person he most admired was his older sister, Inge.

In a letter dated October 30, 1980, and postmarked Toronto, a letter central to my archive, Inge addresses a friend, recalling:

Whenever the farmers sprayed the fields, straightaway our maid was sent out with a bucket of soapy water and a sponge to clean off my swing set in the back garden, so that if I went out to play I wouldn't be poisoned. The day after the tractors left, pulling their tanks of pesticide behind them, I'd slip through the gate, cross the wild area that sloped down from behind our garden to the hops fields, and disappear among the rows of tall, heavy-laden plants. I collected birds from the ground. Those that had only just died lay limp and warm in my hand. I dropped each delicate body into the cloth sack I'd taken from the handle of the kitchen door, the sack my mother filled at the market with vegetables, fruit, sausage, cheese, and bread on market day, which was Tuesday. Every few meters, another corpse lay at my feet. I buried them in the wild area on my way home. But first I sat with them heaped beside me, and examined each one, admiring the colors that came into sudden existence as I twisted a wing so it caught the sun at just the right angle. The hardness of a beak and the softness of an eye—these became mine and could not be taken away. The burial was unceremonious. If, in my eagerness, I'd forgotten to bring a small shovel, I dug up the soil with my fingers.

Our maid was a fat girl, neither pretty nor educated, but hardworking and from a poor family. She was sixteen and I was two years old when my parents hired her to keep an eye on me and to help prepare meals, clean the house, and do our laundry. She remained with us for many years. I must have been about six years old when I started removing dead birds from the fields.

Below the hops fields, in what was called the "little hole," the Italians lived, and the Turks. They'd come to pick the hops and to build sewers and to perform other arduous and unpleasant tasks we Germans preferred to avoid. My parents forbade me from entering the "little hole." To ensure my obedience, they warned me that Italians and Turks ate hedgehogs, and might eat me. To get to the castle on the opposite side of the valley, I therefore had to go the long way around, through the streets of the town. In the central square a freshly painted sign announced: A CORDIAL WELCOME TO TETTNANG. A brief history of the town was followed by a promise that the hops grown in the fields surrounding Tettnang were unrivaled in quality in all of Germany and possibly in the entire world:

> The finest aroma and a delicate bitterness give the beer an unmistakable character and reflect with every mouthful the unique countryside between the northern Bodensee lakeside and the Allgäu.

It was only because of my refusal to eat most foods put in front of me that I was allowed to attend high school, a privilege generally reserved for boys. Most bourgeois girls in Tettnang who completed middle school in 1973 were sent to the Institute of Domestic Sciences, where they were taught cooking, sewing, and how to run a household. My parents feared that, given my peculiar eating habits, were I to attend cooking classes along with other girls my age, I might become the subject of malicious local gossip. So great was my parents' fear of gossip that I was spared the Institute of Domestic Sciences and went instead with the boys to the gymnasium, where I earned my baccalaureate or das Abitur, from the Latin *abire*: to leave.

On very clear days, when everything was bright and hard-edged, as if made of glass, I could see out of Germany and into Switzerland by leaning from my bedroom window. To look beyond Tettnang, beyond Germany, enabled me to breathe better.

I do not know if my brother, Heinrich, felt a similar tightness in his throat and chest whenever he read the sign in the central square: A CORDIAL WELCOME TO TETTNANG, but if he didn't it was because already, in his imagination, he'd left for Canada. Until recently, I liked to believe that I helped him find his way to Canada, but what has happened now has changed everything. I have no clear idea where he is. Heinrich, my younger brother, had a different temperament from mine, yet we were very close. Should I use the past tense when I speak of him? Will any of us ever see him again? I am choosing the present tense: he has a different temperament from mine, yet we are very close.

As a child, Heinrich feared his maternal grandfather.

It was summer and out the back door of his grandparents' house Heinrich went. Someone had given him a pair of roller skates. Abrupt wooden stairs led down to the garden, where a paved path waited for him. On the top step he sat and began to attach his roller skates to his shoes. As he struggled with the stubby metal tongue that had to enter the tiny, uncompromising hole in the red leather strap, his grandfather's legs, or rather the sharp pleats that ran the length of his grandfather's trousers, appeared beside him.

"Wouldn't you do better to wait, and strap those on at the bottom of the stairs?" a voice inquired from above. The voice was not a voice he knew well. He visited his grandparents infrequently, and years later he would forget entirely the sound of his grandfather's voice. The perfectly pressed pleats, however, and the impeccable shine of his grandfather's pointed shoes—these would resist time; they'd persist, totemic, almost legible, the purveyors of Heinrich's inadequacy. He had not thought of descending the stairs before strapping on his roller skates. He did not belong among those who thought ahead.

Throughout his youth, Heinrich's reasoning would undulate rather than slice or pierce, and quite often it would sink out of sight, submerged in murky emotion; it would sway back and forth, pulled by currents of anxiety.

His second memory of his grandfather was of a hunched man in a wheelchair, engaged in the act of disappearing. It frightened Heinrich to have to stand and greet this figure whose clothes fit well but whose skin did not, and whose words fell sloppily from his mouth, a man reaching out with his eyes from within his own uneasy departure.

"You never knew him," said Heinrich's mother, Helene, years after her father's death, in a tone mildly accusatory, mildly angry. Either she was angry at having lost her father or frustrated with Heinrich for having been born too late. Heinrich rarely knew for certain what his mother felt.

"My father was a man of great wit," she explained. "He had style and demanded punctuality. If I lingered in bed, he'd come into my room in the morning, open the curtains, throw open the window, and shake my feet."

Helene stared down at her feet and Heinrich stared at them also. Square, short-toed, they were the only visible part of her that was not beautiful.

How did Heinrich feel about his mother's feet? I too am German (from Munich, to be precise) but this gives me no special insight. I cannot know how he felt about his mother's feet. My search for Heinrich Schlögel began with a photograph. In the newspaper, suddenly there he was—a young man walking down University Avenue. He was in profile, and so I could not be sure of his expression. Determination mixed with confusion? I noted his vigorous stride. Two passersby, approaching from the left, were turning to stare in his direction.

If I succeed in finding Heinrich Schlögel, do I have the right to ask him any question I like? It is mostly through speculation that we exist for others, and for ourselves. That he was being photographed disturbed him, I imagine. According to the newspaper several people pulled out their iPhones to capture him. My tiny Schlögel archive is bursting. I am collecting as much evidence as possible. My search for the truth about Heinrich Schlögel is far from over.

This much I know: throughout his youth, Heinrich's interest in animals neither grew nor diminished; it carried him from one day to the next. He also learned to ride a bicycle and went exploring. Riding was easier than reading but in bad weather he stayed home, shut his door, and arduously pedaled through landscapes of words. He filled spiral notebooks with quickly scribbled quotations from whatever book on animals he was slowly reading:

> Eighty percent of hedgehogs in Germany are born between August and September. Only in the warm Rhine Valley and Saarland are babies born earlier in the year. When hedgehogs are born, their prickly spines lie just below the skin so they don't cause their mothers pain. They are blind at first; they also have baby teeth, just like humans. Hedgehogs leave their nests when they are four to five weeks old. One out of five dies before leaving the nest.
>
> —*Mammals of Germany: A Brief Introduction*

"How much pain," Heinrich wondered, "did I cause my mother during my birth?"

Heinrich's mother's beauty preceded and followed her. Whenever she entered a room, a displacement occurred, conversations shifted, people moved over to give her space. People didn't want to offend, to press up too closely. They confused Heinrich's mother with her beauty, had no idea that she resented and distrusted her own loveliness. They could feel her withheld eagerness. A small mouth, pretty as a bow; her eyes did all the speaking. Though she tried to conceal her sharp thoughts, these glinted visibly from across the room. She appeared calm as she glided among the guests. "It's as if she's wearing a veil," someone said, perhaps someone who'd drunk too much.

When Heinrich thought of his mother, her beautiful head, severed from her body, would go floating through a room full of people who didn't dare move, who waited. They waited for his mother to speak, to offer a revelation.

"Heinrich Schlögel, a name sticky as wet paint," said Inge.

Nearly two years ago, on November 24, 2010, I cut Heinrich Schlögel's photograph from the newspaper. I did so bitten by an intense curiosity, but with little idea of the importance this gesture would have in my life. A week later, I decided to stroll down University Avenue, along the stretch where Heinrich had recently walked. I wandered into the Toronto General Hospital with the vague idea that I might speak with the nurse mentioned in the article that accompanied his picture. Already there was no going back. I have now spent close to two years searching, acquiring clocks, journals, gloves, maps, lamps, and letters, anything that may have belonged to him, that once lay flat in his palm or was flicked open by his fingers.

Tettnang population: 10,236, according to the 1974 census.

On March 3, 1974, Heinrich celebrated his fourteenth birthday, nervously aware that his life was slipping him by. Fourteen took hold of him and shook him upside down, causing hairs to emerge through minuscule holes in his suddenly odorous skin and liquids to escape from his body; sounds twisted and soared out of his throat before plummeting without warning. Heinrich, trapped in his newly alien body, required a story, preferably one in which he played the leading role. But what sort of hero could Heinrich become?

I catch myself smiling each time I think of the delight that Heinrich felt the moment he tore open the gift his sister gave him. On the morning of his fourteenth birthday,

Inge wrapped Heinrich's present carefully. It was a brand-new copy of Karl May's 1875 adventure novel, *Old Firehand*, set in a Wild West eternally crisscrossed on horseback and foot by Winnetou, the wise Apache chief, and his white blood-brother, Old Shatterhand. That May's novels had been made into films and comic strips didn't stop the books from circulating. At Tettnang Middle School for Boys, when you finished one Winnetou adventure you passed it on to someone else who loaned you his in exchange. Like most of his classmates, Heinrich knew that when you were feeling lost you could count on Winnetou or Old Shatterhand to stop galloping long enough to reach out of the printed page and yank you up. Then off you'd charge, in a cloud of dust, leaving school, parents, and any friends who'd betrayed you far behind. Heinrich had loaned his copy of *Old Firehand* to a classmate and not gotten it back. He claimed he could not remember to which boy he'd loaned it but Inge suspected he did not want to have to ask for it to be returned. She also knew it to be his favorite of all the Winnetou adventures. She wrapped her gift in colorful paper and left it on his bed.[1]

---

1 When I lifted the book from its packaging, turned to the title page, and read the inscription, "Für Heinrich zu seinem 14. Geburtstag. Von Inge," I sat down quickly, my heart pounding. The used- and rare-books store in Munich, Antiquariat Axel Grass, had sent me not just any copy of *Old Firehand* but Heinrich's own.

Often, Heinrich felt that he was looking at the world through a kaleidoscope. Glittering ideas, intense images, and random scraps of information tumbled about, fell into patterns—clear, sharply outlined patterns that held for a moment, then disintegrated.

Particulars excited him but he had no idea what to do with them. He was a reasonably good student, never first in his class, yet he showed signs of promise. He was starting to hate the word "promise." He longed to excel at something, anything. Handwriting, neatness, punctuality, organization of content could all do with improvement. He was good at walking. This he shared with his father, Karl Schlögel.

In the company of his father, Heinrich walked for miles, most often without complaint.[2] Karl, on a Sunday afternoon, would set aside the history papers he'd been marking and change shoes. Father and son took the tractor lane

---

2 Can I prove that he did not complain? I've traveled to Tettnang more than once and spoken with people who knew him—the farmer who hired him to pick hops, the music teacher (now retired) who gave up on him, and the town butcher. In assessing all testimonies offered to me, I've relied on my intuition and logic. To determine the truth about someone else's life is a grave responsibility.

that ran between the hay fields to the north of town, then skirted Herr F.'s immaculate apple orchard and crossed the hops plantation recently acquired by Herr R. through an astute marriage.

Father and son. It gives me a burning pleasure to think of them paired, and walking together.

Karl Schlögel listened for birds; head cocked, staring up into the foliage, he searched for the singer. He knew the breast color and head shape, the wing markings that matched each melody. The size of a field determined by song, measured in mating calls tossed between the trees at the perimeter, every bird hidden—at the edge of such fields Karl stopped and waited. Heinrich occupied himself, examining insects and searching for animal tracks.

When he walked behind his father, Heinrich noticed the long muscles in his father's calves, and when they paused for a drink and something light to eat he admired the ease with which Karl slipped the knife from his pocket; muscle and knife wiped the word "father" clean of chalk dust and classroom; the blade unfolded from the deep groove in the handle, sliced through sausage, stabbed a chunk of bread.

"NL," Karl jotted in his notebook. And: "Sunday, April 25, 16h 05, NW corner of P's hay field. Very vocal."

(NL: northern lapwing or *Vanellus vanellus*)

And: "4 ST. April 25, 16h 47, top of lane behind F's orchard. Two singing, one whistling."

(ST: common starling or *Sturnus vulgaris*)

Only now does it occur to me that Heinrich's love of notebooks came from his father. So often, it is the most obvious that escapes us.

A small map and a book—these are the most recent additions to my Schlögel archive. I own them. What giddy happiness! They could so easily have been sold to someone else, someone to whom the name Heinrich Schlögel means nothing. Instead, they sit on my table, mine to pick up and examine whenever I like.

The person who listed them on eBay suspected that the book might be valuable but cared little about the map tucked inside. "1915 edition of *Brehms Tierleben* with reproductions of the extraordinary illustrations done by Gustav Mützel and the Specht brothers in 1876, illustrations praised by Darwin himself. Moderate-to-good condition. Several small stains, no missing pages. Also included a hand-drawn map (circa 1974? date partially erased) of several streets in unnamed German village or town, found inside book."

Mine! The very copy of *Brehms Tierleben* from which Heinrich so often copied passages, and, folded inside it, his sketch of what appears to be his route to school, with places of importance named, his handwriting almost legible. Each time I open Heinrich's *Tierleben* and am confronted by the bright eye of a hedgehog, or, turning the pages cautiously,

I come upon the finely engraved tip of a rabbit's ear, I long to locate Heinrich, to meet him in person. I slip out his little map, unfold it, and turn it around, hoping to spot the detail that will tell me why Heinrich was destined to live such a peculiar life, subjected at the age of twenty to inexplicable experiences that set him irrevocably apart from most others. But the only certainty that is revealed to me is my desire to find him, to know him more intimately—as if knowledge of him could enable me to escape. From my failings or my parents' failings? I very much want to meet Heinrich Schlögel and speak with him, if he is still alive.

The whole town tilts in the direction of Lake Constance but does not reach the shore. The last houses stop, give way to fields at eight kilometers' distance from the broad and beautiful body of water. On the shore of the lake stands a larger, more industrial and important town— Friedrichshafen, birthplace of the zeppelin.

Barn #1: At the sharp bend where Moosstrasse becomes Friedhofstrasse, Heinrich pedaled faster and with all his strength, not because he was late for school but to avoid being ambushed by those of his classmates who enjoyed bullying as if it were a sport and who used the barn for their headquarters.

Norden

Reiterhof

Moosstraße

Scheune

Schlittelberg

Bodensee

Schweiz

Gymnasium

altes Stadttor

kath. Kirche

Metzgerei

Schillerschule

Friedhof

Leichen-
häuschen

Gärtnerei

Gasse

Scheune

Löchle

Kriegstoten-
gedenkstein

Hopfengarten

Schloss

Weg zur
Sonntagsschule

Barock-
Kirche
(Montfort)

The Field behind Schiller Schule: Here the traveling circus parked its trucks and trailers and set up its voluminous tents. During those three weeks that the circus remained in town, Gypsy children appeared in classrooms and were distrusted, but also prized. It was as if the class now possessed a python or tarantula, an exotic creature safe to stare at from a short distance. Heinrich, glancing over his shoulder, saw a delicate earlobe, a dark curl, a sharp nose above pretty lips, and redirected his attention to the floor, resisting the temptation to turn in his seat.

Heinrich's parents wrapped the Gypsies in silence, as did most bourgeois Tettnangers. To speak loudly against the Gypsies felt uncomfortable, as not too long ago, numerous dark-eyed strangers had been herded into trains and disposed of. Nonetheless, accusations slipped from the mouths of some: "Five shirts—that's how many I hung out back to dry, and when I came from watering the garden only three shirts were left." Farmers, when conversing with farmhands, allowed themselves, in such insignificant company, to remark, "The rake I leaned against the shed, it's gone, and I won't be seeing it again, so long as the circus . . ." Suspicions hopped and bit, like fleas.

The Basement of Schiller Schule: Heinrich, after school, followed a long corridor past many closed doors until he came to a room that leaked music. Every week he attempted to learn how to play the flute but showed no aptitude, frustrating his teacher's expectations. The shiny scar that stretched from Herr T.'s left ear to his chin, a gift from the trenches of the Second World War, became an anguished pink as he listened to Heinrich's incompetent efforts. Not for Heinrich's sake but for the sake of those students who possessed musical ability, egg cartons were nailed to the walls and suspended from the ceiling of the practice room, to improve acoustics.

In the month of February or else in early March, with military efficiency, Herr T. would march his students through town, some playing recorder, others flute or accordion or violin. The entire town came out to celebrate. Even the teenagers turned off their transistor radios and straggled into the square, singing under their breath the lyrics to "Miss American Pie."[3] The youngest children, dressed up as roosters, waved inflated pigs' bladders from the ends of sticks and playfully beat passersby with their balloon-like weapons.

The mayor appeared on the balcony of the town hall and tossed the town keys into the crowd of women gathered below, indicating that all order was now tipped on its head, that the women, dressed up as Hops Spiders and Hops Jesters, were now in charge and would remain so until Ash Wednesday.

---

3 Don McLean, the Eagles, Crosby, Stills & Nash—it was from the lyrics of American singers that I first learned English. Perhaps the same was true for Heinrich?

Every year without fail, the carnival came and went, the carved wooden masks—the Hops Jester, the Red Spider, and the Hops Pig—were removed from storage and worn through the streets; they were admired, then returned to cupboards and chests until the following chilly Lent, and so long as the crops grew well, the roads were maintained, electricity flowed, the priest said Mass, the buses ran on time, and one cow a week was slaughtered by the butcher, there was little need for anyone to change his or her ideas.

The Butcher Shop: On a rise overlooking Kirchstrasse, a road made dangerous by the trucks that careened through Tettnang, stood the butcher shop. Heinrich's parents warned him repeatedly to ride with caution along this stretch of his route to school. To arrive in time for the morning bell, which rang at seven thirty, he left home at seven o'clock. Every Monday, he briefly slowed to a halt and lingered outside the butcher shop's holding pen, where a cow stood waiting for its life to end.

All day, the animal's distress swelled in the inner chamber of Heinrich's ear. Bovine anxiety muffled the urgency of historical dates, the beauty of lyric poetry, and the elegance of mathematical calculations. On his way home from school, if the cow had not yet been slaughtered, Heinrich again brought his bicycle to a halt and stared into the animal's eyes—these were liquid, a frantic liquid. He could do nothing to save the cow. Rather than speak words of hypocritical comfort, he pedaled away, and the cow continued tossing its distress from its large mouth. Heinrich rode until exhaustion eclipsed his knowledge of the cow's suffering.

I am tempted to say that Inge felt similarly about the weekly cow that waited for the butcher to lead it indoors to its death, but little documentation remains of the feelings that Inge experienced during her childhood and youth. The one letter that does exist, from which I have already quoted at length, occupies a position of prominence in my archive. I also possess evidence, in the form of a scrap of very old newspaper, that suggests Inge was, at one time, contrary to popular belief in Tettnang, both sly and daring.

Barn #2: The steepest tobogganing hill overlooked the "little hole," where the Italians and Turks lived. At the summit of this hill, Inge slipped inside a barn and became a thief. Where the tiny nails securing the leather seat of an old sleigh had loosened, a shred of newspaper protruded. It caught her eye. She poked at the brittle leather, and it cracked open. She reached in with her fingers, widening the opening as she delved. Old newspapers had been used as stuffing. She tore off a piece and read:

Saturday, May 5, 1880. Family of savages from the Frozen North draws large crowds at the Berlin Zoo.

On Tuesday last, the youngest Eskimo, a girl, six years of age, caught in her mouth and swallowed a raw fish tossed to her.

Inge folded the scrap of newsprint and slid it into her pocket. She imagined donating her find to the collection of a famous museum. She could not, however, reveal her treasure to anyone, as she'd damaged the seat of a sleigh and had stolen her discovery. Only Heinrich she trusted to keep silent. The bit of yellowed newspaper disappeared beneath her socks and underwear in a drawer of her dresser.

The Hay Fields: Every year in late May, before the tall grass was cut and the hay sown, female deer stepped out from between the trees to give birth. The tall grass provided a soft bed for the newborn. The farmers purchased large and modern tractors. Seated high up, they could not see the fawns. When these awkward young animals, uncertain on their stick legs, failed to leap out of the mower's path, the machine cut off their limbs. If the blades severed the limbs without killing the animal, the farmer shot the fawn or called in the town veterinarian, who brought his pistol and relieved the farmer of this act of mercy.

Back Garden: At dusk the hedgehogs rustled in the foliage and Heinrich would set out a bowl of milk. The sharp-nosed, prickly animals investigated. They added this new and delicious liquid to their diet of garden snails. Neither they nor Heinrich knew that cow's milk is not good for hedgehogs. He held his breath and observed their pleasure.

Pellets of blue, slug-killing poison, strewn among rows of plants in the well-tended vegetable gardens that bordered the Schlögels' backyard, endangered the hedgehogs. Karl, Heinrich's father, did not set out poison. He refused to participate in the incidental killing of birds and hedgehogs. He set out glasses of beer in which the *Helix aspersa* and *Theba pisana*, the most common and destructive of garden snails, drowned.

2

The Necessity of Work

This morning, I and several dozen others hurrying to our jobs glided on the escalator down to the subway platform, where we all stood waiting for a train to hurtle into the station. We waited for the rush of air, the sound and suck of it; then out of the station into the dark into the light into more dark we plunged, a segment of our day tubular and buried. In the cold white light of the swaying train I opened my briefcase and read from the diary of the British explorer Samuel Hearne, who, in the late eighteenth century, was hired to travel overland from Fort Prince of Wales on Hudson's Bay to the Arctic Ocean. Hearne was Heinrich's hero.

. . . when perceiving bad weather at hand, we began to look out for shelter among the rocks, as we had

done the four preceding nights, having neither tents
nor tentpoles with us . . .

In the time it took me to read to the end of the paragraph, Heinrich was possibly entering or leaving one of
Toronto's many subway stations, riding in a train identical
to the one carrying me to work. Or was he boarding a bus
in a large European city?

You are a dreamer, I reproached myself. Don't make
yourself ridiculous by imagining you'll succeed in meeting
Heinrich Schlögel. You are living in an age of ecological
crisis, how dare you devote your free time, what little you
have, to researching the life of a young man whose picture
caught your attention in the newspaper? Think instead of
the potato fields.

I felt a rush of grief and shame. One thousand three
hundred and sixteen acres of Ontario's best potato fields are
to be quarried for gravel, if Highland Companies is allowed
to carry out its plan. Over the past several years it has been
buying up farms in Melancthon township a short drive
northwest of Toronto, not disclosing until now its intended
use of the land. They will dig a pit one and a half times the
depth of Niagara Falls. Last Saturday, October 13, 2012, in
Melancthon, yet another protest was held, hundreds gathered, and I was not with them. How was I occupied? With
scouring my archive, frustrated at not being able to lay my
hands immediately on the article about honeybees that I

am quite certain Heinrich Schlögel slipped into his bicycle pannier one afternoon long ago—an article I euphorically discovered, last summer, in a mound of papers sold to me by one of Heinrich's aunts for an exorbitant price.[4]

What can I state with confidence? That Karl Schlögel taught history at the gymnasium where both Inge and Heinrich were enrolled and that it was the only gymnasium in Tettnang.

Evenings, Karl listened to the radio, marked students' (for the most part inadequate) papers, went quickly over his lesson plans, then retreated into the writings of those thinkers he admired most, Goethe, Kant, and Schiller. To Schiller's *Letters on Aesthetic Education* he returned regularly. There, he could count on finding solace.

In Schiller's mind there was no room for doubt that only the experience of art and beauty can offer true freedom, since whenever we leap into political action, the liberty we pursue is destined to founder. We must approach freedom quietly, eye it obliquely.

---

4 In his journal Heinrich mentions an article on honeybees losing their memories when exposed to pesticides—every nerve in my fingertips told me that this was the correct article, as I lifted it from the pile of papers I'd just purchased.

In the gymnasium, when Karl wrote on the blackboard, small objects often flew behind his head from one side of the classroom to the other, so that he had to stop and instill fear in his students all over again, while outside the window pigeons soared across a gray flatness that passed for sky.

Karl would comment over dinner, "Even the common pigeon is better off than I am. For man, the only route to freedom is thought, but my students are not interested in thinking. Long before they arrive in my classroom, they've been taught to fear using their minds. Fear is everywhere. If I were to encourage them to ask questions, serious questions, smoke detectors would go off in the offices of the administration."

And what about my questions? Heinrich wondered. Just that evening, he had asked his father, "If you like birds so much, why don't you use binoculars?"

"I do not own a pair of binoculars because I choose not to," replied Karl.

Behind this unyielding answer, decisive in its evasions, Heinrich sensed the war. What had his father seen, possibly thanks to a pair of binoculars, at the age of sixteen—barely more than Heinrich's present age, but caught in the final, disastrous months of a war that had consumed his youth? Whenever Heinrich's War File became too unwieldy, stuffed with ragged questions, and silences protruding at odd angles, Heinrich would empty it, leaving inside only one frustrated cry, his own "I was not there. I do not care."[5]

When Heinrich woke at night, needing to urinate, he'd stop for a moment in the dark hall, on his way to the bathroom, and observe the light slipping out from under his sister's door. Inge, he knew, was seated at her desk, studying. He stood in his bare feet, in the obscurity of the hallway, and coveted her unwavering sense of direction, her singular passion. Her dictionary open in front of her, Inge was copying out words and their meanings. She was creating columns of verbs, columns of nouns, columns of adjectives. Her talent for learning languages (English and Hungarian so far) had earned her a reputation. She did not want a reputation. Both students and teachers admired her skills. Heinrich had no doubt that Inge possessed heroism. She claimed she

---

5 During the worst years of tension between my own father and me, when I urgently questioned him about the war and, like Heinrich, collided with silence, my mother suffered from a virulent rash, which spread the length of her arms. Would my influence over my mother have been less, and my responsibility less, had I had a brother or sister? I often think how different my life would have been, had I had a sibling.

possessed nothing but the ability to ignore what did not interest her.

Though Heinrich knew he could neither change the world nor equal Inge as a student, he resolved nonetheless to train his mind. He sat in his bedroom and listened to his mind spin like the propeller of a plane, spitting shredded ideas into the atmosphere. There was nobody to remove the blocks from in front of his wheels. He did not dare call out for assistance. Heroes did not call out. He sat in the cockpit, immobilized for hours, the whir of his own stupidity filling his ears, and felt painfully conscious that the very plane in which he sat belonged to some vanished era.

"You're a romantic," said his mother, Helene, stepping into his room. She placed her hand tenderly on his shoulder and he aimed the nose of his plane straight for the ground. Any second, the engine would explode in flames.

No object in my Schlögel archive, not even Heinrich's spinning top (given to him by his mother on his fifth birthday?), for which I paid more than I should have when I saw it in a box of old toys at the Bähnlesfest flea market in Tettnang, can provide me with an accurate measure of the love his mother did or did not feel for him.

I lifted the spinning top out of the box because my hand felt drawn to it. I turned it over, hoping to see his initials. There were none. Possibly this top, which now occupies a place of honor in my archive, never belonged to Heinrich Schlögel, yet I had to have it; my heart insisted that this toy used to delight Heinrich, my fingers itched for it, and I bargained poorly and spent more than was reasonable. It is painted a robin's-egg blue with a canary-yellow stripe around its middle, and it spins for minutes at a time before toppling. Perhaps in a month or two I'll pass Heinrich Schlögel as I am crossing at a busy intersection, or I'll enter a cinema and sit down beside him. It's intolerable to have to rely on chance.

In the one picture of Helene Schlögel that I have successfully acquired for the archive, she's wearing a straw hat that almost completely obscures her face. Perhaps the photographer snapped it by accident or was already inebriated at noon (the sun is high), or he or she simply wanted to finish the roll of film. Perhaps Helene refused to look up when the photographer asked her to. Perhaps the snapshot has survived precisely because it was abandoned, never put in an album with the others.

In her garden, Helene sat, inhaling the words of Krishnamurti. Protected by a wide-brimmed straw hat, she read:

> Truth is a pathless land. . . . In obedience there is always fear, and fear darkens the mind. . . . It is no measure of health to be well adjusted to a profoundly sick society. . . . Knowledge is always in the shadow of ignorance. . . . Meditation is freedom from thought and a movement in the ecstasy of truth. Meditation is the explosion of intelligence.

In these ideas she found strength and comfort, as she did in the fragrant yet unruly lupins and foxgloves, common poppies, field speedwell and bush vetch of her unbridled "English" garden—her horticultural act of rebellion, her discreet refusal to succumb to the carefully arranged narrowness of Tettnang.

Though Inge claimed to be skilled at ignoring what did not interest her, she could feel everyone's eyes watching her.

Her mother's eyes asked: From where have you acquired such independence and discipline? Why Hungarian?

How is it your brother so adores you? How does it feel to be truly loved?

Her father's reprimanding gaze inquired: What use do you intend to make of your intelligence? How do you plan to cure a society given over to mental rot and flatulent ethics? Are you aware that the future is yours to determine?

To Heinrich she confessed, "Sometimes, if I pass Papa's study, I can hear the tapping sound he makes with his pencil on his desk when he's frustrated. It gets louder and louder. At school I hear the sound of chalk—how easily it snaps when pressed too hard. In the garden I hear the hedgehogs scuttling away, in fear. And I can't stop any of these sounds. Everyone wants something from me."

To Heinrich she confided, "If Mama asks one more time if I'm all right . . . You don't know how lucky you are. She follows me around. She watches me. I start scratching at my skin. I can't help it."

Heinrich continued to read about animals.

The whale does not use its ears for most of its hearing but its lower lip, which is tapered and allows a more focused collection of information in the form of sound waves. This data travels from the back of the lip to the inner ear by means of a string. The sound waves that enter by the ear are too diffuse to allow the whale to form the precise pictures that constitute its principal source of vision. In matters of seeing, the whale relies even less on its eyes than its ears, and would be ostensibly blind were it not for its lower lip.

—Amazing Mammals of the Deep

A classmate showed Heinrich a book filled with X-rays. They were of women's breasts. The classmate, whose father was a doctor, explained how these pictures had been taken.[6] A woman, when instructed to do so, placed her breast on a metal shelf while a second shelf was lowered from above until it pressed the woman's flesh flat as a pancake so the camera could make a good image. Some women cried out in pain. Others made no sound. Heinrich wondered how long these breasts retained their flatness. He wanted to know how long the hurting continued. And

---

6 My own father was a doctor, his specialty the human bowel. A spry man with a gracious sense of humor, he spent his working hours bending to probe and to stare into the anuses of men and women alike. My mother was an urban transport engineer. In the institutions where they worked, both were known for their energy and skill. Liquor, fine food, social chatter, and cards—to these they also brought talent and fluidity. A flawless duo, they frustrated and exhausted me. I inherited none of their ease.

was it more or less painful than having your arm twisted behind your back? But his friend was unable to answer his questions. While Heinrich stared at the photos of squashed gray breasts full of white roots and pale blotches, he felt a curious light-headedness. He imagined his penis resting on a metal shelf and a second shelf descending from above, coming closer and closer. "Let's get out of here," he suggested. "Let's ride to Friedrichshafen."

At fifteen, what was Heinrich's relationship to time? Did he think that, if he rode fast enough on his bicycle, he might escape, and from what?

The breasts of the girl who worked on Tuesdays and Saturdays at the Urbach Bakery pressed roundly, eagerly against the white cloth of her blouse. Her breasts filled Heinrich's vision, as if he were at the movies and seated in the front row. No one else having come to see the film, he was alone, except for her breasts, which pushed forward, mute yet hopeful. He did not know her name but she had a pretty smile. What interested him was the secret life that her breasts lived inside the confines of her blouse, a life of soft heaviness, of curved smoothness and pliancy. He could not reach out and touch them. He could only watch them rise and fall to the rhythm of her breathing while she handed him his change.

Heinrich continued to read about animals, and the only trouble with reading about animals was that it didn't take much intelligence, or so Heinrich believed. It was pleasurable, reassuring, and therefore suspect. He couldn't stop himself. He read about animals indiscriminately and in secret, ashamed of his uncontrollable fascination:

> The skeletons you see before you were removed from mummified animals collected by Étienne Geoffroy Saint-Hilaire, one of 150 scientists and other learned men to accompany Bonaparte on his Egyptian campaign. A cat, dog, falcon, ibis, gazelle, and bull—these two-thousand- to three-thousand-year-old skeletons, brought back to Paris by Saint-Hilaire, bore such perfect resemblance to the skeletons of contemporary cats, dogs, falcons, gazelles, ibis, and bulls that they fanned the debate between Cuvier, who believed in fixity, and Lamarck, who defended transformation.
>
> *—An Illustrated Tour of the Paris Museum of Natural History*

There were moments when Heinrich imagined that he was being supported by a huge hand, and that from his perch on the broad palm of this enormous and benign hand he could see in all directions, so that time no longer frightened him. Were a great gust of wind to blow him over the edge, he'd fall willingly, feeling content to have gazed in all directions at once.

One thousand three hundred and sixteen acres of potato fields to be destroyed, and a hole to be dug deeper than Niagara Falls. Streams running dry, trucks hauling gravel to market, to market, to market. To free my mind of these images I am allowing Heinrich Schlögel to occupy an increasingly large portion of my thoughts.[7]

Almost daily, I take Inge's letter from my archive and examine it.

"Heinrich, my younger brother, had a different temperament from mine, yet we were very close. Should I use the past tense when I speak of him? Will any of us ever

---

7 Just as Heinrich did, I came to Canada hoping to discover a pristine wilderness. Having arrived in Toronto, I caught a bus north, and spent three days wandering about the mining town of Kirkland Lake. Beyond the town, forest spread in all directions. I caught a bus back to Toronto.

see him again? I am choosing the present tense: he has a different temperament from mine, yet we are very close."

I should not subject such a delicate document as Inge's letter to too much handling. I ought to scan it, render it eternal. I could create an e-archive. Tomorrow I'll bring her letter to work and scan it. Nearly two years of effort and still I can neither make sense of nor dismiss Heinrich's extraordinary experiences. If he and I were to meet, tomorrow, on the corner of College and University, right where I emerge most mornings from the subway to wait for the streetcar that eventually drops me at the door of Sterling and Schubert: Architects, I expect he himself would be incapable of explaining what really happened to him.

But it's absurd of me to feel that Heinrich is mine, to fantasize that if we met he might reciprocate my feelings of affection and admiration. I am a stranger.

Tomorrow, I'll take Inge's letter to work and scan it. Perhaps I'll even post it on some social media site. So far I've not come across anyone else who is visibly searching for Heinrich; no Schlögel blogs or Facebook page appear to exist.

3

A Language of Uncertainty

Cycling thrilled Heinrich. When sailing down a long hill on a bicycle little else mattered. Cycling convinced him that his father was wrong. Freedom could be experienced by other means than thought.

For his sixteenth birthday, Heinrich received money. Every weekend, without fail, he cycled ten to fifteen kilometers out of Tettnang into a rolling landscape of carefully arranged fields and paths, of sharp steeples and blossoming orchards, and the same distance back. One brilliant afternoon as he was leaving town, a camera, displayed in the window of a store, caught his eye. He brought his bicycle to a halt. A small sign hanging above the camera asked, WHO ARE YOU? And below the camera a second sign answered, A PHOTOGRAPHER!

He went into the store and bought the camera. He'd intended to spend his birthday money on a new set of panniers for his bicycle, a better air pump, an adjustable wrench, and other important items. He took the camera home and hid it.

A week later, his first attempts included the following:

1. Urinal (public but clean)
2. Pair of tennis shoes tossed into the naked branches of a tree
3. Elongated potato resting in a metal bowl
4. Two tractors facing each other on a road
5. Self-portrait, eyes closed

Over time, Heinrich noticed that his photographs were becoming beautiful, and this frightened him, so again he put his camera away. Certain scenes, however, demanded his attention. He brought out his camera, once more moved it an inch to the left, or to the right, tipped it the tiniest bit, and waited for the light's perfect utterance. He took more and more pictures. He could not stop himself. Their beauty fascinated and repelled him. He could not bear too much beauty. Beauty brought his mother into the picture. She slipped herself between the lens and the object poised to express itself. The object went silent, replaced by his mother's lips. Lips that offered a suggestion of a smile, a hint that he might be the cause of something.

Inge's journals from the 1970s, those that I've managed to obtain, contain mostly blank pages. In a rare entry, dated April 15, 1976, she wrote:

"I don't think Heinrich entirely believes me when I explain to him that I don't want a reputation, that I don't like to feel people's opinions stuck to my skin."

Below this she inscribed a fragment of conversation, likely between herself and Heinrich:

"*They* don't know me. Nothing entitles *them* to plan my future. I won't become a diplomat, and I won't become an interpreter."

"Who doesn't know you? Who are *they*?"

"*They* are *they*."

Inge couldn't bear *their* fingerprints on her passion. She could feel *their* hot, inquisitive breath all over her ability. *Their* whimpering, envious admiration disgusted her. *They* could have done as she did, shut themselves in a room and studied and studied and studied, but *they* were unwilling to pay the price. Heinrich, she knew, also coveted her focus and discipline. Unlike *them*, however, he loved her. When he spoke to her, when he looked at her, she almost believed in her own existence, that she was perhaps a worthwhile experiment. Heinrich and the rules of various grammars—these protected her. She was nearly safe from herself.

One afternoon, Helene asked, "Are you hurt?"

"I fell," Inge answered, counting on the anger in her voice to silence her mother, which it did.

When Helene left the room, Heinrich stepped forward.

"What did you do?" he asked.

She told him: animals. When she thought of animals—of hens crammed into coops, dogs used as ashtrays, cats and rabbits put to the test—her body became obscene. She dug out the obscenity using a razor or a broken bit of glass. Skin, after all, was just another lie, a veneer of continuity, a clever bit of packaging. She had so much blood inside her. When she cut through her skin, her blood flowed unobstructed. It tasted of salt, like the sea, and belonged to a larger rhythm. To no longer be sewn into a sausage casing of tight-fitting lies.

If she ceased to exist, Heinrich would remain. He could comfort and satisfy *them*. She was not interested in their silly notions of success. He could do the talking, the traveling, send reports to those who worried and needed to know and felt they had a right to know. Could she count on Heinrich to satisfy them? Was he willing?

Several weeks after learning the source of the scars on his sister's arms, Heinrich asked to take a picture of her. Inge refused. He snapped her anyway. She turned her back on him. He snapped her again. He cycled out of town, photographed a hedgehog, and was overcome by remorse.

In the gymnasium library, without warning, Inge came upon a language learning kit, or rather it came upon her: a rectangular, transparent plastic bag, containing six cassette tapes, a dictionary, a grammar and exercise book, all succinctly titled in English: *Inuktitut for Beginners*. How had she never seen this before?

From that day onward, the kit claimed all her spare time. She stopped carving marks in her skin. Inuktitut did not feature in the gymnasium's curriculum, and, needless to say, in Tettnang not one single person spoke Inuktitut. There was no reason for the gymnasium's library to possess such a language learning kit, and Inge did not intend to return it.

Saali:	*Ullaakkut.* Good morning.
Laina:	*Ullaakkut.* Good morning.
Saali:	*Qanuippit*? How are you?
Laina:	*Qanuinngittunga.* I'm fine.
Saali:	*Tunngasugit, ingittiarlutillu.* Welcome! Please sit down.

Laina:	*ii*. Thanks.
Saali:	*Kaapiturumaviit?* Would you like coffee?
Laina:	*ii, kaapiturumajunga.* Yes, I'd like coffee.
Saali:	*Sukalisuunguviit?* Do you take sugar?
Laina:	*Aagga, sukalisuungunngittunga.* No, I don't take sugar.
Saali:	*Immulisuunguviit?* Do you take milk?
Laina:	*ii, immulisuungujunga.* Yes, I take milk.
Saali:	*Asu. Uvva.* Okay. Here you are.
Laina:	*Qujannamiik.* Thank you.
Saali:	*Ilaali.* You're welcome.

She played the cassettes repeatedly. Her room became a throat. Inuktitut was a language held in, uttered not from the front of the mouth but the back of the throat, a speech that used up as little air as possible. She added a place, a person, a question—each additional affix stretched a word longer and longer until it broke off and a new word began:

> *Qangatasuukkuuimmuuriaqalaaqtunga*: I'll have to go to the airport.

Root, morpheme, suffix. Taking words apart delighted her. She snapped words into units so small they could not be broken any smaller. She collected lexemes, separating out the lemmas.

The affix *-qatau-*

This simple affix indicates that someone is going along or accompanying someone on an activity:

> Umiaqtuqtuq: She goes boating.
> Umiaqtu*qatau*junga: I am going along on the boat ride.
> tuttu + liaq + *qatau* + juq = tuttulia*qatau*juq: He goes along on the caribou hunting trip.

One morpheme drawing another to it, a lexical stickiness, an agglutination that could pass for inevitability, a form of desire she needn't fear.

It was also a language of uncertainty: If it snows, if we survive, if there is food, if the fishing, if the caribou herds, then we will meet again.

If: In this lesson we look at affixes that are used in Inuktitut for the idea of "if."

> *Uqaalaguvit, qailangajunga*: If you call, I will come.

Heinrich stood in the hallway and listened to the tape playing its meaningless sounds over and over. He heard Inge's chair scrape. He watched the light escaping from under her door and wished he could stop himself from envying her. He couldn't. What he desired most, in those moments when he stood outside her door, was to please her or else to be free of her. He did not want to save her. He did not want her to become like other people.

"Here," said Inge, handing Heinrich a voluminous book wrapped in a blue dust jacket. "You should read this."

It was a Sunday afternoon, and she'd come down the hall to find him, bringing with her Samuel Hearne's *Reise vom Fort Prinz Wallis in der Hudsonsbay nach dem nordlichen Weltmeer* (*A Journey from Prince of Wales's Fort in Hudson's Bay to the Northern Ocean*).[8] Heinrich closed his

---

8 As soon as I realized its influence upon Heinrich, I borrowed and devoured Hearne's journal in English (the Toronto Public Library owns three circulating copies), but later, wanting to read the exact German words that had gotten under Heinrich's skin, I sat in the Baldwin Room of the main branch and pored over the two German editions owned by the library. Both were published in 1779, one in Berlin and the other in Halle, and contain only extracts. I turned the pages slowly, carefully.

door, sat down on the floor beside his bed, opened the book, and read:

> On the fifth [July 5, 1771], as the weather was so bad, with constant snow, sleet, and rain, that we could not see our way, we did not offer to move: but the sixth proving moderate, and quite fair till toward noon, we set out in the morning and walked about eleven miles to the North West; when perceiving bad weather at hand, we began to look out for shelter among the rocks, as we had done the four preceding nights, having neither tents nor tentpoles with us. . . . We had no sooner entered our places of retreat, than we regaled ourselves with some raw venison which the Indians had killed that morning; the small stock of dried provisions we took with us when we left the women being now all expended.

The journal of a twenty-four-year-old Englishman, a sailor who left the sea and walked for months on end across harsh and desolate tracts of land, heading farther and farther north, hired by the Hudson's Bay Company to search for copper and also to prove the nonexistence of a navigable Northwest passage—this is what Inge had brought him. Did Inge want him to go there? Did she believe that he possessed courage comparable to that of Samuel Hearne? The weather would be fierce but there would be an abundance of animals. How many of them would he have to kill, and how often? Could he bring himself to eat the raw flesh of a deer? Inge would not want to go with him. She would have no desire whatsoever to set foot in the Far North of Canada, detesting as she did the cold.

Who, Heinrich asked, turning the pages of Samuel Hearne's diary, is Heinrich Schlögel?

4

Soon My Life Will Begin

"Are you sure you don't want to go there?"

"Yes, I'm sure."

The way she shifted in her seat strongly suggested she did not want to answer any more of his questions. He continued with his questions, all the same.

"But why?"

"You go. You'll love it, Heinrich."

"But you're the one learning Inuktitut. I don't speak Inuktitut."

"That has nothing to do with it. I don't want to go there. You're the one who's meant to go somewhere. You're the adventurer. I'm not."

He wanted to believe in her vision of him.

"Why don't we go together? Wouldn't you learn the language faster if you went there? How do you know I'm brave?"

He wanted her to answer. He felt certain she was capable of answering any and all of his questions about anything and everything, if only she'd choose to do so. She turned around and looked him straight in the eyes.

"I want to learn Inuktitut, the language. That's all. The rest doesn't interest me. Just the language."

"What about it?"

"How it functions, its patterns, its sounds and rhythms, how its various pieces act upon each other, that's it, that's all."

"What makes this language so special?"

"Why do you read about animals? Why hedgehogs in particular?"

He blushed. A hot shame spread through him. His only answer was desire. He desired to read about them. Desire was not intelligence.

"Anyone can read about animals," he muttered.

"So?"

"You're the only one learning Inuktitut. There's probably nobody in Munich either."

"So? Don't listen to everyone. They'll poison your mind. You don't need to be better than anyone else."

The subject of the verb.

In English, we often use pronouns to tell us whom we are talking about in a sentence: *I* ate. Who are *you*? *He* left yesterday.

In Inuktitut, we indicate whom we are talking about by using an affix that appears (usually) at the very end of the word:

Niri*junga*: I eat.

To make pronunciation easier, when *-junga* is added to a stem ending in a consonant, the *j* changes to *t*:

Uqalimaaq*tunga*: I read.

Here is a list of the verb endings that indicate who the subject is:

Niri*junga*: I eat.
Niri*jutit*: You eat.
Niri*juq*: He / She eats.
Niri*juguk*: The two of us eat.
Niri*jugut*: We (three or more) eat.
Niri*jusik*: You two eat.
Niri*jusi*: You (three or more) eat.
Niri*juuk*: The two of them eat.

Niri*jut*: They (three or more) eat.

Remember: The *j* of all of these endings changes to *t* when they are added to a root that ends in a consonant:

Isiq*tuq*: He enters.

Samuel Hearne and Heinrich Schlögel—Heinrich allowed himself to believe in such a pairing. Heinrich hadn't the patience to learn Inuktitut but he could walk, and far, without complaint. In his imagination, the two companions walked, they ran, they strapped on snowshoes, they paddled, they fished, they shot, they measured latitude and longitude, they chewed moose flesh, swallowed, then spat.

> The flesh of the moose is very good, though the grain is but coarse, and it is much tougher than any other kind of venison. The nose is most excellent, as is also the tongue, though by no means so fat and delicate as that of the common deer. . . . All the external fat is soft, like that of a breast of mutton, and when put into a bladder, is as fine as marrow.
>
> —*A Journey from Prince of Wales's Fort in Hudson's Bay to the Northern Ocean*

"Have you got a girlfriend?" Inge asked.

Her question hit Heinrich in the side of the head, unexpected as a piece of chalk flung across a classroom. He shook his head.

"Does that mean no?" she insisted.

"It means none of your business."

"All right, all right. I just wondered."

"Well, you can stop wondering. I don't."

But he did. He'd kissed a girl exactly one hour and thirty minutes ago and he could still taste the girl's tongue, which had poked around the inside of his mouth as if determined to find something he kept hidden. Perhaps she wasn't his girlfriend but merely someone whose mouth he'd wanted to feel pressed against his own. How did Inge, so often, know what he'd just experienced, without him telling her?

It was winter when Inge stumbled on the diary of Abraham Ulrikab, an Inuk who was brought, along with seven other Inuit, from Labrador to Germany in 1880.

She entered a used-books store, and there on a shelf stood Abraham's diary, translated into German by a Moravian missionary.[9] She brought it home. After reading a few paragraphs, she got up, crossed her room, and retrieved from her underwear drawer the scrap of old newspaper that she'd found inside the seat of a sleigh. The scrap of newspaper announced: "Saturday, May 5, 1880. Family of savages from the Frozen North draws large crowds at Berlin Zoo. On Tuesday last, the youngest Eskimo, a girl, six years of age, caught in her mouth and swallowed a raw fish tossed to her . . ."

---

9 From the Toronto Public Library, I've borrowed, repeatedly, an English translation of the German translation of the diary of Abraham Ulrikab, but I would like to read the very words that Inge read. I've contacted Antiquariat Axel Grass and several other used- and rare-books stores in Munich, with no positive result to date. I wish that I possessed Inge's knowledge of Inuktitut and could read Ulrikab's diary in the original. Doubtless she wished that the original were available to her. The challenges I'm facing in translating excerpts from Heinrich's and Inge's journals and letters into English make me painfully aware of how much is lost, no matter the efforts of the translator. How tempting to leave all Heinrich's thoughts (and Inge's) in German! Some of his words and expressions are so typically Swabian ("Geschwätz" for "gossip"). But with every sentence of Heinrich's that I translate, I feel I am pulling him out of himself, planting him in the Canada that he came here hoping to discover. Am I? Possibly, of the three of us, Inge knew Canada best, shut in her room in Tettnang, the sounds and rhythms of Inuktitut trickling from a cassette tape, and her mind diligently scrutinizing Inuktitut grammar.

The fact that it was winter when Inge read Ulrikab's diary contributed to what later happened, or so Helene Schlö-gel imagined. Winter, common and unstoppable, was not particular to Inge. Winter could happen to anybody. Only when Helene pictured her daughter's turmoil as a winter of the soul, a naturally dark but transient season, was she able to experience her daughter's pain as bearable.

The question remained: How was it that this diary that Inge had stumbled upon could cause her such anguish?

A painting says: I am. A photograph says: I once was. The small book included a portrait of Abraham Ulrikab, taken with a camera, which is to say a moment removed from the natural flow of time and made to point back-ward.

Abraham Ulrikab, flanked by his wife and children, smiles into the camera. That he is holding a violin to some extent explains why he is smiling. Not only does he hope to pay off his debts with the money he's to receive for crossing the ocean, but he has been told that he is on his way to Europe to visit the art galleries and museums that abound there, several of which have been grandly described to him. On the other side of the ocean, he will attend concerts in halls with balconies trimmed in gold, and he will hear musicians perform on the violin, the very instrument that he has been learning to play. He has not been informed that in Europe he is to be displayed in a zoo, holding a spear and releasing a savage roar from the depths of his chest.

The twentieth century is approaching. It is only two decades away. The Berlin Zoo will sell many tickets; over sixteen thousand curious citizens will pay the entrance fee to stare at Abraham, his young wife, and their two small children. From Berlin, Abraham and his family will travel by train to Prague, where Kaufmann's Menagerie will experience a pleasing rush of financial success until the untimely death of their new exhibit.

First Inge papered the walls of her bedroom with the face of Abraham Ulrikab. Next she focused on his shoulder, his arm, his fingers wrapped around the neck of his violin; these she increased in size with the aid of the school photocopier. She wanted him and his family present when she fell asleep, and witness to her unjustified waking in the morning. She had not earned her right to wake in the morning. Abraham had not earned his untimely death. A brief paragraph on smallpox, provided by her parents' encyclopedia, she pasted on the headboard of her bed. After that, there seemed no point in going downstairs. Clearly, little could be gained from leaving her room.

Last week, I drove from Munich to Tettnang, where I spent a languid and rather futile day, not yet adjusted to German time. I was once again poking about for information regarding Heinrich. The orchards surrounding the town were in full bloom and their delicate beauty made me lazy. I learned nothing about Heinrich that I did not already know, and I got in my car and left.

As the evening was mild and luminous, when I arrived back in downtown Munich I parked my car and wandered with aimless pleasure. In a shop window, a bolt of thickly ribbed cotton fabric was displayed—it made me stop. It was pale green with a pattern of white leaves, and I'd seen it before. But where? In one of Heinrich's snapshots of Inge's bedroom, a curtain hung, half drawn. I recalled the snapshot perfectly. Here on display in a Munich shop window, in the glow of a spring evening, April 13, 2013, was a bolt of the exact curtain fabric Inge'd so often tugged upon to shut the world out, the cloth that had so often prevented Heinrich from seeing into her room as he approached the house, coming home at dusk.

I went into the shop and bought a snippet of the fabric. With my thumb I caressed the very texture of Heinrich Schlögel's childhood—what unbelievable luck. I continued along the sidewalk, wondering if the word "luck" could be applied to a life like Heinrich's. My thumb worrying the bit of fabric, feeling the many threads of its weave, by the time I reached the corner (and had to decide in which direction to further wander), I'd started to hate the word "luck" and its many divisive accomplishments. How easily luck becomes virtue, and there is no end to what virtue allows. The light changed and I crossed the street. I thrust the snippet of cloth deep into the pocket of my dress.

5

The Art of Survival

Every weekend, Heinrich trained for his journey from Hudson's Bay to the Arctic Ocean. Some days he went on foot; other days he cycled. On the days when he cycled, he went the farthest. In the Far North he would not, of course, have the luxury of a bicycle, but for now he allowed himself this small indulgence.

He photographed the footprints of animals—rabbits, fox, deer—and, when possible, he photographed the animals themselves and he hoped they did not realize what he'd done, that he'd stolen a part of them. At home, a thief examining his loot, he arranged their portraits on his bedroom floor, and the more photographs he'd taken during the course of the day, the less vividly he dreamed at night.

He could not ask Hearne if Hearne approved of photography, since the camera did not exist in Hearne's time.

He questioned the explorer on other subjects. He asked if
Hearne approved of Heinrich Schlögel, and Hearne answered, "Yes." Emboldened, lighthearted, Heinrich cycled
farther into the countryside.

"Anyone with information regarding Heinrich Schlögel
or his whereabouts is asked to contact the police." The
article accompanying the picture in the newspaper (the
first photo I ever saw of Heinrich) ended with this request. There was no overt suggestion that Heinrich was a
criminal. The police simply wished to locate him.

Would it anger Heinrich to know that my fascination
with him was first ignited by a snapshot? This evening,
scrutinizing the photo yet again, I catch myself imagining
that Heinrich is one of the anonymous "Just Men" whose
existence, according to Jewish mystical belief, is prevent-
ing the world from being destroyed. There must be, at all
times, thirty-six of them. If one of the "Just Men" learns
that he is one of the righteous, he ceases to be one, and
immediately his role must be assigned to someone else
or the world will end. This story appealed to me when I
read it many years ago, in a volume of essays on religious
myths. The difficult demand of anonymity; the virtue of
undeclared virtue. Were I to find Heinrich tomorrow,
he could not confirm being one of the "Just" without

forfeiting his righteousness. Might Inge be one of the "Just"? Why must the thirty-six "Just Men" be men?

All over Germany, the honeybee is suffering from memory loss. This is caused in large part by exposure to pesticides. Only with increasing difficulty are honeybees able to find their way home. They leave the hive to feed in a field then forget how to return to where they belong.[10]

—*Der Spiegel*

Heinrich, after reading the tiny article, rolled up the newspaper, which he stuffed into his bicycle pannier. He pedaled furiously.

Soon humans, like honeybees, would be unable to find their way home. Soon he would have to shut himself in his room, as Inge was doing, to keep out the terribleness of the world.

---

10 It is this article that I was searching for, six months ago, turning my archive inside out while others marched to prevent a gravel company from destroying over one thousand acres of potato fields. At last the article surfaced, misfiled. I have only myself to blame for its temporary disappearance.

He imagined a world stripped of honeybees and memory: the name of every village and road forgotten, people wandering in circles, examining photographs of faces that others posted in bus shelters and in the windows of restaurants and on the doors of cars as aide-mémoire; everyone, old and young, would consult these faces in the hope of remembering someone or something, some crucial event or person in their life.

Heinrich got off his bicycle, yanked his camera from its case, and shot the fields of tall and trembling hops, shot his feet laced into their shoes and planted on the road; he shot a pebble to the left of his left foot, and a crow in flight; he kept shooting, began running as he shot, breathless, zooming in, retreating, randomly snapping until his film ran out.

At home, in the upstairs hallway, Heinrich tried to photograph Inge but she refused, just as she had the last time he'd asked. She hid her face. She hadn't washed or brushed her hair in several weeks. Her skin had acquired the brittle, translucent appearance of an old person's skin. Even to him she did not look beautiful, not until the lens of his camera told him what to look for. Between her raised shoulder and the knuckles of her hand, which covered her face, a fine tension traveled. He saw it quiver. He caught it. She separated two fingers, and her eye stared at him.

Was his motive to expose her? To pin her temporally into place? He did not know his motive but suspected that he had no moral right to photograph her against her will. He wondered if his desperation diminished his guilt. What he desperately wanted was to know what she was thinking and what she felt.

To Inge, the fate of Abraham Ulrikab sent a single message: How could she trust herself? She was both Abraham and those who profited by him—those who bought tickets to stare at him and, equally, the entrepreneurial German businessman who spared himself the expense and inconvenience of inoculating his Inuit "guests" against smallpox. In her new identity, as everyone and nobody, Inge could not continue and yet there was nowhere to go. Silence refused to let her in. Language performed its mischief in the recesses of her brain. Unwanted sentences kept forming. Voices argued. She could cover her ears but language inhabited her.

"Why did none of my students complete their assignment?" asked Karl Schlögel. He set down his fork and provided his family with an answer. "'Hotel California.' They were out at some party listening to a song called 'Hotel California.'" To Inge, her father's fork became an object of fascination; a trident, a devil's tail, it refused to declare itself definitively. Though it rested on his plate in a state of benign repose, it could not mask that its truest function was to stab, and to do so with beautiful efficiency. In her father's fork, efficiency and beauty of form achieved a harmony that she, herself, could never hope to attain.

When Heinrich was informed that Inge lay in a hospital bed, having attempted to take her own life, he wanted to kill her. This was his first and most immediate desire. He was seventeen. If her aim was to desert him, then let her succeed and get it over with. He'd gladly help her. Live or die; she'd better make up her mind which of the two she wanted most. It wasn't fair to keep him guessing.

Heinrich went to visit Inge in the hospital and found her sleeping. He sat beside her bed. As long as he could remember, he'd believed that Inge knew something she wasn't telling—an important answer to a question he couldn't articulate and therefore couldn't ask. But what did Inge know? Perhaps she knew only that she did not want to live. He stared at her hip. Underneath the blanket it formed a solid mound. How could he have listened to her all these years?

She'd been lying to him, pretending everything mattered when really she didn't believe anything was worthwhile. He reached to pull the blanket off her hip, to expose her, but stopped himself. He hadn't the right to touch her. But he'd brought his camera and he took off the lens cap. She mustn't be allowed to escape, to ruin everything, to destroy the tenuous balance that held their family together. He photographed her feet, the shape of them under the blanket. She was awake now and she curled up tighter, hiding her face from him. He shot her hip, her shoulders, and the back of her head. She shouted at him to stop but he refused. In his fury, he continued to pin her into the world by means of his lens. Her shouting changed to a scream. Her scream continued. The nurse arrived, and Heinrich was ushered out.

Once safely home, and the door of his bedroom closed, he opened *Brehms Tierleben*. Midway down the page, the word "Mole" caught his eye. *M*. He'd always found the letter *M* comforting. Its two solid arches looked capable of supporting considerable weight. The letter *M* could not be easily knocked over.

> The mole's small but muscular body is covered in velvety black fur. Its eyes are very tiny but sight is not important to an animal that lives mostly in darkness.

It does not have a good sense of smell or hearing but is extremely sensitive to touch and can sense vibrations in the soil around it. Each mole has its own burrow system, a network of firm-walled tunnels. The territories of several moles may overlap, but the residents avoid each other if they can, except in the breeding season. If two males meet, they may fight fiercely, which can result in death. A mole can run backward through tunnels and turn right round by doing a somersault! Its velvety fur lies backward or forward so that the mole does not become stuck against the tunnel walls when squeezing through them.

He closed the mammal volume, opened the volume dedicated to insects, and read the word "Monarch." Again, the letter *M*.

The monarch butterfly, in certain regards, defies understanding. Every autumn it flies over three thousand kilometers from its North American home to a forest of pine trees in a mountainous region of Mexico. How knowledge of the route to be taken is passed on from one generation of butterfly to the next remains a mystery, one that the most eminent scientists have failed to comprehend. No single butterfly in its entire life makes the journey more than once, and so cannot lead others along the route but must somehow convey complex directions to be followed. According to the indigenous people of Michoacán, each monarch butterfly is the soul of a deceased person, returning.

Heinrich set butterflies to one side. He flipped through the reptile section. The words "Snapping Turtle" leapt at him. The letter S caused him to pause and consider its sinuous shape.

The common snapping turtle often lives a full one hundred years and can grow up to about twenty kilograms. When angered it is capable of striking as speedily as a rattlesnake. It can reach with its head halfway back along its shell. Should you feel compelled to take hold of a snapping turtle, you are best advised to grab it by its tail and lift it swiftly from the ground, holding it well away from you.

The second time that Heinrich visited Inge in the hospital, he stayed only a few minutes.

Through her bulging eyes, Inge watched a nurse bite the head of a rose from its stem, and the doctor rear up on his hind legs. The sight of the nurse made her laugh, whereas the doctor's behavior sent shivers of fear along her limbs, so that, weeping and giggling, she pulled the covers up to her chin. She peered at the doctor, who thumped his chest while lashing the wall with his tail. It would take several more days before her brain calmed itself from the effects of the pills she'd swallowed by the fistful.

She'd hoped to die, she, the smart one.

Outside the hospital, Heinrich sat on the curb, his feet in the gutter, and became very old. He tried to get up from the sidewalk but was unable to. He'd been alive far too long. He waited, indifferent to what might happen next. Someone from a nearby shop brought him a glass of water. The kindness of this stranger amazed him. It floated toward him in the form of a hand holding out a glass of water. Too tired to respond, he glanced down. His legs looked far away, as did his ankles and feet. Time passed. Cars sped up and down the street. He had no idea who he was, but who he was tried again to stand up and failed. He took a sip of the water. The person from the shop asked once more if he was all right. Naturally, he couldn't answer. Who he was stood up and walked away.

He must have walked in the direction of home, opened the door, and gone inside. He found himself reading *Brehms Tierleben*. He turned to the text on moles and again encountered the letter *M*. As he examined its shape, he remembered that once, long ago, *M* had been his favorite letter. He skimmed over page after page, until a drawing of a tusked and hairy animal made him stop and read:

> The wooly mammoth died out about the time of the last glacial retreat, when a mass extinction of plant life occurred in Northern Eurasia and the Americas. Most mammoths were no larger than the present-day Asian elephant. The biggest mammoth species, however, reached heights of five meters at the shoulder. A four-meter mammoth tusk has been discovered in Lincoln, Illinois. The Siberian permafrost may well contain millions of mammoth remains.

I have created a separate file for all papers, drawings, photographs, and other evidence relating to this very painful and disorienting period in Heinrich's life, when Inge made her first suicide attempt. I go through the contents of this file frequently, doubtless more often than I should. Is my intention to destroy these documents through too much handling? I keep promising myself that I'll bring

81

them to the office of the architectural firm where I work and discreetly scan them; then I fail to do so. I turn these documents over repeatedly, hoping that they will tell a different, less distressing story than the one they told me the last time I contemplated them. I hold them up to the light, weigh them, and examine their texture with my thumb. Once, I tried counting how often certain letters of the alphabet appear in a given passage. I cannot diminish the anguish experienced by Inge and Heinrich; I can do nothing for them.

6

Generative Order

Following her release from the hospital, Inge redecorated her bedroom with Heinrich's help. He accompanied her to the paint store; he assisted her in every way he could think of. She packed her dictionaries out of sight. She returned the language learning kit, *Inuktitut for Beginners*, to the gymnasium library. It had long before been marked "missing" in the catalog.

Her appetite improved and she applied for a job as a typist at a small accounting firm. Her medications she took without complaint. She was hired on by the accounting firm and acquired a routine that she experienced as salutary. Every morning at exactly seven, at the sound of her alarm clock, she slipped promptly out of bed, showered, and pulled on her clothes. Her secretarial duties she performed with a combination of speed and meticulousness that won her unequivocal praise. Too much social interaction she found arduous. Conversation, on the whole, she experienced as a painful exercise. As much as possible, she avoided her fellow workers.

"With you it's different, Heinrich. I know where we're going. When we talk, it's like following a well-worn path. I don't mean I'm bored. Don't look at me like that. I mean that I can trust you not to say something that will suddenly destroy everything. I have to put all the bits of me together so many times a day. Someone smiles, somebody uses a tone of voice I didn't expect, and who I am collapses. A smile can contradict itself in three hundred and fifty ways, in seconds; a tone can suggest a thousand different interpretations. All of these possible messages come charging at me; I try to hide but can't. A comment about politics or the state of the world and I'm lodged inside the hypocritical chaos of someone else's thinking. I'm a mental ligament being ripped apart."

Inge quit her job with the accounting firm. She secured employment as a letter carrier with Deutsche Post and moved into a tiny flat in Munich. To visit her, Heinrich traveled by bus, then by train.

On a sunlit Saturday afternoon, they strolled beside a stream that flowed smoothly through the verdant calm of the vast Englischer Garten.

"It must be great, your new job. You get to walk," said Heinrich, offering his sister a radiant smile.

To the ducks paddling close, Inge tossed bits of stale crust, and to the shy ones on the opposite bank, she threw whole chunks of hardened bread that she'd taken from the cloth sack behind her kitchen door.

"Walking is wonderful," Heinrich insisted.

"And you. Are you still going to Canada?"

"Of course I am."

"When will you go?"

"First I have to go to university."

"Do you?"

"Don't you think I should?"

"I didn't say you shouldn't. I asked, 'Do you have to?' Is there something you want to study? If there isn't, wouldn't you learn more from traveling?"

Home once more in Tettnang, Heinrich shut the door to his room. He was not ready for the North. The North belonged far away. He pressed his back against his bedroom door and behind the door a ravenous wind blew. The gale ripped his tent from its pegs. Rain turned to snow. He felt a numbness spread through him. How could he really leave for the North? Where would he find the necessary courage and skills? Perhaps, once he'd earned enough money for a plane ticket and supplies, he'd discover bravery? Inge would not miss him.

He grabbed from the floor beside his bed Samuel Hearne's *Reise vom Fort Prinz Wallis in der Hudsonsbay nach dem nordlichen Weltmeer*, and from the page where the thick volume fell open he read:

In this deplorable condition, he was laid in the center of a large conjuring house. . . . The piece of board [which was to be swallowed] was prepared by another man, and painted according to the direction of the juggler, with a rude representation of some beast of prey on one side, and on the reverse was painted, according to their rude method, a resemblance of the sky. . . . After the conjurer had held the necessary conference with his invisible spirits, or shadows, he asked if I was present; . . . and on being answered in the affirmative, he desired me to come nearer; on which the mob made a lane for me to pass, and I advanced close to him and found him standing at the conjuring-house door as naked as he was born. . . . When he put it [the piece of board] to his mouth it apparently slipped down his throat like lightning, and only left about three inches sticking without his lips; after walking backwards and forwards three times, he hauled it up again, and ran into the conjuring-house with great precipitation. . . . And notwithstanding I was all attention on the occasion, I could not detect the deceit. . . . It is necessary to observe [however] that this feat was performed in a dark and excessively cold night; and although there was a large fire at some distance, which reflected a good light, yet there was great room for collusion: for though the conjurer himself was quite naked, there were several of his fraternity well-clothed, who attended him very close. . . . As soon as our conjurer had executed the above feat, and entered the conjuring-house, as already mentioned, five other men and an old woman . . . stripped themselves quite naked and followed him, when they soon began to suck, blow, sing, and dance round the poor paralytic; and continued so to do for three days and four nights without taking the least rest or refreshment, not even so much as a drop of water. . . . And it is truly wonderful, though the strictest truth, that when the poor sick man was taken from the conjuring-house, he had not only recovered his appetite to an amazing degree, but was able to move all the fingers and toes of the side that had been so long dead. In three weeks he recovered so far as to be capable of walking, and at the end of six weeks went a hunting for his family.

Heinrich set down the book and opened his bedroom door. He nearly ran down the hall to ask Inge, "Do you believe in miraculous cures?" He almost burst into her room to ask, "In Canada, will I be cured of my doubts and confusion? Or is it you who will be cured, if I go there?" But Inge was in Munich and not in her room at the head of the stairs. He returned to his bedroom, sat back down on his bed. He opened his spiral notebook and copied out the passage he'd just read in Hearne. Then he wrote:

Inge believes that I can become an adventurer. But is this what I want? I hope that in Canada I'll see lots of animals. Perhaps in Canada, I will also make a few friends? But my English is not good like Inge's and I don't know any Inuktitut. I'm not like Hearne; I'll have no guide and I won't know in what direction to walk. I will have to find a guide. I am good at walking and not afraid of long distances or of carrying a large weight on my back. Maybe in Canada I will succeed in becoming the person Inge thinks I can be? What is it, if anything, that she wants from me? Who knows what will be possible in Canada? In any case, I am going there. It is too late to turn back.

Heinrich's thoughts, his doubts and assertions, advancing across the page of his notebook, surprised him. He was unaccustomed to valuing his own ideas enough to keep a record of them. The ideas of others, the insights and facts that he came upon in books, on museum labels, in newspapers and magazines—these deserved to be inscribed. The written word was a territory he entered in order to pilfer, to borrow, to place between quotation marks. Yet, suddenly, he'd declared, in ink on paper: "I am going there. It is too late to turn back."

Disconcerted, he closed his notebook, picked up Hearne's diary, and continued to read:

Cos-abyagh, the Northern Indian name for the Rock Partridge . . . since that time [of his cure] . . . always appeared thoughtful, sometimes gloomy, and, in fact, the disorder seemed to have changed his whole nature; for before that dreadful paralytic stroke, he was distinguished for his good-nature and benevolent disposition; was entirely free from every appearance of avarice . . . but after this event he was the most fractious, quarrelsome, discontented, and covetous wretch alive.

The outcome of Cos-abyagh's story disappointed Heinrich. Irritated, he once again opened his notebook and wrote:

Should I trust Hearne? He sounds pleased that Cos-abyagh's personality changed, pleased that the healers partly failed. They cured their patient's paralysis, but his character soured. Hearne claims that Cos-abyagh became nasty. Hearne calls the healers "conjurers" and he's convinced that their skills involve deception. I've always accepted Hearne's observations as accurate. He sounds so certain of his objectivity. But can I rely on his perceptions?

Heinrich stepped into the hallway and lingered at the top of the stairs, painfully conscious of Inge's absence. He could not imagine what she might be doing at that moment. Her Munich habits and routines were a mystery to him.[11]

---

11 After I left for Canada, my parents' habits, I assumed, underwent little change. I was the one embarking on a new life. They carried on, engineer and doctor, inspecting and diagnosing, admired for their expertise at work and, in their spare time, for their talent at drinking and dealing cards. Then, without warning, they died within weeks of each other, he from bone cancer, aggressive and undiagnosed, she from a heart attack. Together my meteor parents fell burning from the sky. I was stepping back to catch my breath when I opened the paper and there was Heinrich Schlögel.

A list formed in his mind of several necessities to be packed for his journey to the North, and he went back into his bedroom and jotted down: "Take with me: thick wool socks, matches, the warmest jacket I can buy, a wool hat, scarf and mittens, and also a knife. In what month will I be going?"

He opened Hearne's diary and was confronted by catastrophe:

The wind blew with such violence, that in spite of all our endeavours, it overset several of the tents, and mine, among the rest, shared the disaster, which I cannot sufficiently lament, as the but-ends of the weather tent-poles fell on the quadrant, and though it was in a strong wainscot case, two of the bubbles, the index, and several other parts were broken, which rendered it entirely useless. This being the case, I did not think it worth carriage, but broke it to pieces, and gave the brass-work to the Indians, who cut it into small lumps, and made use of it instead of ball. . . . I cannot sufficiently lament the loss of my quadrant, as the want of it must render the course of my journey from Point Lake, where it was broken, very uncertain; and my watch stopping while I was at the Athapuscow Lake, has contributed greatly to the misfortune, as I am now deprived of every means of estimating the distances which we walked with any degree of accuracy, particularly in thick weather, when the Sun could not be seen.

I must take the best maps available, Heinrich told himself, closing Hearne's account of how easily wind and weather had destroyed his ability to measure. I must not lose my way, I must advance cautiously, Heinrich warned himself. He pictured Hearne's delicate instruments of calculation cut into pieces and shot from a gun. He jotted in his notebook:

I do believe that Hearne recorded his experiences as honestly as he was able to. I am not more honest than he is. My journey will be so much easier than his, and still I am frightened. I must select a route that has been clearly recorded and marked. If no marked routes exist, I will have to abandon the idea of going.

The year was 1979, the month, March. Heinrich celebrated his nineteenth birthday and Inge presented him with a gift—a compact volume, titled *A Pocket Guide to Arctic Plants*. His date of departure as yet uncertain, he thanked her and placed the book on his shelf.

In the year 1979, as Deutsche Post employee, Inge delivered a great many bills, requests for charity, personal letters, and other printed material. All too often the words concealed inside the envelopes that she handled appeared in her mind's eye. They imposed themselves upon her imagination:

"As you are aware, there are millions of children around the world whose bellies . . ."

"Your father feels strongly . . ."

"I didn't want this to happen. Please believe me, you've got to believe me . . ."

"If we do not receive payment by the end of the month . . ."

"Soon, soon I'll be holding you in my arms again . . ."

"Even a small donation will go a long way . . ."

"Listen, pussycat, if my music hurts your ears . . ."

She tried to clench her mind shut against these linguistic intrusions but couldn't.

Only once did she intentionally unseal someone's mail. The envelope was releasing a heat that threatened to burn her palms. She tore it open, causing the scalding sensation to stop. She read:

Dear David,

I am now quite convinced that the implicate or generative order is primarily concerned not with the outward side of development and evolution in a sequence of successions but with a deeper and more inward order out of which the manifest form of things can emerge creatively.

Regards,
David B.

A letter from one David to another. It was postmarked 1969, suggesting that the message must have begun its journey a decade ago. She went into the nearest store and bought a roll of tape. Having taped the envelope shut, she dropped it in the mail slot of Professor David Peat, Brotstrasse 32.

David Bohm's words, addressed to David Peat, filled her with a relief that spread through her body, reducing the intensity of her solitude. After that, she was tempted to open other letters but did not do so. Nothing, in her opinion, could match the content of David B.'s note to David P.

7

The Importance of a Plan

The time came for Heinrich to enroll at the university, but he could not decide what to study.

I can sympathize all too well. It's not easy to select a path. Until a passion finds you, all is speculation. Had anyone, when I was nineteen and an architecture student at the University of Munich, suggested that one day I'd devote my spare time and resources to doggedly piecing together the life of a stranger named Heinrich Schlögel, I'd have laughed or wept. I might even have leapt on my bicycle (in Munich I had a beauty, a red one with perfect handlebars) and pedaled away, in the manner of Heinrich.

✴

The year was 1979 and Heinrich wondered who he was about to become. Karl Schlögel assured his son he would make an excellent historian. Heinrich's mother happened upon a box of his photographs and urged him not to waste his artistic talents. Heinrich, lying on his back in bed, stared at the ceiling fan's slowly rotating blades. Then one morning he got up and went to see his neighbor, the hops farmer, Herr Glück. Heinrich hired himself out as a picker. It was late July, and, the hops having ripened early that year, the harvest was about to begin.

"Like a Greek or an Italian," remarked Helene.

"Yes?" Heinrich asked.

"My son."

"Yes?"

"My son," Helene repeated, and smoothed the skin on the back of her hand.

"Work," he told her. "Haven't you always said work is what matters?"

In the ensuing silence, she removed the bread crumbs from the table. She did so using a small silver-handled crumb brush that had belonged to her grandmother, who'd hated her.

At age seven, Helene had stood outside her grandmother's bedroom door, listening.

"You could easily have made a better marriage. If you'd picked a more capable man, you wouldn't have these worries, would you?"

Behind the closed door, silence gave way to sobbing.

Helene slipped into the bedroom. Her gaze traveled from her mother's damp and reddened face to her grandmother's pursed lips. She stared into her grandmother's eyes—eyes that fixed her in her place. Helene tossed her loathing across the room and it burrowed like a tick into the old woman's flesh. Between the young girl and the old woman no affection was possible from that moment onward.

"When I die," Helene's grandmother specified in her will, "my silver-handled crumb brush is not to be given to Helene. It must be given to someone else."

Helene's younger brother inherited the crumb brush, which he did not want. He offered it to his sister. Helene accepted the crumb brush, so as not to forget the crime she'd committed against her grandmother, a crime of knowledge.

The painful knowledge now confronting Helene concerned neither her mother (long dead) nor her grandmother (even longer dead). It concerned her son, whose entire future lay ahead of him, her son who had no intention of going to university, who was choosing instead to work in the hops fields and then to risk a pointless, solitary trek into the Canadian North. Helene watched her son leave the room. She could feel her grandmother's eyes observing both her and Heinrich. Helene put aside her cleaning, went into the garden, and read from Krishnamurti, "Truth is a pathless land. . . . Knowledge is always in the shadow of ignorance."

His first day on the job, while anxiously waiting to receive his instructions, Heinrich spotted a pamphlet left lying on the window ledge in the farmer's office, a pamphlet that Heinrich took without thinking and did not read. Distractedly, he rolled the pamphlet into a tight tube between the damp palms of his hands. Had he read the glossy text, he would have learned:

According to our sources the first reliable mention of hops growing in Tettnang dates from 1150 AD, though commercial use did not commence before 1844. Today, hops growers elsewhere in the world use the name "Tettnang," but only those hops labeled "Tettnang Tettnanger" may safely be assumed authentic. Rich, flowery, and spicy, true Tettnanger hops contain alpha acids from 3.5 to 5% and are used for bittering, aroma, and flavor.

All through the month of August, Heinrich cut and loaded vines, heaving them in awkward armloads into a cart pulled by a tractor. The vines were four meters long, and heavy with hops that made his hands itch whenever he pulled off a cluster of the sticky cones. The tractor spluttered slowly through the heat, squeezing between the rows of towering, leafy growth. Left behind were bare, vertical wires, and the sky—a sky made newly visible, at once shocking and familiar.

Heinrich also worked in the vaulted hangar, feeding the ravenous picking machine. In the hangar, the sun could not beat down on him, but the dense and biting scent of hops crammed itself up his nostrils and filled his mouth. Into his ears, the machine stuffed its voluble grinding.

After twelve hours of labor, interrupted by one brief hour of rest at noon, his legs and arms carried him home on his bicycle, as if his body were an awkwardly shaped parcel that his exhausted limbs had discovered in a ditch and didn't dare leave behind.

Heinrich had a plan. By living at home, he could set aside most of his pay and in September, the harvest over, he would drive a brewery truck delivering crates of beer. Midwinter, he'd buy a plane ticket for Canada, and in July he'd fly away.

This was his plan. To have a plan frightened him. By imagining the future, surely he was inviting fate to obstruct his desires? Yet in order to see beyond his present days of repetitive labor in the stagnant heat he required a plan. His plan was a good plan, as far as it went. How he'd proceed once he reached Fort Prince of Wales remained to be seen.

According to the atlas in the Schlögel living room, Fort Prince of Wales stood across the river from Churchill, Manitoba. Would there be marked trails indicating Hearne's historic route? Might he be required to travel by canoe, shooting rapids and crossing wide lakes? He kept intending to do the necessary research, to send away for maps and information. He wanted to act but did not act. He dreamed he was already there, in Canada, and walking.

Then, without warning, one afternoon, in the hops hangar a Canadian appeared.

"Jeremy!" shouted Jeremy.

"Heinrich!" yelled Heinrich.

They were each holding a rake. They leaned toward each other in an effort to hear over the gnashing of the machinery. Around their feet lay the scraps of leaf and vine they'd been assigned to gather and remove from the smooth, concrete floor of the hangar.

"Where are you from?" Heinrich shouted.

"Canada!" yelled Jeremy.

"Canada?" asked Heinrich, wanting to hear Jeremy say it again.

"Yeah. From Montreal."

Jeremy Burton, twenty years old, was crisscrossing Europe by rail. Several days earlier, he'd struck up a conversation with a local farmer while waiting for a train in the industrial town of Friedrichshafen, birthplace of the zeppelin. Jeremy's cash was running low and soon he would have to find work. He told the farmer that he'd be happy to land any kind of job. By the time the train pulled in, the man had offered to speak with his neighbor, who might need more pickers. The following day, Jeremy caught a bus to Tettnang to start work in the hops fields. He caught a bus because train service to the small town had been permanently suspended by the railway administration the previous year, in an effort to eliminate those routes considered underused and particularly unprofitable.

Jeremy, raking vines from the concrete floor of the hangar, was not surprised by his luck. That he'd so easily found work, in a country he was merely passing through, did not cause him to reflect on his good fortune. Wherever Jeremy went, people took pleasure in helping him. Perhaps doing so gave them the impression that some small portion of Jeremy's physical ease and glowing confidence might become theirs? He looked as if good luck followed him about, and it did.

"How long will you be staying in Tettnang?" asked Heinrich, shouting over the machinery.

"Another few weeks. I dunno. Something like that."

Jeremy grinned, reached into the pocket of his jeans, pulled out a packet of chewing gum, and offered Heinrich a stick, which Heinrich accepted and unwrapped carefully—it was the first gift he'd received from a Canadian. With the back of his arm, Jeremy wiped the accumulating sweat from his forehead.

"Lugging these vines around from six in the morning, it really sucks," he yelled. "But I get why you keep growing this stuff. Fantastic beer. Really fucking fantastic."

"I have also plans to travel," declared Heinrich.

"Cool. Where you headed?"

"To Canada."

"No shit."

"I hope to follow part of the route of Samuel Hearne."

"Hearne?"

The name Hearne meant nothing to Jeremy. The North, however, he knew quite well, a small corner of it. Heinrich could not have encountered a Canadian better suited to his needs.

"When I was twelve years old, my father got posted in a place called Frobisher Bay, on Baffin Island. We stayed there two years. At first I thought I'd die of boredom, and it was so fucking cold. I took my model helicopter, my favorite one, outdoors. The plastic froze and split. Then I started making friends. They got me eating raw seal meat."

"What was the taste?"

"Thick and bloody. When you cut a seal open, steam pours out. It stinks. But I got to like it, even the stink."

Heinrich nodded and listened.

"All summer," said Jeremy, "we never came inside or slept, we ran around all night. Or that's how I remember it. Nobody's parents really cared. By the time we left I didn't want to go back south. So, July, next year, I'm headed north, Frobisher Bay, here I come. I would have gone this summer, but I wanted to see Europe. It was one or the other."

"And I," interjected Heinrich, "next summer, I will visit Churchill, Manitoba, on Hudson's Bay. Also Fort Prince of Wales, from where Hearne began his expeditions overland. I am hoping there will be trails for hikers to follow along part of his route."

"Could be. I've never been to Hudson's Bay. You should check out Baffin Island. Come to Frobisher Bay instead. We could fly to Pangnirtung together. There's this hike out of Pang that I've heard is amazing. You should forget Hearne and Hudson's Bay. I'm telling you, Baffin Island's the best."

Next to the two young men, the picking machine continued its violent chewing and spitting. First it tore the hops free, rolled the sticky clusters aside; next it dropped the hops into the drying-and-sorting room. And all the while, with a vigor and indifference that Heinrich envied, it ejected malodorous mulch into the yard behind the hangar, a spew of leaf and vine that accumulated in a mountainous heap called the "reek."

"Tettnang," said Jeremy, leaning his rake against the wall and stretching his arms. "It's straight out of a fairy tale. Not this big metal monster we're feeding, but the rest, the streets and houses, the castle. I keep expecting a donkey to appear with a dog and a rooster, balancing on each other's backs. 'The Musicians of Bremen,' right? I always loved that story. Wasn't there another animal? A cat? I should check out Bremen. If there is a real Bremen?"

They both stood there, laughing, and not until a year later would Heinrich wonder if they'd been laughing for the same reason.

The blue jay is a songbird that has no song. Native to North America, it has a wide variety of calls. Its most frequent call sounds both harsh and jeering. The blue of the jay's wings does not result from pigmentation, but from the internal structure of its feathers, which causes a particular light refraction. If crumpled, its feathers lose their striking color. The blue jay sometimes attacks the eggs and the young of other birds. Captive blue jays have been witnessed using strips of newspaper as a rake to draw scraps of food closer to their cage.

—*Raach's Illustrated Birds of the World,* sixth edition

In addition to this information about the common blue jay, Heinrich jotted in his notebook, "I have made my first Canadian friend."

The two friends labored side by side, cutting, hauling, and loading the vines. A flow of questions poured from Heinrich. Jeremy, in response, provided stories. A snowmobile sailed over a rise, broke through the ice on a frigid river, and the boy who was killed was the cousin of a school friend of Jeremy's. It was this same friend's older brother who taught Jeremy how to track and shoot a fox. It was summer and Jeremy and his girlfriend were out on the land. They lay down on the moss, and she was fantastic. A polar bear wandered into town; Jeremy stepped out his front door, then stepped back inside. The father of Jeremy's best friend shot the bear. Jeremy was out on a boat, his friend's cousin steering between drifting slabs of ice, when a dense fog rolled in. By the time they found their way back, the engine had so little gas it could barely push the boat through the dark waves.

Weeks elapsed and the harvest was nearing its end. Jeremy spoke of his grandmother and of how he'd been nearly expelled from school the year that his grandmother died—"Old history," he said. He pulled out a map. "Here's where I'm headed next." He planned to hitchhike to Bremen, check out the North Sea, possibly cross over to Denmark, or head east to Berlin. Had Heinrich been to Berlin? No. Had he been to Denmark? He hadn't. Once more, Jeremy urged Heinrich to join him on Baffin Island the following summer.

"You gotta come. It'll blow your mind. I'll get the gear together. It's not like we'll need much. So long as you know what to take, that's what counts, knowing what you need, not loading yourself down with all sorts of extra shit. All we do is follow the Weasel River. A friend of mine did it last year. You gotta come. Glaciers, moraines, waterfalls, caribou, fox, lots of animals. You'll love it, man."

Heinrich traveled to Munich, and opposite the opera house he entered a narrow café where Inge sat waiting for him. Having arrived early she'd immersed herself in a novel, but she got up and embraced her brother warmly. She hoped he wouldn't stay long. If there was a person she loved, it was Heinrich; nonetheless the unpredictable rhythms of his breathing and his indecisiveness made her nervous. She could feel her edges becoming murky as soon as the skin of his cheek touched hers.[12]

"I'm going to Canada next July. To the North, Inge. I'm going to do it. I'll have the money by then. But I'm not going to follow Hearne's route."

He sounded as if he'd been running. She felt sure it was fear not exertion that caused him to be out of breath. Or, she wondered, was the fear inside her?

"Where will you go instead?" she asked.

"Baffin Island. Pangnirtung, Mount Asgard, the Penny Ice Cap."

"Because?"

"I've heard it's wonderful, and a friend of mine is going, a Canadian. We met working in the hops hangar. Jeremy Burton. I think I told you about him the other day, when we spoke on the phone?"

"No."

"Didn't I?"

---

12 According to his aunt, Heinrich's hands were smooth and delicate for a boy, his skin very soft. She mentioned this to me twice, when we spoke. I once had a boyfriend who couldn't stand to have his ears touched. When I think of Heinrich's skin and Inge's skin touching, of Inge's vulnerability and confusion, the image of this boy's ear flashes through my mind.

"You didn't."

"Well, his name is Jeremy, and I've agreed to meet him in Frobisher Bay, on Baffin Island."

"You'll have a fantastic time."

Heinrich felt his throat tighten. He had half hoped that Inge might experience a twinge of regret, a part of her yearning to go with him. But it was his journey, not hers, he knew this. Travel didn't interest Inge. Travel was only what she wanted for him, and her eyes and mouth expressed neither regret nor longing.

"You'll love it," she insisted.

"Jeremy and I are going to meet in Frobisher Bay and buy supplies, before flying farther north."

"You'll have an incredible time."

"Will I? I'm abandoning Hearne."

"I expect he'll survive without you."

"It's a year away. But I've said I'll do it. I've agreed. Does this make sense?"

"Heinrich. Just go."

"And you?"

"I'm staying here."

He caught the evening train from Munich, then the bus to Tettnang. Upon arriving home, he went directly upstairs to his bedroom and pulled *Reise vom Fort Prinz Wallis*

in der Hudsonsbay nach dem nordlichen Weltmeer from his bookshelf. The heavy blue volume fell open at page 185.

He sat on the floor and read how Hearne's native guides had walked quickly and steadily, days on end, stopping neither to rest nor to eat. The soles of Hearne's feet bled, small stones lodging themselves in his raw flesh. He staggered on, as best he could. He feared being left to die if he could not keep up with his guides, who pressed on, impatient to rejoin their wives. The wives had been instructed to wait at a certain campsite. Hearne hobbled on, a lacerating pain shooting up from his feet.

> On seeing a large smoke to the Southward, we immediately crossed the river, and walked towards it when we found that the women had indeed been there some days before, but were gone; and at their departure had set the moss on fire, which was then burning, and occasioned the smoke we had seen.

Heinrich pictured Inge crouching, setting dry moss on fire, signaling to him her presence and imminent absence, sending by means of smoke her wordless decision to move on and the direction he must take to find her. He continued to read:

> By this time the afternoon was far advanced; we pursued, however, our course in the direction which the

women took, for their track we could easily discover in the moss. We had not gone far, before we saw another smoke at a great distance, for which we shaped our course; and, notwithstanding we redoubled our pace, it was eleven o'clock at night before we reached it; when, to our great mortification, we found it to be the place where the women had slept the night before; having in the morning, at their departure, set fire to the moss which was then burning. [July 25, 1771]

On July 2, 1980, Heinrich Schlögel boarded a plane in Munich, and seven hours later arrived in Ottawa, Canada. From there he flew farther, in a smaller plane, to Frobisher Bay.

PART TWO

ᐃᖃᓗᐃᑦ
Iqaluit
(Frobisher Bay)

Place of Many Fish

1

The Fox Stepped Back into the Fog

The two friends met at the airport—a single, low structure, at the edge of the sea.

"There's something I've got to tell you," said Jeremy, as they walked along the wide dusty road leading out of the airport; and Heinrich wanted to listen but he could not take his eyes off the town, a haphazard scattering of squat buildings that gave the impression of waiting to be removed, to be replaced by something better.

"My plans have changed. I would have called you, but it all happened just two days ago. Nothing was definite, then it kinda fell into my lap. Shit. It's just that opportunities up here . . ."

Heinrich turned his attention to his urgent friend.

"A chance to do research and production, and be on the air, the whole fucking thing, all of it. This would never have happened to me in Montreal. And then there's this girl, Lisa. I keep thinking I'm dreaming, man. I'm gonna wake up and she'll be gone. But it's not about her, it's about the radio station. Honest to God, I'd have been crazy to turn them down. I couldn't say no. Shit. I'm really sorry, man. I never, honest to God, shit, I was so looking forward. You've gotta just do it. Just take my equipment and go on your own. My friend who went two years ago, he did it solo. The hike will be astonishing, right up the valley, all the way to Mount Asgard and the Turner Glacier, there's no reason for you not to do it, just because of me screwing up, shit."

They stood, side by side, in the middle of the broad road. The young man named Jeremy Burton leaned eagerly into the wind, hands thrust deep into his pockets, as if to anchor himself while waiting for a response.

So, thought Heinrich, nothing is going to happen as planned. I have come all this way. I have abandoned Hearne and his route for the sake of this person who is telling me to hike alone. Now it is my turn to say something. This person whom I thought I knew, he hopes I'll forgive him, but just in case I don't forgive him he's already forgiven himself. He needs nothing from me. He's not the person I came here to meet.

"I have nothing to say. Not right now," said Heinrich.

"Fair enough. I understand. I fucked up our plans. Look. Do you want to dump your pack? We can go grab a bite to eat?"

"Later. Maybe later. I'll see you."

Heinrich walked away, his large knapsack on his back. Leaving the main road, he followed a smaller one, equally dusty, that led down to the sea. He came to a gathering of wooden crosses that faced the open water. The rough crosses were painted white, their austerity alleviated by gaudy wreaths of plastic flowers. At the edge of the grave-yard, a path enticed him out along the rocks, climbing; the bay widened and across the water there was no visible end to the folds in the treeless land, no end to the barren, brown slopes and deep pockets of snow. The buildings of Frobisher Bay fell behind him.

The sound of a stone landing in water made him turn. A raven stood perched on a large rock. It released from its throat the noise he'd just heard, followed by a series of scrapings, clickings, and tappings.

"Ravens have an extraordinary vocabulary," Heinrich noted in his journal. Then he walked back into the town to speak with Jeremy Burton, who he'd imagined was his friend.

The next day he wrote in red pen:

I have lost my blue pen. That's not all I've lost. According to Jeremy, I "need more ego." I don't allow myself to act on my desires. He says that I shouldn't have changed my plans to fit with his, not if what I really wanted was to follow Hearne's route. "Look, I wanted to travel with you. I asked you to come. But hey, life changes. Nothing's ever certain. That's why you've got to go for what you want most. Sometimes, you've just got to go for it."

This person, called Jeremy Burton, has accused me of having no faith in myself, of distrusting my desires. Perhaps he is right. I will go on my own. I will prove him wrong. If hiking alone into the wilderness has anything to do with ego, I'll show him. Is it ego that I lack, or character? What is it I'm missing?

Heinrich set down his pen and flipped backward through the pages of his journal. Paragraphs about animals greeted him—sentences that preceded Jeremy Burton: facts taken from an informative text posted beside a display of mammoth tusks in the Munich Paleontological Museum and a detail lifted from a descriptive label beside a gibbons "exhibit" in the Hellabrunn Zoological Gardens of Munich.[13]

---

13 That he explored those very rooms where I spent so many hours in the company of my father makes me smile. I picture Heinrich peering through the glass of the huge case that encloses the mammoth tusks, and I feel that we have already met and that surely we will meet again.

At the Hudson Bay store, he bought nearly weightless, dehydrated food, one plastic bowl, one cup, a spoon and fork, bottles of liquid fuel for the tiny camp stove that he was borrowing from Jeremy, who was also lending him a tent and two cooking pots that nestled inside each other.

"These pots are fucking fantastic," Jeremy promised. "It's amazing what a difference a lid makes, I mean a really good, tight-fitting lid. The water boils in seconds. I'm envious, honest, man. I wish I were going with you."

Between two racks of clothing, at the back of the Hudson Bay store, Heinrich came upon the closest thing there was to a bookstore in Frobisher Bay: three unsteady shelves, attached by crooked brackets, supported a small selection of paperbacks and hardcover volumes. He examined a few of the titles, wondering if his English was good enough to make purchasing one of the books worthwhile and, if so, which one. *Stories and Legends from Cape Dorset. Never Cry Wolf. One Man Alone: A Kayak Journey. An Introduction to the Geology of Ellesmere Island. Weather Station: Memories of Resolute Bay. People of the Deer. Land of the Midnight Sun: An Inward Journey.*

A photograph on the cover of a slender paperback caught his eye. It showed a group of children seated stiffly behind wooden desks. Not one of them was smiling.

A Brief Study of Residential Schools in Northern Canada:
Evolving Approaches to Educating Indigenous Populations.
New Critical Perspectives Series: number 67. Copyright 1975.
University of Chicago Press.[14] He took the book to the cashier and paid for it.

Outside the store, he opened his new book and, turning the pages, he started to walk. What he read landed like a stone in his belly. He stood still, wondering if he could trust his English, hoping his English was at fault and misleading him. The children were beaten for speaking Inuktitut. They were underfed and housed in overcrowded dormitories, where disease spread easily. They were taken, against their parents' will. Some escaped and froze to death trying to find their way home. Were these schools still in existence? He flipped ahead a dozen pages but saw no mention of them being shut down. He continued to walk until he came to the sea and the wind slapped him, and he could taste the salt in the air. He looked down at the photograph on the cover of the book, at the faces of the children behind their desks. They all had dark hair

---

14 Only last year did I succeed in purchasing a copy of this out-of-print academic work. Possibly, by traveling to Chicago, I could have consulted a copy earlier, had the University of Chicago granted me access to one of their libraries, one with a copy in its collection; but the expense of yet another trip felt unjustifiable and the prospect of more travel made me anxious.

and eyes, identical haircuts, and were dressed in similarly shabby clothing.

That they are individuals, easy to distinguish from each other, is not what the photograph wants to say, thought Heinrich.

The children stared at Heinrich, or rather through him. Their individuality was a secret that hovered. Who they were seemed to leak into the picture despite the picture's intentions. Again, Heinrich opened the book. It began to rain. He slipped the small paperback under his jacket, not knowing what else to do, and continued to walk, aimlessly. With each step, his thoughts acquired if not an order at least a rhythm.

A sign read FROBISHER BAY CAFÉ. Heinrich climbed six wooden stairs, pulled open a door, and stepped into the tea-colored dimness of a room furnished with several tables and chairs, a room with a bare plywood floor and a low ceiling. On these hard, straight chairs, people sat with a loose yet decisive heaviness. Heinrich, glancing about the room, felt that he ought to know what he intended. Glued to the tops of the tables, newspaper clippings overlapped, yellowing under several coats of varnish. He would have liked to try to read the stories contained in the clippings but his discomfort would not allow him to approach, to intrude on those seated at the tables. From a man standing behind a makeshift counter at the back of the room, he bought a dense ring of deep-fried bannock, and, still not knowing what he intended, he went back outside into the steady, gentle rain.

The rain stopped but the wadding of thick clouds remained. The clouds were the same gray as the sea and inhabited by a same stillness. Heinrich sat on a rock, in the company of ravens, and wrote in his journal:[15]

I have bought a book. It is surrounded by silence. The ravens keep talking. I cannot think of anything to say. I am adding to the silence. My friendship with Jeremy, if it ever existed, is over. He liked me. In Tettnang, he told me: "I like you, man. You're kinda different, but you're a good guy." He told me stories and I mistook his stories for friendship. He described his grandmother's hands. They were always busy and

---

15 Had the young anarchist who worked at the hostel in Toronto not been on duty that afternoon, over two years ago, when I turned up asking about Heinrich; had she not, a few days earlier, slipped several of Heinrich's notebooks into a drawer when the police came looking for information about him; had she, the young anarchist, not decided to entrust me with his notebooks, would they have been recycled or become landfill by now? I don't know why she gave them to me. I am exceedingly grateful to her.

covered in liver spots. She drove recklessly, backing away from the sidewalk without looking. She died in bed. The sheets went up in flame when her cigarette dropped from her mouth. Jeremy suffered from fits of anger, the year that his grandmother choked on the smoke from her burning bed. They sent him repeatedly to the principal's office or kept him after school and he became known as "that one." He destroyed another student's work. The student had seen him crying. Jeremy's parents moved him to a different school and his behavior improved. He told me all this, as if it were natural that his parents had had the power to rescue him, as if all parents are able to protect their children. I listened to all his stories. I did not think such openness could exist in the absence of friendship. But there was no real openness. Does his endless need to perform make him feel exhausted? I will return his equipment in three weeks' time. That is our understanding. That may be all we understand of each other. I believed that someone called Jeremy Burton was my friend. There was a Jeremy Burton who worked in the hops fields, and he used to grin at me, and insist I had nothing to worry about. This radio commentator with his gorgeous girlfriend also grins, and tells me I have nothing to worry about; and at the same time he informs me that I "need more ego," that I am an incomplete person. Does he

think his beautiful girlfriend makes him gorgeous?
The Jeremy I met in Tettnang knew all about the
North. I wanted to believe the North existed. Now
I am in the North, and this radio commentator is
lending me his stove and tent, his cooking pots.

The night before leaving Frobisher Bay, before boarding the
small plane that would carry him to Pangnirtung, Heinrich
woke from a vivid dream and composed a letter to Inge. It
was the first and last letter he would send to her. He experienced pleasure as each word took shape. He had the distinct
sensation that she was present in the same room and reading
his sentences as quickly as they appeared on the paper:

> In the dream I just had, it was summer, Inge. There
> were no trees. I wasn't ready. The wind blew and day-
> light spread. The sea came in and out. The length
> of the fjord doubled, under the authority of violent
> weather. That the fjord's length was measured in hours,
> not kilometers, I didn't question. Fog erased the high
> hills in minutes. So, I thought, this is Pangnirtung. I
> was quite sure that I'd at last arrived in Pangnirtung. A
> truck, spitting dirt and gravel, veered into the yowl of
> generations of dogs; children ran, kicking something
> in the road.

"Ajiliurut?"[16]

I turned to see who was speaking.

"Ajiliurut?"

The word wasn't coming from a tape, playing in your bedroom, Inge, but from the mouth of a young boy dressed in jeans and flip-flops, gesturing to indicate that he wanted me to take his picture. I reached for my camera but couldn't find it. The fog was thickening. The fog stank of burning garbage.

"The dump fire at the end of the bay," the young boy's sister explained. She'd come along the road and now the two of them formed a pair. "When the wind blows in this direction," she said, "it stinks, for days."

An arctic fox trotted out of the fog and lifted its leg on a stop sign. The girl and boy went home to get a gun, so they might shoot the fox and give it to their mother to skin. As soon as they'd gone down the road, the fox stepped back into the fog and disappeared.

I found myself in a quiet room with a large window. I'd been waiting for two days in this room. It was open to anyone who wanted to come in but nobody came, and it was peaceful. I remained there, quite alone, and content to be alone. I looked out the window, which had a fine, unobstructed view of the harbor.

---

16 The Inuktitut word for "camera."

In the harbor a boat was ready to leave, and I watched everyone clamber on, including a girl who could not find her parents. The boat set off. Perhaps the girl had no parents. The others, seeing that she was alone, pushed her overboard to make more room. She held on to the side of the boat. With a knife someone cut off her fingers. She sank, rose to the surface, then sank deeper. Her severed fingers bobbed on the waves. They became ringed seals, and her thumbs two larger seals. So, I thought, this is Sedna. I knew the girl's name.

How did I know her name? Was she in one of your books, Inge, and you told me about her, about a spirit called Sedna, who rules the ocean's movements and the animals that live in it? I'm sure that I am not inventing her. Two stories about her arrived in my dream from somewhere, and the first story kept repeating itself, the boat carrying the little girl leaving the shore, over and over. Each time I wanted to warn her to hide her fingers, to make fists of her hands. A scream climbed in my chest. But if she hid her fingers, then there would be no seals.

In the room, where for days I'd been waiting, a thermos of coffee and a package of crackers sat on a small table. I helped myself. I felt grateful for the coffee. When I'd drained my cup I bent down, reached under the sofa, and pulled out a box of books. The one that I opened and started to read had a picture of a girl on the cover. It told a second, slightly different, Sedna story. A young woman had just come of age. The young men from her camp, and from neighboring camps, approached her openly, but she couldn't love any of them. Though they were kindhearted she couldn't forgive them their awkwardness. Her imagination had promised her a different sort of man, confident and well-spoken.

She waited, and sure enough, one afternoon just such a young man glided close in his kayak, paddling effortlessly. As he slipped near to the shore, he called to her. "Beautiful furs and many other riches will be yours, if you come with me to my home across the sea."

She hesitated.

"You will never know another day of hunger," the young man promised.

His words rippled across the smooth surface of the water as he paddled closer. The young woman climbed into his kayak and for three days she and her lover traveled over the sea, blissfully happy together. Farther and farther they went.

Land appeared, the land where she'd agreed to live as his wife for the rest of her days. The moment their kayak touched the shore, a giant bird snatched her up in its beak and flew with her.

I tried to close the book, Inge, I didn't want to be exposed to more suffering. I slammed the covers shut. But the story, of course, continued, and I could see you smiling, Inge, amused at my attempt to change the course of events.

As the ground fell far below, the young woman called desperately for her husband. "I am your husband," declared the bird and he placed her in a nest made of sharp sticks and branches. The nest in no way resembled the home that he'd promised her. Leaving her in her new and uncomfortable dwelling, which perched on the edge of a cliff, her husband flew off, saying that he'd soon return. She cried bitterly but no one could hear her.

Across the water, in her village, her father paced the shore. "She's gone off with a stranger," people told him. "We saw her climb into a kayak. She has been taken to the land of the birds." Her father, hearing this, got in his kayak and paddled without rest until, on the third day, he heard his daughter wailing. Her anguish fell into his ear from a place high above him. He climbed up into the nest, and he took her back down to his kayak.

You do own a book with this story in it, Inge. Now I remember. I took it without telling you. You didn't care about the book (it was only a story, not grammar), but you were furious that I'd gone into your room. I felt ashamed, and then, when you wouldn't forgive me, when you persisted in not forgiving me, I felt angry. I felt you were incapable of ever entirely forgiving me, and that was an unbearable feeling.

When the bird in my dream, in that part of my dream that I took from a book, which I took from you, returned to find his nest empty, his fury was terrible. He flew swiftly and soon caught up with the kayak. "Your daughter is my wife and has agreed to live with me. She has given her word," he warned the girl's father. The father refused to relinquish his daughter.

The bird, seeing that he had lost his wife, flew far away. But first he made his rage felt. The sea gathered into towering waves that tossed the kayak, as if it weighed no more than a feather or a blade of grass.

The father regretted having angered such a powerful bird. Fearing for his life and determined to calm the sea, he tried to push his daughter out of the kayak. She resisted. Again, he attempted to force her out. This time she fell into the water, but would not let go of the boat. Her father took out his knife and cut off her fingers. As the girl sank to the bottom and became Sedna, her severed fingers floated to the surface, and each finger became a seal. The girl's father reached the shore, exhausted. He pulled his kayak up onto the beach, staggered home, and fell into bed. While he slept, Sedna, his daughter, lifted the sea into an immense wave that crashed down on the village, sweeping away him and his house, and the houses of many others.

In my dream, I felt pleased that Sedna had gotten her revenge (even if innocent villagers had lost their homes), and I looked about, Inge, wondering if you agreed with me and were also pleased by Sedna's actions; but you weren't anywhere to be seen. I slid the box of books back under the sofa and got up to stretch my legs. These books are full of stolen stories, I thought, and that's why they're hidden under the sofa. (I'm not quite sure what I meant, in my dream, by the word "stolen." Here, in Frobisher Bay, I feel like an intruder, not quite a thief but almost. I'm sorry that I went into your room without asking, all those years ago. I've just read a very disturbing book—a short one, the right length for me—that I bought here. But I'll tell you about that another time.)

I wanted to leave, to escape the room with its sofa and its books filled with stolen stories. What was I waiting for? I opened the window and stuck out my head; the fog had been replaced by wind. I was waiting for the wind to die down. Once the sea quieted, I would be taken by boat up the fjord to begin my long walk into the interior (in my dream I seemed to know I was going on a hike).

I waited. Again, I looked out the window. Snow was falling. For three days it snowed ceaselessly. I grew tired of crackers and coffee. I left the room. I walked out of Pangnirtung (tomorrow I'll see how the real Pangnirtung compares with my dream of it!) and climbed a nearby hill.

Behind the hill, I walked farther. The snow continued to fall. Two quickly disappearing sets of boot prints were headed out across the land. I followed as best I could, and soon I saw a young couple trudging through the blowing drifts.

This story, Inge, the last in my dream, I've no recollection of reading but I'm just as sure it's not my invention. Is "alliok" a word you know?

The woman trudging through the snow was pregnant. She stopped and crouched down. Against the edge of a snowbank, she gave birth to twins. She and her husband spoke together. She hadn't eaten in days and her breasts had dried up. "You cannot feed our infants," said her husband. "They must stay here." The woman and her husband dug a hole in the snow, placed the twins in the hole, and continued on their way. I followed. For a long time they trudged through the deep drifts. I did as they did, straining to overhear the few words they exchanged. They hoped to reach, quite soon, a camp where they might be given some food. I looked over my shoulder and saw the twins emerging from their hole, as one creature. The creature had short legs and arms, a wide mouth filled with sharp teeth.

An alliok—the word came to me, Inge (from one of your tapes?). An alliok had entered the twins. The creature bounded through the snow until it caught up with its parents; then it jumped into the air. The alliok landed on the heads of its parents and stomped until the man and woman lay dead. I turned quickly away from the horrible scene. I plodded on through the deepening snow. As I approached a group of houses that I felt must be Pangnirtung, bright headlights and the roar of a snowmobile rushed toward me out of the whiteness.

What do you make of all this, Inge?

Last summer, on yet another trip back to Germany, I wasted several days in Tettnang, unpleasantly hot days under a searing July sun, asking questions, hoping to uncover some piece of information perhaps overlooked on my last visit.[17] Exhausted by the weather and jet lag, I

---

17 So often my parents urged me to visit them in Munich and I delayed, reluctant. Now that they are gone, Heinrich lures me there regularly.

imagined that Heinrich might suddenly appear on Kirchstrasse or in the garden beside the Schloss. Nothing. I got in my rented car and drove off.

In Friedrichshafen, I stopped for gas and noticed a small furniture store on the opposite side of the road. As it was Sunday, I nearly didn't cross over, quite certain the store would not be open. There was a sudden lull, however, in the flow of cars and trucks. I crossed the road. I turned the handle of the shop door and stepped inside. Immediately the owner tried to interest me in a lamp. It was made of brass, in the shape of a donkey's head. I told him I did not want a lamp. A box of papers caught my eye. The papers were not for sale. FORSTER METZGEREI— Forster Butcher's Shop—in bold blue letters was printed on the box, and in smaller red letters: KIRCHSTRASSE 1, 88069 TETTNANG. I offered to buy the lamp if the owner would throw in the box of papers. He agreed. Several minutes later, seated in my parked car, I let out a yelp of joy. Heinrich's letter to Inge. The long letter that he sent her from Iqaluit—there it was.

How do I define pleasure? The search for, and wondrous discovery of, each new artifact? Decipher, elaborate, speculate, turn upside down, reconsider, arrange, classify. Am I leading an irresponsible life, given how little time is left? Storms decimate one coast after another, while inland, tornados and earthquakes devastate. But what if my research leads successfully to Heinrich? My archive now includes the letter he sent to Inge from Baffin Island, several of the sporadically legible notebooks that he kept during his long hike, and much else. That these documents, however fragmentary, have survived is remarkable. That I've acquired them further astonishes me. Were someone else to delve into my archive, they might tell Heinrich's story differently than I do, what they'd want from Heinrich would be different. What I want from Heinrich is immense. Something immense is required and time is short.

PART THREE

ᐊᐅᔪᐃᑦᑐᖅ
Auyuittuq

Land That Never Melts

1

The Longer I Wander

July 6, 1980

I thought of Inge. I woke in the morning and immediately thought of her. She did not want to come to this place.

I stood looking down at the quiet arm of the sea where slabs of bright ice were drifting. The air felt crisp and clear. Mosquitoes gathered on my arm and crowded around my head, one flew into my open mouth, then the breeze lifted the rest of them away.

Last night, I pitched my tent on a wooden platform in the campground behind the town. Night never came. Instead, teenagers came, loud, on three-wheeled machines. They brought old packing crates.

Outside my tent, they left their machines and continued on foot, lugging the awkward crates along the
narrow path that winds between clumps of heather,
overlooking the turbulence of a river. "Are you going
to make a fire?" I asked. "Yes," they nodded.

The river raced and frothed, down through the settlement
and into the sea. The bungalows sat, as if by accident, along
the broad, unpaved roads. How would Inge respond to this
place? Heinrich wondered. Pale dust from the road had settled on the snowmobiles that waited for winter, in the grass
between the houses. It was a place of accidents. The same
dust coated the crushed pop cans, plastic bags, torn clothes,
battered strollers, discarded toys, scraps of metal and old
carpet lying in ditches, under back stairs, in babbling brooks
of clear glacial water. Footpaths led out onto the land.

The startling cotton grass. Heinrich couldn't take his
eyes off its whiteness. As for the ice down on the shore,
it wasn't white but turquoise—enormous pieces of it,
sculpted by the sea, then stranded at low tide. The ice
lured him down onto the mud and rocks, and when he
got close enough the slabs of ice became eight and ten
feet tall. Every hollow glowed turquoise. Heinrich peered
into the narrowest slits and these were filled with an alto-
gether different light, with a blue intensity he'd only ever

come upon in the tiny alpine flowers called gentians, and in the lapis lazuli earrings worn by his mother. He wandered, slipping on the mud, regaining his balance among the slowly melting giant forms carved in shades of blue.

In his notebook, he wrote:

July 6, 1980

The park warden stands very straight, his hands behind his back. He is comfortable observing me. Several minutes pass before he decides to speak:

"Before you go off into the park, there are a few things you should know."

I wait. I would like to know all he is willing to tell me. This room, where he's brought me to sign the necessary forms, is full of maps and records. I was counting on Jeremy to be my guide. Now I must count on this man, the warden. I can do nothing without his help and consent. He is arranging for a fisherman to take me by boat up the fjord so that I can begin my walk. But he is not yet ready to tell me what to expect in the park.

"I was born on the land, brought here as a boy. They made us come here, to Pangnirtung, so it would be easier to teach us, and to offer us medical treatments."

He watches me, to see what I think of his explanation. The amusement in his eyes suggests he is willing to offer me a different explanation, if I like; that there is no single story, and which story I choose to believe does not matter to him. He continues his tale.

The smile in his eyes acts like a paper cut; at first I feel nothing. My discomfort in his presence is the only measure I have of what I imagine he has lost. He uses silence to make his incisions. I am standing before a surgeon. He says that in the park I can expect winds traveling at over one hundred kilometers per hour, or no wind at all. There will be blowing sand, or perhaps blowing snow. I will not see a polar bear, but if I do, I must avoid it. Right now, the bears are busy, along the coast, hunting for seal. In the valley there is very little for them to eat—arctic hare, arctic fox. If I do see a bear, I must not attract the bear's attention, but once the bear notices me, and approaches, which could happen, I must make as loud a noise as possible. Guns are not allowed in the park. I am to be ready, on the rocks behind the visitors' center, in an hour's time. I hold out my hand and we shake hands, though I'm not sure why. It is possible we will never see each other again. A man named Joavee, the warden explains, will come in his boat and take me up the fjord to the mouth of the valley.

Once more Heinrich rummaged through the contents of his backpack, removing anything that he could do without, determined to carry as little as possible. He was glad his mother could not see how lightly he was packing. That he was discarding so much might have frightened her, and this pleased him. He felt free of her. Of Inge's approval he could be certain; spareness delighted Inge. On a long hike, what mattered was not to be weighed down. He had the weight of twelve days' worth of food, his tent, and other essentials. She would forgive him for leaving behind her gift, *A Pocket Guide to Arctic Plants*.

For the ride up the fjord, he extracted his down jacket, pulled it on, and was happy to have done so. The moment they separated from the shore, the air became bitterly cold, the boat navigating between drifting slabs of ice. On the mountain slopes grew dark patches of green, wild sorrel. "That," said Joavee, pointing. "That plant is very good to eat."

Too quickly, they reached the valley at the end of the fjord. He'd been enjoying the ride, the landscape sailing past while he sat and now and then turned his head, the wind tearing unsuccessfully at his hat and scarf.

Heinrich jumped onto the beach, and his backpack was handed out. Though this moment is not described in those pages of his notebooks that I possess I can picture it exactly, and have the impression I've seen it in a photograph. Once or twice, I've even gone meticulously through my archive, intent on locating a snapshot of the moment Heinrich's journey truly began—a snapshot I feel ought to be there.

He waved goodbye to Joavee, who was eager to head off, away from the shallow river mouth while the tide remained high. There was nothing for Heinrich to do now but to walk. He followed the Weasel River.

Some considerable time later, the light in the sky became delicate, felt more distant, and shadows glided up the face of the mountains on what had to be the east side of the river. He had no compass. The proximity of the magnetic North meant that no compass could function reliably.

Heinrich consulted his watch, which confirmed that evening had arrived, and he set up camp and cooked his meal.

Several hours passed, according to his watch, and there remained an abundance of fragile light. Nonetheless, he crawled into his tent and lay down. He wanted to stay outside longer, to try to convince himself that his surroundings were real, that the staggering beauty of the valley was not imaginary, but whenever he sat still mosquitoes closed in and he was too tired to evade them; his lower back, his knees and feet felt too weary for him to keep moving.

Because it felt odd to stretch out in his sleeping bag when it wasn't yet dark and would not become truly dark for at least another month, not until winter began its rapid return, he rolled up one of his shirts and used this to cover his eyes.

Shortly afterward, or perhaps many hours later, he woke and remembered that he was alone. He crawled out of his tent to check the weather, felt his watch in his pocket, retrieved it, and looked at it. It was morning. He made tea. Doing so warmed and occupied him. The immediacy and simplicity of the task alleviated his anxiety. Stiff but rested, he cut some bread and sprinkled it with sugar. There were no visible clouds in the sky. No storm was approaching. The river flowed beside him and his solitude pleased him.

Some peanut butter and a thick slice of sausage completed Heinrich's breakfast. His excellent appetite confirmed that he'd been working hard the previous day, and this gave him satisfaction. He felt that he'd covered a fair distance since being dropped off, especially given the tricky terrain under his feet and the substantial weight on his back.

Confident, eager to move farther up the valley, to discover what lay hidden beyond the next bend, he washed his spoon, cup, and knife in the smooth-skinned river. The tug of the river's concealed current told him how small he was.

He took out his camera and attempted to photograph his awe. Immediately he felt certain he'd failed, and he buried his camera deep in his pack, but he could not take his eyes off the river, nor could he stop thinking. An idea came to him. Again, he extracted his camera. He positioned the small apparatus, looked through the lens, and his idea failed. He'd brought only two extra rolls of film and he chastised himself. Another angle proposed itself.

Minutes, maybe two minutes later, when he looked through the lens he saw and caught the river's secretive strength, then he put the camera away quickly between layers of clothing and food. He took down his tent, strapped it to his pack, which he swung up and onto his back. Within an hour, any separation between him and the act of walking disappeared. He felt he'd always been walking and would forever continue to do so.

Sometime later he glanced at his watch and saw that over two hours had passed since he'd broken camp. Around midday he rested and ate his lunch beside the river. He hungered to photograph the mountains but did not want to use up his film too quickly.

His days unfolded smoothly. The good weather held. He did not want rain, but its prolonged absence worried him. He might be asked to pay a high price for such extended good luck. But who was there to demand that he pay? Perhaps he would not have to pay, and his luck would simply continue.

When he needed or wanted to rest, he sat on a hummock of moss, other times on a boulder, on sand, on gravel, but always he sat beside the river, as it was always beside him.

In his journal he wrote, "Would Inge hate it here?"

Day after day the river flowed, and the valley slowly climbed, twisting with the river. When the protruding tongue of a glacier or the trembling of a small flower stopped him, then he wished that Inge or even Jeremy Burton were standing next to him on the path, that one of them might also look up and see the ice compressed into the shape of a whale's tail, or peer down at the yellow petals of the arctic poppy, so finely cupping the warmth of the sun; but his were the only eyes, and he could not know if others would have seen what he saw. His true desire was for someone to feel exactly as he did, so perhaps it was best that the others were absent, leaving him free to imagine the precise quality of their delight.

The eyes of the animals were watching him, the fox and hares. They took great care not to reveal themselves. He guessed at their existence. When they'd left marks in the sand or mud, he crouched beside these proofs. When they'd left no marks, he imagined their presence.

The mountains thrust straight up on either side of the river. But because he had nothing against which to measure them he could only guess at their immensity; he could not fully perceive what he stood in the midst of. Later, however, he spotted an emergency shelter on the opposite bank, a tiny orange hut, crouched at the base of the rock face, and in that moment he understood that hugeness surrounded him.

July 12, 1980

This afternoon I saw my father standing beside the river. He had something in his hands and he was fiddling with it: a tiny motor. He set it on the ground, adjusted the belts, took a can of oil from the breast pocket of his jacket and squeezed a drop or two, then pulled the cord and the miniature pistons lurched into motion. What the motor was meant to drive or accomplish, I couldn't tell. There it sat, attached to a plank of wood. Papa was dressed in a three-piece suit, and, having cleaned his fingers on his handkerchief, he adjusted his necktie and collar. My mother came along the path, one hand holding down the skirt of her dress as the breeze kept lifting the hem. My father took her by the hand but then he let go of her hand; he extracted an envelope and the stub of a pencil from his pants pocket. On the envelope, he began jotting down explanations, sketching diagrams, until he'd covered both sides. All the while, he was speaking to Mama, but I could not hear what he said, nor could I make out her intermittent responses. She listened attentively or appeared to do so, sensing perhaps that if she denied Karl her attention, his abandonment would be complete. When he'd covered both sides of the envelope with his jottings, she took it from him and saw that it contained a letter she'd written long ago. Papa sat down on the ground and covered his face with his hands. She crouched beside him and spoke at length, but again I couldn't hear what she said. He started loosening his necktie, unbuttoning his shirt, but she stopped him. Meanwhile, beside their feet, the little motor nailed to its piece of wood continued to splutter and cough. I walked toward them, but, naturally, once I reached the place where they'd been standing, they were gone. Even as I write the word "hallucination," I feel convinced it does not accurately name what occurred.

In his next entry, which is undated, Heinrich makes no mention of his parents.

The sound of water is constant. The glaciers only appear to be motionless. Their silence is untrue. They speak in ropes of blue water. When the water reaches the edge, it falls straight down the mountainside, crashes whitely, plunges farther, lower, babbles, soft-edged at last, between mossy, flowering banks; it spreads out over vast beds of gravel. As for the Weasel River, I walk beside its green and milky width but cannot hear it flowing, my ears full of the roaring mountainside.

Suddenly, Heinrich wondered if, upon his return to Frobisher Bay, he ought not to ask Jeremy to help him find a job. That way he could stay a bit longer on Baffin Island and delay going back to Germany. The idea startled him. He lay in his sleeping bag, listening. Outside his tent, water was gushing, and gravel inaudibly shifting. To ask a favor of Jeremy Burton would be humiliating, though doubtless Jeremy would leap at the chance to redeem himself, calling up friends, setting things in motion. Already, Heinrich was using Jeremy's camping stove and cooking pots. These would be simple to return. To repay Jeremy for finding him work would not be so easy. On the other hand, a job would mean that Heinrich could stay in one place and attempt to understand what was expected of him. Here, nothing was expected of him. He lay on his back, listening.

July 14? 1980

Immensity is a form of silence. The movement of shadows is the closest I've had to a conversation in days. There are, of course, the conversations in my head.

Happily, after only one day of fog and intermittent rain the fine weather resumed. The sky cleared and the mountains returned. He hoped to spot a hare or a fox. The complete absence of trees in no way bothered him. He felt disloyal, however, for not missing the presence of trees. Surely it was ungrateful of him to forget them so easily? He tried to remember all that trees had given him—shelter from the wet, the pleasurable sound of leaves rustling, the relief of shade, the beauty of dappled light. His efforts met with resistance. If he conjured a general idea of a tree it felt unconvincing. If he started to recall a particular tree, one he knew well, its presence became too real and intruded.[18] In this valley, no tree belonged. Did he belong? He felt he did until he lifted

---

18 Is the large pear tree in the Schlögel back garden still alive? On my last visit it appeared healthy, towering above the fence, a breeze caressing its uppermost leaves, and already some of its fruit had fallen and rolled. I did not go around to the front and knock. There was no point in my speaking a second time with the new owners.

his backpack and its new lightness reminded him that his supply of food was diminishing. How many days had he been walking? He tried to line up the precise areas of landscape through which he'd passed; he attempted to arrange in chronological order the exact locations where he'd pitched his tent each night, and to count the number of nights, to enumerate the meals he'd eaten, but failed.

In his journal he noted:

Survival requires that we remember, but adaptability demands that we forget. There are moments when I hear Jeremy Burton's voice without particularly wanting to.

Of Inge he makes no mention. Page after page of his journal excludes her from his thoughts. Or perhaps she was such a constant presence in his mind that he felt no need to comment?

Late one afternoon, his grandfather appeared from behind a rock. The old man's shoes were impeccably polished, his pants carefully ironed. He pointed to his shoes and said something to Heinrich, but Heinrich could not hear him properly. Again the old man tried to make himself understood and the effort caused a small vein to pulsate in the side of his neck. Heinrich stared at him, uncomprehending. His grandfather removed his shoes and tossed them into the Weasel River.

Later, Heinrich wrote:

His shoes were riding the water, one in the lead, the other spinning, caught in a whorl of the current. I turned, gathering my courage to speak to him, but he was gone. I ran along the bank. The spinning shoe sank. I watched the other shoe shrink smaller and smaller, then disappear where the river bent.

In his next entry, the word "Inge" appears, and her name leaps off the page. He is pressing down hard, his pen digging into the paper. He writes:

Her exacting eyes, the clarity of her gaze—I can feel these always, they accompany me without her being here. Eider ducks have landed in a flurry on the seamless water.

He stared and stared at the ducks drifting on the river.

Boulders thundered down the rock face in a balletic shroud of dust, and at the sound he rushed from his tent. The dust continued dancing in the air. The following day, farther along the path, he found a thick, stiff snowmobiling glove left over from winter. It lay on the ground behind a rock. This second event did not relate to the first. When he found himself trying to connect the falling rocks and the appearance of the glove, he wanted suddenly, fiercely, to speak with someone.

To walk was not enough. He wanted to see animals. For animals, he had chosen the wrong valley and it was too late to turn back. He'd assumed that the North would be full of animals—caribou, wolves, fox, and bears. He'd been misled by Jeremy Burton, who'd confidently assured him: "There will be animals. Hey, man, it's the wilderness."

July 1980

Jeremy Burton was wrong about the wildlife, but he was right in accusing me of not having enough ego, not having enough independence of will. I should have followed Hearne's route, gone to the Western Arctic. But Hearne's path would still not have been my own path. How am I to find a route of my own?

He had a path and it was under his feet, and for the most part clearly marked by inuksuit.

The snowmobiling glove that he'd spotted a while back—why hadn't he photographed it? He'd wanted to. He should have taken the time and done so. Each step forward now took him farther away from the glove that he'd not photographed. Quickly, almost running, he retraced his steps, followed the path back to the exact spot. The glove lay where he remembered it. He fished out his camera and removed the lens cap.

The curled, rigid fingers he brought in and out of focus, playing with the composition. Without touching the glove, he moved around it, hoping that each new shot would better express the glove's abandonment and endurance. The setting obstinately refused to provide any clues as to why the glove had been removed or what had prompted it to be forgotten. Nonetheless, he tried to make these questions present in his shots.

He was about to return the camera to its place of safety in his pack when he experienced a strange sensation, as if the device in his hands no longer belonged to the present but was a vestige of some earlier era. He examined his camera carefully, touching but not opening the little door at the back that concealed the film. He ran the tips of his fingers over the narrow sliding panel that kept the batteries in place. In none of its features had the camera changed. He continued his examination, which served only to intensify his impression that in some invisible yet irrevocable way the familiar object had become a relic. Confused, he wanted all the more urgently to speak with someone.

He wrote:

Soon, I'll reach Mount Asgard, but how soon? Unless I've been misreading the map, Glacier Lake can't be more than two days away. Of course it all depends on the river crossings.

The land had much to communicate. There were times when he allowed its vastness to reach a scouring hand inside him. But its details, the stories it articulated, he couldn't read. He'd become illiterate.

He observed with curiosity the position and shape of a stamen or leaf, the presence or absence of lichen, the texture and distribution of rock and sand. Behind each plant's structure and presence, in the positioning of every stone, lay a story, a long sequence of delicately hinged events leading to the present and pointing to a possible future, yet none of these botanical and mineral narratives could he comprehend. He lacked knowledge. He walked beside the river, unable to read its movements. Never had he imagined he would so intensely miss the act of reading.

When his body declared it was night, he crawled into his sleeping bag. Once, when he opened his eyes a violent, rainless wind was tearing at his tent. The cloth walls pressed down on him, the poles bent. He lay in the center of his own howling fear, listening to every note. A rope snapped free. The rip-resistant, synthetic lung that contained him collapsed. He remained motionless, and a silence grew inside him.

The storm passed. In his journal he noted:

> To my relief the tent has not suffered any permanent damage. My supplies are intact. I am able to continue.

Before packing it away, he photographed his collapsed tent, as it comprised his only evidence of the storm's occurrence. In a second shot, he documented the nonexistence of the storm's passage: the absence of fallen trees or broken branches. He ate, reorganized his supplies, swung his pack onto his back, and walked.

The weather shifted; the air reeked of rain.

Jeremy Burton is with his girlfriend, in Frobisher Bay, and when he's not in bed, fucking her, he's producing radio shows. Inge is delivering mail, and when she's not doing that, she's shut in her room studying Mandarin or Ancient Greek or some other language she's fallen in love with, and that she finds less distressing than Inuktitut, than Abraham Ulrikab's language. A lost snowmobiling glove, the broken runner of a wooden sled, a scrap of rope— the Inuit travel this valley only in winter; right now they are out on the sea, fishing, or collecting the eggs of shore birds. Everyone except me is busy, purposefully occupied.

Rain and more doubt arrived together. He sat down on a rock. To remove his pack for even a few minutes brought a sense of relief, but to keep warm required motion. He waved his arms about. If he allowed his neck and shoulders too much freedom, the constraint of the pack and its weight when he put it back on felt all the more oppressive. Keeping up a good steady rhythm was essential.

He berated himself for not pushing hard enough, for ambling forward, admiring the flowers, delighting in the shocking red of a stretch of moss. A quicker pace, a clearer focus on what lay ahead, on what waited around the next bend, and his sense of purpose would return. He was on an adventure, after all.

The rain though steady was not heavy. Rain meant no mosquitoes. He should have reached Mount Asgard days ago. Thor Peak was long behind him. He'd passed a tiny lake that was not on his map. There were errors in his map. The curves in the river did not precisely correspond, nor did the moraines. His supplies were dwindling and every day his pack felt lighter. Possibly, by tomorrow, Mount Asgard would come into view. He pressed on.

Hearne appeared.

This afternoon, I came over a rise and saw a figure on the path ahead of me. I knew him immediately, though he did not recognize me.

This statement is followed by several lines that have been scribbled over. The next legible sentences express an irrational disappointment:

All that time, when I was reading his diary, Hearne did not feel me devouring his descriptions and his courage, my admiration and sympathy going out to him. For him, I did not exist.

Two blank pages follow; then he writes:

I introduced myself. Hearne asked about my life.

Heinrich and Hearne walked along a narrow path beside the Weasel River, Hearne in front and Heinrich following.

I told him that my sister had given me his book to read. Then quite without warning he wanted to know if I'd ever seen a soldier run through with a bayonet. I hadn't. Had I been forced to drink my urine? Had I received a lashing? No, none of these. He gave me a searching look, as if I were, perhaps, a woman disguised as a man. He was, I think, assessing how reliable a traveling companion I might make.

The rain stopped. We climbed another rise and came to a lovely spot, suitable for making camp. To have pressed on would have meant crossing a large moraine likely to prove tricky underfoot, and we agreed to save that challenge for the following day. While I pitched my tent, Hearne brought out his pipe. We smoked, and the smoking relaxed me. I hadn't felt so lighthearted in days. He promised that if we sighted a hare or a fox, he'd teach me to shoot and would show me how to skin an animal. I excused myself and walked off, a short distance, as I needed to urinate. I hoped that no hare or fox would show itself. Behind a large rock, I relieved myself. I imagined killing and eating a hare and, to my surprise, the hunger in my gut became more insistent.

I returned to find Hearne examining the zippers on my tent. Next he ran his fingers along the fabric and touched the netting in the doorway with fascination.

"A most singular notion," he announced, "to construct a tent from silk and veils." He tapped the taut surfaces with his fingertips. "If indeed this fabric is silk, it sorely lacks in sensuality and yet it does possess, I think, surprising strength."

I assured him that his assessment was correct, that the tent had withstood several violent storms and was of excellent quality. We smoked a second pipe. I brought out the last of my whiskey. He spoke with admiring affection of his guide, Matonabbee, to whom he owed the success of his third and final expedition.

The next few pages of this notebook have gone missing, with the exception of one half page, which I've recovered.[19] I can only hope that I'm inserting this half page correctly. It is filled to its very edges with a single word repeated over and over: "Inge Inge Inge Inge Inge Inge Inge Inge Inge Inge Inge Inge Inge Inge Inge Inge Inge Inge Inge Inge Inge Inge Inge Inge Inge Inge Inge inge Inge Inge . . ."

After his obsessive inscribing of his sister's name (if my chronology is correct), Heinrich's next entry reads as follows:

The wilderness is perhaps the worst place to risk complete honesty, though ultimately it demands it. I turned and confronted Hearne. If what I said caused a falling-out between us, I'd again be alone—I knew

---

19 This half page was posted on a site called "Did You Lose This?"—a site dedicated to returning mislaid journals, notes, letters, and portions of diaries to their rightful owners. It was one of a dozen fragments described collectively as "lost handwritten texts of unknown origin and authorship, mid to late twentieth century, mostly German." I immediately recognized the handwriting. I contacted the person who'd posted the fragment and explained my interest in acquiring it. She was reluctant. She would have preferred to be contacted by the actual owner of the journal. I explained my role, and she relented.

this. I addressed him more loudly than I wanted to. Some regulating valve inside me had ceased to function. "During your third and successful journey," I shouted at him, "the native women accompanying your expedition were treated little better than pack-horses." I did not want to be shouting and I tried to calm my breathing, but my leg began to tremble. I waited for Hearne's response. He indicated his agreement with a sorrowful smile and a slight, sideways movement of his hand. The shaking in my leg increased. I felt a painful pressure behind my eyes, as if someone's fist were thrust inside my skull. I yelled at Hearne, gesticulating: "When a deer was shot, it was the women who were sent running to haul back the kill. They prepared the animal, they gutted and skinned it, they rubbed the animal's brains into the hide to keep the hide from stiffening, and they cooked the flesh and stuffed, then boiled the bladder. After all this work, they were given nothing. They had to wait until every man had eaten his fill before they were allowed a scrap to chew on, and if no scraps remained they went hungry. For any defiance they were beaten." I was panting, as if I'd just run up a hill. Sweat was pouring from my skin. I could feel another wave of rage advancing through me, a rage too large to contain, a rage I did not feel belonged to me. Was this Inge's rage? Did she need or want me to express it for her? I tried to calm my breathing. The muscles in my neck throbbed.

Hearne leaned back on his elbows and stretched out his legs, making himself comfortable before offering his thoughts. At last he spoke:

"As it was their primitive practice to use their women in this fashion," he stated, with composure, "they saw no error in their actions, and upon those occasions when I gave expression to my concern, they laughed outright at my dismay. I thought it wise not to further interfere, lest their amusement turn to anger. And yet, to conceal my pity proved most difficult at times. A young wife was forced to change husbands against her will. I bore mute witness to this barbarity. I could do nothing to alter her circumstances. Nor could I lessen the suffering of a woman obliged to slog through snow and water up to her knees, only days after giving birth, and this with a heavy load on her back and her infant strapped to her."

With a few deft gestures Hearne refilled his pipe. I stared at him, my neck throbbing and the ache in my brain threatening to split my head open. I felt as I imagine a tree must feel when another tree is struck by lightning and fire travels underground to lick the roots of the tree not yet in flames. Fire was traveling up my legs, filling my chest. Words and spit flew from my mouth: "Who do you think you are? What about women in Germany and England? Isn't brutality a European specialty as well? Have you seen the women in your fields and alleyways and stables and bedrooms? You disgust me. I despise your arrogant certainty that you've been somehow chosen to understand the world, to brutalize the world with your self-interested understanding, to ram your laws in place, here, there, and everywhere you like. You're so busy making sense of the universe, aren't you? Have you looked behind your haystacks or lifted the bedroom sheets? What ground do you have to stand on? I've walked for miles with you. I've tried to see through your eyes. You've noticed everything: the details of plant life and the behavior of animals. What have you done to me? Where are the answers you promised?"

I could no longer look him in the face. Gasping for breath, I stared down at my feet. There was a hole in the ground, and someone was inside the hole. I knelt. It was Inge, at the bottom, her legs folded like a grasshopper's. Razor in hand, she was slicing gashes across her thighs. She staunched the immediate flow of blood with a piece of torn sheet. I felt sickened, and did not want to see more, and lifted my head. Sounds were coming from the hole. She was talking. I held my breath and listened:

"If I bandage this carefully, and pull on my jeans, will they know? Let them know. They won't dare speak. Each time I cut, I can feel. First comes the pain, quick and precise, then the warm wetness spreading. They'll know, but they won't dare ask. Will they find it painful to be unable to speak about what they know? Let them see how that feels. Do they feel anything? Do they see anything but what they want to see?"

I looked up at Hearne.

"She's talking," I told him. "She's describing what she does. How do you suggest I help her? Have you any suggestions?"

I grabbed a large stone from the ground and hurled it into the Weasel River. I grabbed another stone and threw it with all my strength, then another. Each rock that flew from my hand vanished into the milky flow of the broad river.

I took hold of my notebook. I would have tossed it into the water but Hearne reached out and stopped me. I turned and saw the exhaustion in his face.

"Have you ever been shown something you weren't ready for?" I asked. "A violence and a suffering you've tried to run away from ever since? A part of you stops and can't go forward. You're too busy pretending everything's normal. It happens to all of us. It happens very early on. We discover the taste of ruthlessness, the cold arbitrariness of the world. But we have to continue. We all know far more than we want to, and so we create elaborate schemes."

I looked down at the ground. The hole was gone. I raised my head and already Hearne had reached the steep moraine farther upriver, the moraine we'd planned to climb together on the following day. When he arrived at the top he did not look back but started his descent down the other side, the side not visible to me, and he was gone. I lowered myself onto a mossy hummock and held my head between my hands.

The mosquitoes gathered quickly, both at the back of my head and on my face and arms. I swatted at them hopelessly as I unpacked my cooking stove and supplies. I busied myself preparing my evening meal. Mosquitoes settled on my nose; they landed on my forehead and cheeks. I tried to brush them away, but needed one hand to hold my bowl and the other to lift my fork. I ate, barely taking the time to chew, then cleaned my bowl in the nearest stream and at last slipped into my tent. I lay on my back undisturbed, and through the thin fabric observed the luminosity of the outdoor world.

After this entry, for many pages Hearne and Inge go un-
mentioned. At what pace Heinrich's days elapse is hard to
say—no dates delineate them. His days are neither placed
in a clear order nor prevented from flowing into each
other. Past and present tense become interchangeable.
He seems to be approaching Mount Asgard, his arrival at
the base of the Turner Glacier feels imminent, and then
nothing happens; both landmarks vanish from his map.
He deliberately or unconsciously shrinks his handwriting,
perhaps in an effort to conserve space within his journal. I
assume that he fears running out of paper.

He writes:

If this is a photograph, I am that tiny detail that
serves only to reveal the overwhelming proportions
of the whole. I am part of the composition. As soon
as a composition makes itself clear, everything stops
moving. If a composition is less than perfect, however, the picture quickly fills with expectation; we
eagerly anticipate a shift, a return to movement. A
perfect composition, on the other hand, makes motion hold still in such a way that we do not need to
see the movement to know it exists and to sense its
presence; the elements do not yearn for a better or
different alignment, as they are already in a state
of ideal balance, and this lack of yearning creates
a calm, a calm that brims over with energy. Such

utterly harmonious compositions I could stare at forever; forever lasting several seconds or several years;
a perfect composition allows the experience of time
as indivisible.

I continue along the path, go a few feet farther,
and immediately I long to recover what I've just left
behind. Sometimes I go back to look for it. But it is
never there. Perfection is loyal only to itself.

He had to contend with river crossings and did not always
time these crossings well. The best and safest spot to cross
was rarely self-evident. It could be where the river braided
out, separating into several strands, or higher up, before
this dividing occurred. Very early in the morning, when
the day had not yet warmed, or on a cloudy day, the volume of melted glacier pouring into the river was less and
the river less forceful.

He thought he heard thunder, but it was the rumble
of concealed rocks being carried toward him by the silty
white current. He placed a foot blindly. He remembered
to undo the chest and waist straps of his backpack so he
could escape from its weight, were he to lose his balance.
His second foot touched the stony bottom. The rumbling
that wasn't thunder continued. But the loose rocks being
carried by the current did not touch his legs or feet as

they passed. He forgot that he mustn't look down, and he glanced at the churning surface. Dizziness overtook him. Quickly, he redirected his gaze to the solid bank.

I rested on the gravel and ate, surrounded by carpets of purple flowers. This is more than happiness—this shout of purple, reverberating in all directions. The river is a verb, Inge, and so are the flowers. Knowing this, would you agree to come here? Rock and ice are verbs. The weather, at times, settles heavy as a noun. Would you feel at home in this grammar, Inge?

She was the only person with whom he wanted to speak—once more the only one who he imagined might understand him. As for the burning rage that had raced through him earlier, as for her presence at the bottom of a hole in the ground, and the accusations he'd hurled at Hearne—of these disturbing matters he said nothing to her in his journal. He stared at the purple expanse of fire-weed growing out of the gravel, a shimmer of blossoms that seemed to hover in the evening light, and he no longer felt charred inside but capable once more of supple emotion.

Inge, again the river has widened. The mud has cracked into reptilian patterns, so that I'm advancing across a huge skin. I've been walking with this magnification under my feet for hours; mud is a story that begins: "Once, long ago." In places, the mud unexpectedly gives, sucks, and grips my foot, its silky mouth pulling hungrily at my ankle. I move away from the river, return to the hummocks of resilient moss. These sink and rise with each step I take, so that my knees ache. My camera lies buried in my pack. You understand? A picture would transform all of this into some sort of trophy, a sign of victory. Do you agree, Inge? You do, don't you? Victory wants to make everything stand at attention and salute. It is hateful. But nothing in this valley salutes. Honor is for humans to figure out—an honorable relinquishing. Rocks break off and crash down the mountainsides, every hour or so, raising huge flags of dust that twist and drift without honor. My watch has stopped, and yet I persist in thinking in hours and minutes. It's as if I were a blind person sticking stamps on an envelope. To whom am I sending my envelope stuffed full of time? My dear Inge, when I next see you, I will be carrying a thin layer of the North inside me. You, who have always understood my thoughts and feelings better than I could, what will you make of me, of this immensity from which

I can no longer separate myself? I hope I am altered. Will you strike me as very small, seated at your desk, with your dictionary beside you?

Late one afternoon, he arrived at the base of the Turner Glacier, and he pitched his tent on a high moraine of stones that were mortared together by ice, then covered in sand. The slightest breeze lifted a delicate gray powder into the air, a powder that clogged the zippers of his tent and found its way up his nostrils, a powder that coated his tongue and settled on his clothes and boots. When he stepped out of his tent and brought his foot down hard, a deep reverberation revealed that the great mound of ice-mortared stones and gravel supporting him was hollow.

Not one single plant had succeeded in taking hold. Out of the opaque, green waters of the lake emerged a steep pyramid of stones heaped upon stones. This construction culminated in a summit, which Heinrich, having scrambled up, found he could balance upon. He looked across the lake, and Mount Asgard came into view—a square tower of brown rock jutting out of the Turner Glacier. He stared at the peak's improbable shape; only the blade of a knife could explain such squareness. The tower felt intentional and therefore human. Yet its gigantic indifference made it godlike. Ice, several hundred meters thick, advanced upon it from behind and spread out in front of it.

Heinrich reached up to scratch a mosquito bite at the back of his neck, and the movement of his arm caused a shift in his balance. His foot nudged a stone that gave way. The stone rolled fast, then faster, unstoppable, down the steep incline. He watched the stone slip silently into the cloudy waters of the lake. Ice had scraped out, then filled the lake; ice had pushed into shape the structure of stones upon which Heinrich perched and from which he looked nervously down; ice had acted with seeming neglect yet according to precise rules of resistance and force, of angle and weight, rules unknown to Heinrich. He felt troubled by his ignorance of certain rules, and the more visibly the stones shifted around him the more uneasy he became, his ignorance of physics an ache inside his belly.

He noted:

> I am camping in a construction site. It is neither beautiful nor welcoming. This is a place of difficult austerity.

Under the banks of sand, the walls of ice were melting; ice-turned-to-water went hastening into the lake; every day the shoreline shifted, the lake acquired a subtly new shape. The tongues of the glaciers were becoming smaller. How much smaller? At what pace were they diminishing? Heinrich couldn't say for sure. He wanted to leave. He craved moss and flowers. Grit and sand surrounded him. He wrote in his notebook quickly, brushing the gray powder off the page with the side of his hand.

Hearne appeared.

I ran down the sand bank to speak with him, but before I could reach the place where he stood, I came upon an old woman busily trying to catch fish. I approached and saw that she was blind. Immediately I knew who she was. I'd read Hearne's description of her suffering more than once. I urged her to leave. She showed no sign of having heard me. I turned my back on her and scrambled up the moraine to where my tent stood.

Already I could hear the old woman screaming in agony. Looking quickly behind me, I saw that she lay crumpled in the sand, pinned in place by several spears. They'd plucked out her useless eyes. Blood trickled from her ear also. Farther along the shore stood Hearne. He was no longer alone. A young Inuk, a woman, clung to his ankles. Spears were being thrust into the flesh of her arms and legs, great care being taken not to strike any internal organ. Clearly, Hearne's Northern Indian companions, her torturers, were playing with her, denying her the relief of death, for however long their amusement lasted. Hearne tried to move his leg, to lift his foot. The young woman, in her writhing, tightened her grip on his ankle. Hearne shouted above her moaning, demanding that her tormentors finish her off more swiftly.[20]

I turned away from the scene and started to dismantle my tent. Laughter came from the lakeshore.

---

20 Like Heinrich, I've read Hearne's depiction of the slaughter at Bloody Falls. On the subway one morning, I came upon his graphic passages, read them once, then a second time, wondering how much of it was true. Hearne's memory insists that what he witnessed made him feel like weeping, and that he risked speaking out in defense of the girl being tortured. But did the young girl exist or did he add her in for his readers? She's absent from the notes he made directly after his journey. It is not always easy to describe immediately what has been unbearable to witness, and this could explain his failure to include her in his early notes. According to Hearne, a number of the Northern Indians, the Chipewyans, who accompanied him on his expedition, did so hoping for an opportunity to murder some Inuit. The hatred they felt for the Inuit had deep historical roots. On the banks of the Coppermine River, near a waterfall, they came upon a vulnerable Inuit camp and spared nobody.

I tried to block the sound from my ears. It was the triumphant laughter of those inflicting suffering. I wanted to escape the churning landscape that surrounded me—a landscape of broken rock and melting ice that was releasing sickening events from the past, events that did not belong in this valley. I packed my gear as fast as I could.

One of my tent poles fell and immediately vanished beneath a layer of gray dust. I snatched up the nearly weightless pole and cleaned it off as best I could on the dusty sleeve of my shirt. The slaughter at Bloody Falls, on the Coppermine River, had occurred on Hearne's route through the Western Arctic, not here beside the Weasel River. What was the meaning of such geographic illogicality? Was the purpose of these scenes to reinforce my distrust of reason and order? Perhaps these apparitions had no purpose and were the random offerings of an ongoing and violent confusion—my own. I wanted only to walk, to walk quickly away, to hurry back down the valley, to be among hummocks of moss and babbling brooks edged with purple flowers.

The screaming by the lakeshore ended as I stuffed the last of my gear into my pack. Considerably lighter than at the start of my long walk, it swung up easily onto my back. I took one last look at the lake. I surveyed the shoreline. No trace remained of the old, blind woman, murdered while fishing, or of the younger woman being pinned to the ground by spears while she grabbed at Hearne's ankles. The tortures endured by these two women had left no discernable mark on the landscape. My eye traveled from the lake to the Turner Glacier.

A line of schoolchildren was crossing the glacier's pale expanse, herded by a man dressed in a dark suit. Though they were far away, I could see them as clearly as if I were looking through a pair of binoculars. The man wore a clerical collar. The children's hair had been cut short and their faces scrubbed. The boys were dressed in work shirts and shapeless pants held up by suspenders, and the girls wore woolen dresses. Their scuffed shoes were either several sizes too big or else fit so tightly that they splayed open. Some had no laces. So as not to slip on the ice, the children stepped with evident caution and precision, none of them glancing right or left or speaking a word.

I made my way down, off the gravel moraine, and entered an area of large boulders through which I had to navigate slowly. Midway across, I paused, turned, and looked back at the Turner Glacier. The children had stopped walking and were kneeling on the ice.

I continued to pick my way between the massive boulders until I reached the base of the next moraine and began climbing. Once I'd reached the crest I turned again and looked back. The children were now naked from head to toe. While they knelt, bare-kneed on the glacier, the priest, fully clothed, paraded back and forth in front of them, his hand clutching his exposed, erect penis. Despite the violent wind, which must have made it difficult for him to aim with precision, he was depositing from the tip of his penis onto each child's waiting tongue a drop of ejaculate. "With this holy milk, I anoint you," he repeated. "With this holy milk . . ."

The wind died suddenly. The sun beat down on the small area of the glacier occupied by the kneeling children and the officiating priest. Their parcel of ice, without warning, broke free from the body of the glacier and advanced down the mountainside, grinding and churning the stone beneath it, carving a trough in its wake. A slab of brilliance, the ice entered the lake at the base of the mountain and floated. The children got up from their knees and started to hop from one frozen foot to the other, while the priest, having put away his penis, stood in silent prayer. The great slab tilted, and the children slid into the frigid, opaque waters of the gray-green lake. One by one, they disappeared beneath the surface, while the priest continued to drift on his island of ice.

A sound formed. I could feel it in my belly and I opened my mouth to hear what might emerge but not even a small cry came out. To stop myself from numbly staring at the lake I turned my back on it, put one foot in front of the other, and walked.

Heinrich made his way across a second expanse of boulders. An entombing silence surrounded him. For the first time in days, he could hear no waterfalls, no brooks or river. He looked in all directions for an inukshuk but there was none. He proceeded in what felt like the right direction. A boulder shifted under his boots, the tip of his metal walking stick struck against stone. Dryness and silence closed around him. When at last he stopped to rest, questions poured out of him. He searched urgently in his pack for a scrap of paper. He addressed his questions to Inge in the form of a letter that he would never send, and that would remain tucked into his notebook.

July 1980

Dearest Inge,

There's a book I bought in Frobisher Bay. I read through part of it before beginning this long walk, from which I'm about to return, unless I don't succeed in returning. The book discusses conditions in boarding schools. Many Inuit children were and are sent to these schools. The book was published only five years ago. I'd recommend it to you, but I'm not sure I'd want you to read it. The cruelty that Ulrikab experienced, it continues taking on new forms. But perhaps you already know this? Perhaps, a long time ago, you found and read a similar book? Perhaps you were aware of far more about the North than you told me? Perhaps you wanted me to come and see for myself? You stayed at home with your dictionaries and sent me to Canada in your place. What is it you want me to figure out, Inge? How all these terrible actions, this cruelty and suffering, relate to you and me, and what we are to do about them, or if we are free to do nothing? I can only think the obvious. Pain, however cleverly stored away, will find its way out. Suffering, like water, cannot be frozen permanently. But when anguish escapes its confines, who is to be held accountable for the violence of its release? Is it all a question of timing, of what we choose to ignore and for how long? You didn't want to come here, did you? Have you any answers for me? It is good that you stayed home. I am good at walking. You sent me to Canada hoping that adventure would bring me the relief that you find in studying grammar. That is the best story, Inge: your desire for my happiness. That is the story I'm selecting as the truth.

Heinrich crushed yet another mosquito. With his pen he formed letters on the page, and the movement of his hand forming each letter relaxed him. When he imagined Inge reading what he was writing, his exhaustion diminished, though his legs felt heavy and his shoulders ached. It was evening, and he'd escaped the silence of the boulders. Moss and flowers surrounded him. The earthy sweetness smelled familiar. To his right gushed a fast-flowing brook. He dipped his cooking pot in the tumbling, cold water. He managed to light his stove (which was Jeremy's stove) and he cooked his dinner. After his meal, his belly full, he wrote with one hand, the other swatting at mosquitoes.

The degree of his weariness surprised him, given the beauty now spreading out in front of him. What he'd witnessed, in the overturned and shifting landscape at the base of the Turner Glacier, had exhausted him more thoroughly than he'd realized. Each movement he made demanded a great effort. By evening an impression of failure overcame him. As he looked about, observing the abundant pink flowers that bordered the brook, his heart filled with gratitude and happiness, and he understood that the impression of failure invading him did not belong to the present moment; yet it felt inescapable in its familiarity. He wrote in his journal, quickly, as if hoping to outrun some perpetual shortcoming.

Inge, would you call our father a Disappointed Man? I know that I have added to his disappointment. But is it fair to call him a Disappointed Man? Should such a category exist? Whenever he has a student who shows promise, who does not disappoint him, he ceases to be a Disappointed Man. Every label misleads. To those students in whose abilities he believes, he gives fervent, unwavering encouragement; and several of these students have not let him down.

In the morning, Heinrich woke early and, while drinking his tea, again he wrote in his journal, taking care to keep his handwriting compact:

Half a dozen caribou are racing along the opposite bank of the Weasel River but I can't see them because my eyes, like those earliest cameras, erase anything that moves. Imagine, Inge, if this were true! Let's suppose my eyes required such a long exposure time that they eliminated all waterfalls and moving animals. The crashing of water and the pounding of hooves would be heard inside a scene of complete stillness, a scene from which they appeared to be absent. This could be the case, Inge. So much is vanishing, and so much is hidden, and so much we choose not to see.

All of the next day he walked calmly, admiring the mountains and the river, which seemed in its narrowing and widening to continually reinvent itself. Every patch of lichen pleased him. Evening came, and Heinrich ate a cursory meal while shadows climbed the mountains. They climbed on the east side of the river, and the luminous sky remained cloudless. He washed and stored his cooking gear, packed the last of his food, checked the ropes of his tent to be sure they were secure, and set off to explore his surroundings more closely.

Something unexpected caught his eye. It moved. At first, he could not tell what it was. Because of its long, tapered ears, because of its size and markings, he mistook it for a small goat. But it was not a goat. It was a large hare, a hare much larger than he'd ever imagined a hare could be.

Heinrich crept closer. He got down on his belly and wriggled forward. The hare held its pose, then disappeared behind an erratic. Heinrich sat in the heather and waited. He was no longer alone; from a safe distance behind a rock a fellow animal was observing him.

The next morning, just as he did every morning, he took down his tent, collapsing its poles and rolling up the fabric tightly. He swung his pack onto his back and checked the ground to be sure that he was leaving nothing behind. Every morning, he left nothing behind but his surroundings, and though it felt good to be leaving he walked away slowly, attempting to memorize every detail.

The second time that he spotted the hare (though possibly it was not the same hare) it appeared to be waiting for him. When it bounded off, he followed. The hare arrived at an immense erratic that was split in two. Three or four powerful leaps carried the hare through the slot between the rock's two halves. The rock stood taller than Heinrich and was shaped like a rounded hill. The hare emerged out the other side of the passage through the center of the giant stone. Sniffing the air, it held still, as if waiting for someone or something. Heinrich entered the slit. No sunlight entered with him. He passed between the two smooth walls of stone. Just as he emerged into the daylight, the hare dashed off. A few yards away, the long-eared animal stopped. It turned its head and gazed at Heinrich, who stopped moving also, uncertain how to respond. The two contemplated each other.

Maybe it is in order to meet this giant hare that I have traveled from Tettnang to Baffin Island and walked the length of this valley? What is more certain is that I am running out of food, that my knees ache, and that my map is falling apart from repeated folding and unfolding.

He continued to walk. As he descended the valley, the riverbed widened decisively. The tongues of the glaciers did not reach so far down as before, or so it seemed to him. Close to the river's mouth he came upon four backpackers. Two of them were cooking while the other two walked about, choosing the flattest spots to pitch their tents. Heinrich approached and asked if they were entering or leaving the park. A fully formed, comprehensible sentence came out of his mouth. The sound of it surprised and relieved him. It felt like years, not weeks, since he'd last spoken with anyone, anyone besides Hearne. The hikers answered him:

"Leaving," one of them said. "We're headed back to Pang tomorrow morning."

They'd arranged for a boat, which would be coming to collect them.

"There should be enough room, if you need a ride," another offered. They were friendly, and didn't seem to find him peculiar.

"How far up the valley did you get?" the first who'd spoken now asked.

"To Mount Asgard."

"Fantastic. We had to turn back at Thor Peak. We only had four days. Are you from Germany?"

"Yes."

"The mosquitoes here are pretty awful, eh?"

"The mosquitoes? Yes, there are many of them."

How do I smell? Heinrich wondered. How do I look? He went some distance off, farther along the riverbank, to pitch his tent. That night, he lay awake, visited by images of Hearne fingering the fabric of his tent, Hearne filling his pipe and the two of them smoking, Hearne shouting over the anguished cries of a young woman being murdered. He saw Inge at the bottom of a deep hole, and a row of naked children kneeling on the ice of the Turner Glacier; his father appeared, cradling a small engine attached to a board, and his mother listened to Karl or pretended to listen while the breeze played with the hem of her skirt. He knew he must not tell anyone what he'd witnessed or speak of his strange encounters. He could not explain, therefore he must keep silent. Was he going soft in the head?

He did not feel as if he were losing his mind. Perhaps his recent experiences could be explained. What he'd seen and heard had been tossed to the surface by the melting ice and the slowly shifting moraines. Tossed to the surface of his consciousness? Surging from where? This was the closest he could come to an understanding. It was incomplete and not an understanding he could expect anyone else to accept as proof of his sanity. He rolled up one of his T-shirts, placed it over his eyes, and listened to the sounds outside his tent, to water falling down a rock face, and to the quiet flow of this same fresh water spreading wide at the river's mouth. He heard the salty sea. It advanced and retreated, tugging at the mouth of the river.

PART FOUR

ᐸᖕᓂᖅᑐᖅ

Pangnirtung

Panniqtuuq

Place of Many Bull Caribou

1

A Woman's Knife

There were more houses, more cars and machinery than he remembered. This did not surprise him. He'd anticipated a shock. He'd foreseen that his return to "civilization" would feel like a head-on collision: his interior world confronted by a noisy place that claimed to be real and felt vaguely familiar but was wrapped in an aura of strangeness.

As the boat glided closer, headed for the harbor, he stood in the stern, exposed to the icy wind, and watched the roads, where cars and all-terrain vehicles raced people and objects from one fixed dwelling to the next.

The roads had widened and multiplied during his absence. Or perhaps his memory of them was inaccurate. Before setting out, he'd stayed barely twenty-four hours in Pangnirtung. As before, there were buildings with solid roofs and walls; there were front steps and back steps;

there were glass windows and metal chimneys. The long, low Hotel Pangnirtung, which crouched at the water's edge, was now painted blue rather than brown. Possibly it had never been brown? The Hudson's Bay shed, with its unmistakable white clapboard, its red roof, and black lettering that stated its year of construction, 1926, had not moved.

The boat bumped against the shore. Heinrich jumped onto the rocks, along with the other hikers. The packs were passed out and the boat's owner paid.

"Are you staying in Pangnirtung awhile?" the others asked.

"Yes," he answered. "Yes, I think so."

They were headed for the hotel.

"We'll see you then, at the hotel?"

"I'll come by later. I don't have a room reserved. The parks office, I must go there first, I think. Aren't we meant to tell them that we are safely returned?"

"In theory."

That was the idea, the others agreed, but before anything else they wanted a shower and a hot meal. He also longed to shower, to dress in clean clothes, to sit at a table and be served food that he'd not pulled from the bottom of his knapsack, measuring it out nervously, aware of how little remained.

"See you 'round."

"Yes. See you later."

Heinrich looked around him. Just as before, in the grass and flowers between the houses, snowmobiles waited, and heavy wooden sleds on runners waited; children's bicycles, battered toys, scraps of metal, discarded carpet, plastic, and shards of glass waited. There were char, headless and gutted, hanging out to dry on the front porch of the house nearest to him, and beside the back stairs of the next house over, two sealskins were stretched on frames and drying.

He remembered his immediate purpose and walked up to the visitors' center. The drab, single-story building overlooked the harbor. A large sign, above the door, stated: ANGMARLIK VISITOR CENTRE. He tried the door. It was locked. A broken window had been boarded over with a scrap of plywood cleaner and newer than the rest of the building.

A few meters to his left stood an unfamiliar structure with a cathedral ceiling and immense windows. An outside deck offered a panoramic view of the fjord, its drifting slabs of ice, and the high hills descending into the ocean. He could just make out the far-off entrance to the river valley. From there he'd emerged a little over an hour before. Heinrich contemplated the picture-perfect vista and tried to imagine himself still wandering inside it.

PARKS CANADA OFFICE, the sign above the door informed him. This was not, however, the "Parks Canada office" that he remembered. Could there be two? He pulled on the door, which opened, and he stepped into a narrow mudroom. On a low bench, he sat and removed his boots.

In his stocking feet, he entered a spacious foyer dominated by an information desk. Panels, mounted on the walls, displayed large photos of local flowers and lichen, of arctic fox and hares, of Mount Asgard and the Turner Glacier. There were photos of rushing streams and steep moraines. A teenage girl stood behind the information desk, quietly observing him.

"I've come to report my safe return."

The girl offered him a quick, shy smile, as no doubt she'd been instructed to do. Then she waited, silent and awkward, avoiding his gaze. Heinrich realized that he hadn't told her his name. He said his name, then spelled it. He explained that he'd been hiking in the park, though this seemed obvious.

She had short hair, and small breasts hidden under a loose T-shirt. For a moment he'd been uncertain if she was a girl or a boy. She was perhaps sixteen, he guessed. It must be a dull job, to sit behind a counter all day, waiting for hikers to walk in and ask questions, probably the same questions over and over.

Her eyes on a small screen that looked like a TV screen but wasn't one, she was typing hurriedly on a keyboard that appeared to be connected to the screen. What was this machine? As she typed, words appeared. From his side of the curved counter he could see only a portion of the screen and before he could stop himself he leaned forward, staring. She stopped typing.

"I've made a mistake. I must have entered a letter wrong, or I didn't hear your name right," she apologized. She slid a pen and a slip of paper across the counter. He wrote out his name.

"I hope my handwriting is not too bad."

She smiled.

"Not bad like mine," she assured him.

Again, she tapped on the keys. A list of people's names slipped into existence, slid up and down the screen, then vanished, replaced by more names, also numbers, indicating dates. He wanted to ask her about the machine she was using, but could feel himself blushing at the thought of revealing his ignorance to her.

"I can't find you. You're not in here."

"I'm not in where?" he asked.

"In these files. When did you enter the park?"

"On July 6."

Again, she tapped on the keys, searching. Then she shook her head, to indicate that she'd not succeeded, and he felt tempted to reach out and touch her thick, dark hair.

"Nope, not under July. I'll have to check with my supervisor when he comes in."

"Will that be soon?"

"Could be. He said this afternoon."

"Is there another thing I must do? May I leave, if you can't find me?"

She looked at him, amused.

"Do you want to watch a movie?" she asked.

"A movie?"

"Yup."

"Maybe. Thank you. Maybe later."

He looked once more at the strange typewriter, then glanced around the unfamiliar room, with its high ceiling and illustrative panels.

"Can I ask you something?" he said.

"Okay."

"Is there another parks office, somewhere else in Pang-nirtung?"

"Nope."

"It's just that this building, I don't recognize it. I sat at a table and signed the forms to enter the park, but in a different building."

Her warm, incredulous laugh softened the sharp edge of his unease. Some of the tension in his neck and shoulders loosened. Nonetheless, the room where they stood continued to make no sense to him.

"These ceilings, they're much higher than I remember, and the windows, and the platform outside . . ."

The girl was listening to him intently.

"I must be thinking of somewhere else," Heinrich concluded, overcome by shyness and confusion.

"We have some movies you can watch," she offered again. "Do you want to see a movie? They're about the park. There's a new one called *The Asgard Project*."

He declined. He thanked her for her patience and stepped outdoors into the brightness, into the midday dust and mosquitoes. A truck slowed, rolled down its window. There were people approaching on foot, talking as they made their way. There were people repeatedly stepping aside for passing cars and other traffic. There were frenetic vehicles, without doors, roofs, or windows, charging here and there, riding high on four big wheels, confident as military tanks yet driven by grandmothers and children. From the harbor came the dull, steady roar of more machinery, scraping and gouging.

Heinrich stood where he was, where he happened to be, on the shoulder of the road, and listened to the incessant, motorized travel linking one end of the village to the other. Movement and noise braided the gathering of houses into a whole, while just beyond the last dwellings spread the treeless silence of the wind-scoured land.

Heinrich walked to the hotel. The door of the hotel was locked. He tugged on the door. Through the glass, he could see that nobody was inside the small lobby, not one guest or employee. What met Heinrich's eye were a wooden bench, a stretch of muddy carpet, a collection of boots and shoes, the window of a small interior office, a pay phone attached to a wall, and, facing the phone, a stiff chair on metal legs. At the very back, four steps led up and out of sight. He banged on the door.

The wind blew in off the ice-clogged sea. His back to the frigid waters, he stared through the door's glass pane and waited. A heavy man wrapped in a large white apron came slowly hurrying until the width of him filled Heinrich's view. The door swung open and Heinrich stepped into the warmth.

"You want a room? Something to eat? A shower? What is it you want?"

The man had a soft face, clouded by worry. The pouches of loose, delicate skin under his eyes spoke of exhaustion. Heinrich swung his backpack off his shoulders. He wanted everything—a bed, hot water, food. He was about to ask the price but the man in the apron took a cigarette from his breast pocket, tapped the tight paper tube of tobacco on the back of his soft, pale hand, and continued to speak, a raw irritability rushing his words.

"I don't want to be rude. I am not a rude man. But I am upstairs cooking, and now I am down here with you, and I can't be in two places at once, not even I can do that. So you tell me. What is it you want?"

"I would like a room for tonight, and what is the price, please?"

The price shocked Heinrich. It was more than twice what he'd paid in Frobisher Bay. From the bottom of his pack he pulled out his wallet and counted the necessary sum.

"Tabarnak!" the man swore. "Where did you get those?"

The man in the apron lifted one of Heinrich's bills to the light. It was a fifty.

"At the bank. In Ottawa."

"I haven't seen one of these since twenty, twenty-five years. Maybe thirty years? But you don't remember that far back, you weren't born. Could be you found this somewhere?"

"I'm sorry? I don't understand."

Heinrich found the man's accent difficult to decipher. What was he saying about the money? Was he accusing him of theft or of counterfeit?

"Twenty years, thirty, that's how old these are, and you say you got them from the bank? How long ago was that? I take these to the bank, they will say to me: 'Go visit a collector of antiques or use them, peut-être, to blow your nose.'"

"I'm sorry. I do not understand. There is a problem with my money? In Frobisher Bay, two weeks ago, I paid for my room, my money was good, nobody told me I must return it to the bank."

"Nobody told you? Maybe you were handing out something else? Maybe someone had a bit to drink in Iqaluit? How should I know? All I know is that these dollars, a museum can use them, not me. I can't use them. Frobisher Bay, Frobisher Bay—nobody told you, the name it changed since seven years to Iqaluit?"

"Please, this is the only money I have. Is there a bank here, where I can exchange them?"

"You think I am inventing a little game?" The man in the apron opened the drawer of the cash register, took out a fifty, and slapped it on the counter; its design was markedly different from that of the bill in Heinrich's hand.

"Please, I believe you," Heinrich insisted, articulating carefully, hoping to calm the man, and to calm himself as well. "This is all I have, I have no other way to pay you for a room, or food, or anything else. But once I go to a bank. Is there a bank?"

The man in the apron put away the fifty-dollar bill that he'd taken from the drawer of his till. Then he took one of Heinrich's fifties and slid him some change in the newer currency across the counter.

"I am upstairs cooking. If I am not cooking, there is no lunch; and you have just paid for your lunch. Your room, she will cost you more. There is a bank machine in the Northern Store. You can go there, after lunch. The bank machine will still be there, after lunch. I am putting you in room fourteen. You will use the shower at the end of the hall, past the kitchen, please. There is one shower for men and one for women, and you will use the men's shower, please. I don't want any trouble."

His large hand placed a key on the counter. With a nod of his heavy head, he indicated the four steps leading out of sight at the back of the lobby.

"You will climb those steps, and up there, past the freezer, you will turn left. The door to your room, number fourteen, you will see it right away. Your name, please?"

Heinrich gave his name. "Do you need my passport?" he asked.

"I don't need your passport. I have my own."

"Thank you."

"Don't forget to take your boots off. Lunch will be at one o'clock, if there is any lunch. Am I cooking? Do you see me cooking? No, I am standing here talking with you, while my soup . . . Maudit, quelle vie, des piasses d'y a trente ans, on aura tout vu . . ."[21]

The key turned easily in door number fourteen, and Heinrich stepped into a room not much larger than a closet. Nailed to the blank wall facing the bed hung a calendar, advertising snowmobiles. It had the year wrong: 2010. The snowmobiles looked sleek and powerful. They were likely more reliable than the distracted person who, in

---

21 I may be exaggerating the shock expressed by the hotel's cook and manager at the sight of Heinrich's outdated money. If I'm exaggerating, it's because I've not been sleeping well. My neighbor is in a state of distress and I wake, worrying about her. When my nerves are on edge my sense of proportion becomes

distorted, or so I've been told. The Schlögel archive contains limited descriptive evidence of Heinrich's exact experiences on his return to Pangnirtung. Documentation has been difficult to come by. During his stay in Pangnirtung, Heinrich failed to make substantial entries in his notebooks. I don't blame him. He had a great deal to contend with, and the act of keeping a journal presupposes a degree of trust—perhaps not trust in others, but in the possibility of imposing order on the flow of days and weeks. A person who records regularly and meticulously believes in the desirability of pinning something down by careful notation. A person who records events is often (and I confess that I am generalizing) a person who believes that time can be relied on to abide by certain rules of chronology, and Heinrich, shortly after arriving in Pangnirtung, ceased to be such a person. Through the wall I hear my American neighbor talking on the telephone. Her tense voice pleads for news of her niece. The officials or volunteers on the other end of the line have no precise information to give her. Information is trickling out of Moore, Oklahoma—24 dead, 377 injured, and 1,150 homes destroyed—but none of it mentions her niece in particular. I turn on the radio and the morning news repeats, "Winds of unprecedented strength reached 340 kilometers per hour. Rescue efforts continue . . . cars lifted and tossed . . . six minutes' warning, then the elementary school collapsed . . . the number of dead uncertain . . . a boy pulled from beneath the rubble . . ." *Oklahoma* is the name of a musical. My parents saw it performed on their one trip to North America. This was before my birth. It was their first extravagant holiday. They flew to New York, stayed there a week in a fancy hotel. When I was a child, my father would often hum the melodies from *Oklahoma* but knew none of the lyrics.

doing the layout of the calendar, had leapt thirty years into the future. Or perhaps the error was intentional—a joke, a form of French Canadian humor? Possibly the reaction of the man in the apron to Heinrich's money was part of this same joke? The logic behind it all would become clear once Heinrich took a shower.

The bedroom's one window did not give onto the sea, but offered a view of the vinyl-sided house across the road. The room's vista also included an empty oil drum, a wooden sled, and a brilliant patch of blue sky.

Heinrich opened his pack and reached deep down. At the very bottom he'd saved a clean shirt, underwear, and socks, all tightly rolled together and crammed into a plastic bag. The bag was gone. He emptied his pack onto the bed, and the missing bag reappeared. He smoothed and spread out the T-shirt. He admired the socks and clean underwear.

In a few minutes, he'd walk down the hall, strip, and stand naked under a shower of hot water; hot water would hurl itself at his skin. He'd arrived at the end of his journey; he'd returned to civilization. He sat on the soft hotel bed and tried to picture the valley he'd just left. Already, the river and mountains were losing their precision. Only in the sore and swollen joints of his knees, in the fissured tips of his fingers, in the cracked skin of his lips did the valley and mountains feel fully present. His memory was hard at work, favoring certain images, ordering these, layering them, creating contrasts and connections, combining sounds, attributing smells. Not until this task of sorting and of assigning meaning was complete would the terrain through which he'd walked stop hanging in limbo, neither forgotten nor retrievable, capable of expressing itself only in the movements and aches of his body.

In the bathroom, tiles and taps confronted him; also, two sinks and a toilet, two shower stalls. As there was nobody else in the room, Heinrich undressed slowly. He turned on the water, adjusted the temperature until it was as hot as he could bear. The heat pummeled his shoulders and neck; he stepped a few inches forward and the intensity of it struck his lower back.

The hot water removed the relentless effort of the past weeks; it took away his fear of high winds, of cold and violent rain; with a washcloth he scrubbed from his skin the trembling, exuberant purple of fireweed and the milky green flow of the Weasel River; he cleansed his chest of the anticipation of fast-moving currents that might grab and hold him under. The shower cleaned him indiscriminately. The need to wait until such a time as he could cross a river safely was washed from his body, along with the grit from between his toes and the soreness in his calves; he could not choose what to keep and what to lose: patience was removed as well as fear. The jets of water cleansed his skin of mudflats and of the granular surface of the Turner Glacier; the heat dissolved set rhythms that his movements had acquired—the repeated bending and reaching in order to unfasten the numerous clips on his pack, and the continual stuffing and compressing of clothing and food into the pack's interior.

When he could clean nothing more from his body he stepped out of the shower, refreshed and emptied. It had been a necessary emptying. Later the valley would reenter him, but first this hotel was making itself known, and he felt ready to receive it.

Past the kitchen, through the lounge and dining room, down a short flight of steps, past the freezer, around the corner he went, and came once more to room fourteen— his room. He slipped the key into the lock and the door opened easily.

He dropped his dirty clothes on the floor, then hung his damp towel over the back of the chair beside the bed. He took the wall calendar down from its nail. AURORA SNOWMOBILES, IQALUIT.

No mention of Frobisher Bay, instead the Inuit name for the town, the name that the man in the apron had used. Iqaluit. A rumbling sound, escaping from his stomach, reminded him that he was hungry. He returned the calendar to its place on the wall, left his room, and headed for the dining room.

Already, the men who spent their long days dredging and expanding the harbor had come in and were eating, their laughter and talk reverberating under the room's low ceiling. Heinrich spotted an empty chair.

"This is not taken?"

A rawboned young man looked up from cleaning his bowl with a piece of bread. He used the edge of his napkin to wipe the soup from his moustache. His wide smile revealed tightly packed teeth. He gestured for Heinrich to sit down, and Heinrich did so. A woman wearing heavy-rimmed glasses appeared at their table and served them each a plate of char.

"Bertrand," the lanky young workman announced, and he thrust out his hand, which Heinrich shook with deliberate vigor.

"Heinrich," said Heinrich.

They spoke between mouthfuls of the succulent fish.

"Chicoutimi, Québec. That's my hometown. And you? You are from Germany?"

"Yes. I come from a small place. Not so big like Munich or Frankfurt. A town for making beer."

A picture window ran the length of the dining room's western wall. Outdoors, the sea was gently rocking its cargo of ice.

"You are working on the pier?"

Bertrand nodded. "It's a big job. They spend lots of money for this, the government."

"The man in the apron."

"Pierre?"

"I don't know his name. He runs the hotel, I think, and he does the cooking. Has he ever told you your money is no good, it is too old?"

Bertrand lowered his fork, a roar of laughter rising from his chest.

"That my money is no good?" His words exploded. "My money, I tell you what Monsieur Pierre, he do with my money, he put it in his pocket. You tell him, if he don't want yours, if your money is too old for him, he can give it to me! Eille, Pierre, tu m'entends, Pierre?" Bertrand, twisting in his chair, called in the direction of the kitchen, his voice traveling over the heads of the assembled men, most of them bent to the task of eating. "Eille, Monsieur Pierre . . ."

Pierre came from the kitchen, balancing two plates of fish, and paused long enough to see who was calling him.

"Oui, Monsieur Boisvert," he answered. "Et, qu'est-ce que je peux faire pour vous? My soup, it's not to your taste? Et mon excellent poisson non plus? Maudit!"

"Ta soupe, Monsieur Pierre . . ." Bertrand began. But already, Pierre had set down the two plates and disappeared back into the kitchen.

"The food is very good," Heinrich remarked.

He gazed around the room, his eyes surveying the walls. Somewhere, there must be a calendar, he thought, but he could see none.

"Eh oui. Pour ça, oui. Vous avez raison. Nobody cooks like Monsieur Pierre. I been all over the North. You don't get meals better, not even in Chicoutimi. What Monsieur Pierre says, well, you can't always believe, you gotta remember he's a joker, but his cooking, you know it will be more than good, always."

At the back of the room sat a television set with its sound turned off, mute images parading across a screen far larger than any television screen Heinrich had ever seen. At least I know what it is, he thought. Perhaps the news will come on, and even though I won't be able to hear anything, a date will appear. He shifted his attention from Bertrand Boisvert to the figures on the screen.

Dressed in a pale blue suit, a stout man, smiling, was leading a young couple through an apartment. He paused to open a closet door. He pointed joyfully at a light fixture, then swept his arm in an expansive gesture. Across the bottom of the screen in bright letters glided the words: *Via Luigi Pirandello,19*, followed by a price. No year or month. Again, the address and price slid by, as the salesman ushered his clients out onto a tiny balcony. From there the camera swooped down, took in cars, cafés, and shops, circled a fountain, followed a pigeon up into the azure sky. Rome? Heinrich wondered. Milan? Without warning Italy was gone, replaced by a long-legged woman with an exceptionally prominent chin, leading a new, more sober couple through a different apartment. *56 Rue Descartes* flashed across the screen and a price. France had ousted Italy. Paris, City of Light, or one of its many suburbs? Still no month or year. Discouraged, Heinrich redirected his attention to his table companion, who was once more wiping his plate with a piece of bread.

"Do you have this in Germany, the real-estate shows?" Bertrand asked.

"I don't think so. I've never seen one."

"Paris, London, Rome, they are good for some people. Me, I choose Lisbon."

"Can you tell me, please, what year it is?"

Heinrich knew how strange his question must sound, but he couldn't wait any longer. Bertrand Boisvert looked him in the eye.

"What year it is?" Bertrand echoed.

"Yes, please, what year?"

"2010."

"2010?"

Bertrand laughed, and Heinrich tried to laugh with him, but his heart was racing and his mouth felt dry.

"You wanted, maybe, that last year should go on forever?"

He could feel Bertrand Boisvert's eyes studying him with open curiosity.

The voices of the hotel guests, in cacophonous unity, twisted and moved through the room like a cloud of birds. Birds, thought Heinrich, reveal the sky for what it is. The shifting shape of their flight shows that the sky is not flat, just as voices rising and falling in the confines of a room reveal time for what it is, a gathering and parting of movements seeking direction and shape.

These thoughts did not comfort him. They did nothing to alleviate his confusion and fear. "2010" continued to reverberate in his ear, a future year pronounced into immediate existence by Bertrand Boisvert.

There must be some misunderstanding, Heinrich told himself. Perhaps Bertrand Boisvert knows about the calendar in my room and he's pulling my leg? Does every room have a calendar with the same mistake? Or have I been singled out? Singled out for what? The girl at the parks office couldn't find me in her files, inside her typewriter that was not a typewriter. Already while I was hiking my sense of time felt off-kilter. Did I really meet Hearne? I saw my grandfather toss his shoes into the river. I thought it was all happening because of my solitude, and the shifting rocks and melting ice. I thought that once I left the valley I'd stop witnessing strange scenes, and time would unfold as usual. Am I not hearing correctly? Not seeing properly? I expected that everything would settle into place, once I was less alone. Am I less alone? For Bertrand, time appears to be flowing quite predictably. Can he see what is happening to me? Does it show?

Heinrich excused himself and got up from the table, pushing back his chair more violently than he'd intended. He hurried from the dining room and down the hall to the safety and privacy of his room.

He sat on the bed, facing the terrible wall calendar, and questioned himself further. He tried to slow his breathing and to follow each of his thoughts through to a logical outcome. How could thirty years have possibly elapsed while he'd hiked to the Turner Glacier and back? He'd have run out of food. He'd now be fifty years old. What year was it in Germany? Could his father be eighty-two? Was Karl still alive? And Helene? And Inge? How was he to replace his passport?

"Aurora Snowmobiles: The Best Buys in Iqaluit," the calendar promised. His head throbbed and his throat felt constricted. He grabbed the calendar from the wall and tore it into pieces. By doing so, he achieved nothing. Questions, reproductive as flies, buzzed and proliferated inside his head. Though seated, he felt he was losing his balance.

I must call Jeremy, he decided, and he stood up. I'll return Jeremy's tent to him and his cooking pots and stove. He started looking around the room for Jeremy's pots. The contents of his knapsack lay in two heaps, one heap on the floor and the other on the bed. He rummaged in the heap on the bed, felt his camera, and extracted it. The familiar object lay in his hands. If I call Jeremy, he'll tell me to relax. "Take it easy, man." He won't take what I say seriously. There's no point calling him. Instead, I must photograph every detail. If I photograph what is happening, later I will have evidence.

Clutching his camera, he ran from the room, his feet pounding along the corridor. Outside, he stepped into the sun's brilliance and the wind's strength. Behind the hotel, sheltered somewhat from the wind, he tugged off his hiking boots and socks. He photographed his bare feet and the rock beneath his feet. He rolled up his pants and shot his knees. If he'd not been scared that someone might come around the corner, he would have undressed completely and shot every inch of himself. He lifted his shirt and photographed his navel. The skin on his stomach and chest had neither loosened nor wrinkled. His body looked thinner but no older than when he'd started his long walk. His socks he stuffed into his boots, and his boots he tied together and hung around his neck. His hands were now fully free to operate the camera, and he ran.

He looked around as he ran. A set of tire tracks veered across the road. He shot these tire marks, and the cotton grass, and the pristine sky. He raced down the road, ignoring the pain of haphazard, sharp stones under his bare feet. He photographed the rusting husk of a snowmobile, shot a satellite dish, then slipped between two houses and trotted beside the wire fence separating the airport runway from the town. He shot the fence, he shot the runway, then he turned and saw the sea. Slowing his pace because of a stitch in his side, he jogged left then right, between more houses, and came upon a church. Balancing on tiptoe, spying through a window, he framed the pews. He trotted around to the front of the church, and through the vestibule window he zoomed in on a baby's bottle left on a shelf. Pinned to the wall hung a display of large brown leaves mummified in transparent plastic. The leaves caught his eye and held his attention. They'd been used, perhaps, to teach the names of trees that grew in the south of Canada, trees hard to imagine: oak, maple, cedar, and birch. He shot the leaves. A brief pressure applied to the correct button, the shutter closed, and off he ran. He jogged past the Northern Store, picking up speed, ignoring the soreness of his feet and the invisible blade that jabbed between his ribs. He collapsed on the rocks and meager grass behind the hotel.

His efforts were wasted. Taking all these photographs proved nothing. What if he was dreaming all of it—the camera in his hands, the dirt and stones under the soles of his feet? It struck him that time had tried to turn him into a photograph. Time had behaved like a camera, snatching him from the regular flow of months and years, so as to set him apart. Would people start staring at him, would they put him on display, as they'd done long ago with Abraham Ulrikab, and sell tickets? "Step right up, see the German who slipped through a hole in time."

Not one of his shots proved his sanity; not one of the images captured by his camera could explain what had happened to him or diminish his solitude. He yanked open the back of his camera and allowed the brilliant light to devour everything. He sat on the ground, arms wrapped around his knees, and sobbed.

Sobbing exhausted him. The name Jeremy Burton surfaced in his mind. I must call Jeremy Burton and give him back his stove, his cooking pots and their lids, he thought. With this as his goal, he lifted his head from his knees. In the hotel lobby he'd seen a pay phone. His money might be out of date, but he had the change given to him by Monsieur Pierre. He pulled on his socks and boots, stood up, and walked around to the front of the hotel.

In the palm of his hand lay a few nickels, pennies, and dimes, also several quarters and dollar coins. The telephone accepted all but the pennies, said the information on the front of the phone. He hoped he had enough for a brief long-distance call. He punched zero, followed by the set of numbers he'd written on a scrap of paper and tucked, decades or perhaps two weeks ago, into the tiny pocket of his camera case for safekeeping. The cost per minute for an Iqaluit call appeared in bright numbers on a small screen above the coin slot. He counted out the correct amount. The coins, accompanied by a metallic sound, disappeared through the slot. He heard them drop, one by one, inside the telephone's collection box, and he waited. He'd bought himself one minute of time.

In Iqaluit, or whatever place Frobisher Bay had become, a telephone rang. The ringing persisted, and Heinrich hoped fervently that Jeremy would be at home, that Jeremy would be the one to answer. The ringing continued, and then it stopped.

"Hello?" said a woman.

"Could I speak to Jeremy Burton, please?"

"There's no Jeremy here."

"Will he be in later?"

"You have the wrong number."

"I am looking for Jeremy Burton."

"You don't hear so good?"

"I'm sorry."

"No problem. Your friend gave you the wrong number, that's all."

"Thank you."

"You sure he lives in Iqaluit? I never heard of him."

"He works at the radio station."

"You could try there. But my cousin, she works at the station, and she never spoke of no Jeremy Burton."

"Thank you. I am sorry, so sorry to bother you."

"Like I said, no problem."

"Goodbye. I thank you."

Heinrich lowered the receiver from his ear. Jeremy had moved and probably didn't work at the radio station anymore. But did that prove that thirty years had disappeared? A dull humming emanated from the plastic object in his hand. How much proof do I need? he wondered. Too tired to think, he sat down on the stiff chair next to the phone, the receiver still in his hand. After a few seconds, he stood up and hooked the object in its cradle.

For Germany he'd have to call collect. He punched zero, and a recorded voice spoke to him. He asked to place a collect call to "Tettnang, West Germany." He enunciated clearly, giving the correct number and his father's name, then his mother's. He waited. Far away, a telephone rang. He pictured his father getting up from his reading chair to cross the living room, his mother coming in from the garden. The ringing stopped abruptly.

"Allo?" asked a voice, an old voice but unmistakably his father's.

"Papa?"

"Who is speaking, please?"

"It is me, Papa. Heinrich."

Something solid shifted. An ashtray or perhaps a book was knocked over onto a hard surface.

"Papa?"

Heinrich waited, listening. He could hear his father's labored breathing.

"Whoever you are," said his father's voice, "you are not my son, and I am not your father."

The voice went silent. Then it spoke again, with the same authority.

"I have read about people like you in the paper."

Far away, air entered and left his father's lungs. Heinrich could hear the rasping.

"Don't you recognize my voice, Papa?"

"You amuse yourself by stealing and intimidating. You try to confuse the old and the weak. But I am not so weak or so easily confused as you'd like me to be."

Silence.

Heinrich's palms were now sweating, and he wiped his free hand on a leg of his pants. With his other hand he gripped the receiver as tightly as possible.

"I took the plane from Munich, Papa. You and Mama saw me off."

The leg of a chair scraped across the floor.

"Do you remember? July 2, 1980. Inge was there also. I flew to Ottawa, Canada."

The silence at the other end of the line thickened and spread.

"Please, Papa, I want to explain. I wish I understood, then I could explain. I am staying in a hotel in Pangnirtung, on Baffin Island. I am in room number fourteen. Two weeks ago, I left on foot, I crossed the Arctic Circle, I walked for two weeks, or maybe for thirty years."

Again the leg of a chair, or some other piece of furniture, scraped, and his father's breathing was audible once more.

"What year is it in Tettnang? 2010? But you see, I'm not any older. No, you don't see. How can you? How long have I been gone? You must have come looking for me. Did you? I am so sorry, Papa. Did you come all this way? Will you say something?"

Heinrich held perfectly still. Somewhere, perhaps in his father's house, or outside an open window, a dog barked, then stopped barking. Heinrich listened. He could no longer hear his father's breathing. Had his father set the receiver down on a table or chair and gone out into the garden? Maybe he'd gone to get Helene, to get Mama? Heinrich perched on the edge of his chair and waited.

"Heinrich?"

It was his father's voice, the same voice as a few minutes earlier but more tired, and with a new hesitancy.

"Yes."

"Is it possible?"

"Yes. Yes it is possible."

A wild hope seized him. He felt intensely eager and his pulse quickened. He heard water rush from a tap, then stop rushing. He pictured a glass being set down, and heard silence surround it.

"I would like to think so."

"Shall I tell you your nickname? Your nickname is Gi-raffe. Your older brother gave it to you."

A fit of coughing, then slow, careful breathing.

"How did you find this out?"

"Schiller is your favorite, or one of them, Schiller's *Letters on Aesthetic Education*. Chocolate is the only candy you like, and you don't let anyone else polish your shoes."

"Whoever you are, you have done your research well."

Heinrich pressed on.

"On our hikes together, we took dark chocolate and apples. I know that you brought the chocolate to please me and to reward me. I didn't need a reward. I always loved to walk. It was what I did best. It was the only way I could please you."

Heinrich waited. Perhaps, he thought, I've said too much? He held perfectly still so as not to scare his father away.

At last his father spoke.

"I do not know why you have chosen to make me the object of your nasty little game. Your prank is not amusing. I may be an old man but I am not so old that I have forgotten how to report a crime like yours to the authorities. You have been trying to find things out about me, but you don't frighten me. You won't succeed. The police know very well how to stop people like you. If you assault me in this way again, you will be stopped."

"Papa, I have frightened you. I've said too much. I am sorry."

Again the barking of a dog. Was it the same dog? Did his father own a dog? What did it matter if there was a dog or not?

"I understand that you do not believe me. But you must, Papa. I know things about you, things a stranger could not know. I am not saying this to frighten you but so that you will understand. How could a stranger find out your nickname and know that you have read, over and over, Schiller's *Letters on Aesthetic Education*, or that your son lost your knife with the walnut handle when he was thirteen years old? I did that, Papa. I am the one who lost your knife."

The line went dead. Had his father hung up the phone and if so, on purpose or inadvertently? Heinrich, the muscles in his throat tightening, again punched zero and stated his father's name and telephone number. Far away a phone rang. It continued to ring. Someone lifted the receiver but did not speak.

"May I speak with Helene Schlögel, please?"

"Who are you?" asked his father.

Heinrich repeated his request.

"May I speak with Helene Schlögel, please?"

"No."

"I want to speak with my mother. Even if you do not believe me, perhaps she will listen. I can tell you about her also. When she was a child she was made to stand on a dock for hours because she refused to dive headfirst into Lake Constance."

"Your research has been inaccurate. Helene Schlögel no longer lives here."

"I have not done any research." He could no longer keep the anger and frustration from his voice. "Where has she gone?"

"I will not tell you."

"You must tell me."

"I don't have to tell you anything."

"And Inge? What about Inge?"

"I'm sure you will make inquiries. Extensive inquiries. You seem to be very good at finding things out about people."

There was a sharp bang, not metallic but wooden, as if a small drawer had been shoved or knocked into place.

"I am Heinrich Schlögel. I am your son."

There was a sound of papers shifting, followed by silence, next a throat being cleared of phlegm. More elastic silence stretched. It was stretching between what fixities?

"What is your reason for doing this?"

"I have no reason except to speak with you."

Again, the line went dead.

For several moments Heinrich sat without moving, all coherent thought erased from his mind. Again he punched zero, gave his father's name and number, and once more he heard ringing. The ringing continued, it persisted. He's not going to accept the call, thought Heinrich, and he wanted to walk out the door of the hotel lobby, to keep walking, but he was clutching the receiver in his hand and the ringing would not allow him to leave. Then the ringing stopped. He heard a cough escape from deep in his father's chest.

"Papa?"

"Why have you chosen my son? Why is it me you are attacking?"

"I want to speak with you."

"I wish to know your motivation."

"I've told you. I want to speak with you. You are my father. Please do not look for a logical explanation. You must choose to trust me. If I tell you that I broke my left arm at the age of ten, what use will that be? You'll just accuse me of doing research. What if I tell you that I slipped through a hole in time? Will that do as an explanation? I do not understand any more than you do. I know only this: you can choose to trust me. Please, Papa. I need you."

Once more the barking of a dog. His father's dog?

"My son disappeared thirty years ago. People do not reappear after thirty years of absence except in books and films. People do not claim to have slipped through a hole in time unless they are unwell."

"Perhaps I did not slip through a hole in time. I was only trying to offer an explanation. The truth is that I don't understand. I only know who I am, I am Heinrich Schlögel, your son, that's all I am certain of."

A fit of coughing, quickly stifled.

"Are you all right, Papa? You don't sound well. Are you alone?"

"Why do you ask if I'm alone?"

"I want to be sure you are safe."

"You sound just like my son."

There was tenderness in his father's voice. Heinrich felt he'd been punched in the stomach. He listened for the slightest shift in his father's breathing.

"You are a very troubled young man."

"Yes."

"My son had a gentleness, a deep sympathy for all living creatures."

"Yes."

"It took me a long time to accept his death."

Heinrich leaned against the wall beside the pay phone.

"We are all animals. We die."

"Yes."

"For a long time, I imagined that one day my son might reappear. There would be a knock on the door, or I would be crossing the town square and I would see him."

"And then?"

"At last, I accepted my son's death. I no longer fought against it."

"Papa, from Pangnirtung, I took a boat to the end of a fjord and for two weeks I walked, the way you and I used to walk on Sundays in the countryside, only this time I was carrying a tent, a camp stove, and twelve days' worth of food. I never ran out of food or lost my way; at the end of my long walk I met up with some other hikers, and the fisherman that came for them gave me a ride also. That was early this morning. This morning I arrived back in Pangnirtung. Until a few hours ago, I did not realize that anything was wrong."

"I can tell that you believe in your story. And you want something from me. My help? What sort of assistance are you hoping for? I am not the right person for you to ask. Your invention has nothing to do with me or with my son. You have robbed my son, taking parts of his life to fabricate your elaborate tale. Why you've chosen to include my family in your fantasy, I don't know. There are many things that I do not understand. Soon enough, it will be my turn to die, and when I do so I will perhaps come to understand more than I do now. Until that time, I wish to be left in peace."

Heinrich let go of the receiver. It dangled from its cord. He snatched it up again.

"I am sorry, Papa. I am sorry to have disturbed you."

"I don't want you to call again. I cannot help you. What you need is a good doctor."

"Papa."

"I am tired. Goodbye."

A click, followed by a dull humming, a meaningless drone that would have continued indefinitely had Heinrich not put an end to it by hanging up the receiver. A profound exhaustion overcame him. Only once before had he felt this tired. He'd sat, that other time, on a sidewalk, his feet in the gutter and cars speeding past, while in a hospital bed his sister raved and hallucinated. Now, he slumped on a stiff chair, facing a pay phone attached to a wall.

Night refused to come. At last, Heinrich Schlögel, who was no longer Heinrich Schlögel according to his father, stood and made his way upstairs to the hotel lounge. On the sofa under the picture window, he stretched out and waited. He did so without asking himself what he was waiting for. The calm surface of the sea glowed pink and orange, reflecting the gaudy sky that would not darken for another month or two.

On the shore, a figure stood on a wooden dock that jutted out into the water. Heinrich sat up straight to get a better view. The small person appeared to be his mother. She was about ten or eleven years old, dressed in a bathing suit. He pressed his face up to the glass of the window, which was designed not to open. He watched her curl and uncurl her bare toes. Her toes came into sudden, unexpected focus, as if he were observing them through a pair of binoculars.

For several minutes all she did was curl and uncurl her toes. The water lapped. Through the closed window he could not hear the water's soothing, repetitive murmur. He contemplated, however, the small waves rumpling the surface of the ocean.

It pleased Heinrich that his mother's bare feet remained firmly planted on the dock and that she did not dive. Those children who had already dived sat on the shore and observed her. He imagined his mother's fingers breaking the surface, her head entering the sea, the sea that concealed large, silently approaching fish.

Minutes passed. The girls who were gathered on the shore stared at the plump, plain girl who was his mother, his mother as she'd been when she wore thick glasses that might at any moment shatter and blind her, were she to run or try to catch a ball, his mother before beauty pounced.

The girls on the shore observed his mother's plainness and feared it; they observed her solitude and feared it. They were united by having already dived. Helene's refusal to dive, her refusal to join in, offended them. They did not want to witness weakness and strength inextricably intertwined within one solitary girl. Heinrich, watching them through the window, sensed their fear. The girls on the shore, the girls united by having dived, felt insulted by the thick round lenses of Helene's glasses. Often, at lunch, when she sat in silence, looking down at her plate, they felt that she was passing judgment on them, as if she were an owl or an old woman. Heinrich understood this.

Heinrich watched his mother's toes curling and uncurling on the wooden dock. She was visibly deciding that between her and those who had dived no compromise was possible. A breeze, delicate as a surgeon, lifted the skin of the sea and folded it back.

Somehow, thought Heinrich, I must find my mother. I must rescue her.[22]

Close to midnight, Monsieur Pierre appeared in the hotel lounge, and Heinrich asked him for a job.

"I think that I must stay here for a while, in Pangnirtung. My plans have changed. Do you know where I could get work?"

"You want to work, eh? Tu me laisses un moment? I need a moment, a little moment. We all need a bit of time, no? I can't do everything at once."

Monsieur Pierre disappeared into the kitchen, and Heinrich found himself once more alone in the lounge. Three mismatched sofas surrounded a low coffee table, and in the back corner, a half-sized refrigerator kept liters

---

22 Why was Heinrich plucked from the year 1980 and deposited in the year 2010? Was it so that he might bear witness? To our collective madness? Through my wall I hear music. My neighbor's niece has been found and taken to a hospital. They predict that she will recover well from her injuries. Yesterday, my neighbor knocked on my door to bring me the good news. Impulsively, I threw my arms around her and felt my neighbor's unfamiliar body pressed against mine, the warmth of her happiness. Then I closed my door and washed my dishes.

of milk and plastic pitchers of orange juice cool, its motor humming steadily. Someone had set out a plate of freshly baked butter tarts, accompanied by a note that read: "$4.00 each. Help yourself. Put payment in jar."

Heinrich eyed the tarts and considered stuffing some of his outdated money into the jar. Monsieur Pierre returned with an unlit cigarette clamped between his lips and a pitcher of lemonade in his hand.

"You could try the fish plant, or the Northern Store. What can you do? Have you worked before? You want a glass of my lemonade? No smoking in here. Too bad for me. There is the balcony."

He removed the cigarette, which had stuck to his lower lip, and tucked it in the pocket of his apron. He glanced inquiringly at Heinrich.

"At home, in Germany, I worked picking and preparing the hops for making beer. I also have completed high school. And yes, please, I would like lemonade. Thank you."

"At the fish-processing plant, the work, he comes and goes. I tell you how it is—if you are an Inuk and have a job, the government it is charging you more for electricity than if you don't go to work. When you work, they are increasing your rent. You are better to go fishing for yourself, if you have a boat. Or you carve stone for the tourists. The fish plant is often short of workers. You go there, tell them Monsieur Pierre sent you."

"Thank you, Monsieur Pierre."

The cook, dismissing Heinrich's thanks with a weary gesture, sat down on the sofa nearest to the windows and closed his eyes. He asked, "Dites-moi, do you know *The Glass Bead Game* by Hermann Hesse?"

"Yes. I have heard of it."

"This is my favorite book. It is one of the best books ever written. Hermann Hesse. Hermann Hesse is a very good writer, a huge writer."

"I have not read it. I read very slowly."

"How slowly?"

"I have read *Narcissus and Goldmund*."

"That is a good start. C'est mieux que rien."

"And you, Monsieur Pierre? What makes you stay here, managing this hotel, cooking all the meals?"

"Ten years, tabarnak. It's like this. How should I say? I arrived at this place and I never left, I am too busy working to leave, too tired to go somewhere else. Besides. Did you see? Did you notice?"

With a sweep of his arm he indicated, through the window, the glowing pink and orange sky.

"Such luminosité. There is nowhere else. Ten years in this room, and never a night exactly like this one, never. Incroyable. You are looking at it? You see it? Wait here, I'll bring you something, wait. Incroyable, un ciel de même."

No sooner had Monsieur Pierre left for the kitchen than Heinrich sank into the sofa and allowed his exhaustion to overtake him. Somewhere to live—the thought formed behind the closed lids of his eyes. I'll need a place to live, a room cheaper than my room in this hotel. He heard his father's voice: "You are not my son." He kept his eyes firmly closed.

Monsieur Pierre returned, bearing a plate of carefully arranged delicate slices of char, wedges of lemon, rings of onion, and tiny green capers.

"Eat, eat. One hundred platters of gravlax, I once served, on the main street in Boston, to the big delegation, one hundred platters, tabarnak, and they wanted more, so we gave them more, on the main street in Boston."

He held out a fork, which Heinrich accepted.

"Eat, eat my gravlax. What was the name of that street, the main one in Boston? I don't remember. But my gravlax you will not forget. The name of a street—it goes; the taste of my gravlax—it stays. And out there, regarde-moi cette luminosité." He threw his arms wide, revealing the beauty of the world.

Heinrich ate; he forked the tender fish into his mouth, pools of lemon and salt gathering on his tongue.

"Is there a room?" Heinrich asked. "Do you know, please, in town, in someone's house maybe, a room that would cost me not so much to stay?"

"You don't like my gravlax? Ostie. And I thought, here is a young man of education, of finesse, with him I will discuss Hermann Hesse, we will eat my gravlax and talk of *The Glass Bead Game*, of *Siddhartha*."

"I am sorry. I am a slow reader. Please, Monsieur Pierre, I must earn money to buy a plane ticket home. Your cooking is very good, so good, and I cannot stop myself from eating, you see?"

With the tines of his fork Heinrich speared the last morsel of fish and lifted it eagerly into his mouth.

"Ha! So you do like my gravlax? Good. You will go speak with Sarah, Sarah Ashevak. She will tell you if she has a room. You can go see her tomorrow."

"Tomorrow, yes. Thank you, thank you so much, Monsieur Pierre. Sarah Ashevak, I will go see her. Where will I find her?"

"I will tell you the way to her house, tomorrow. Now I am tired. I am going to bed. One day I won't get up in the morning. They will come find me in my bed and complain, 'Monsieur Pierre, your crêpes, your delicious crêpes, we are waiting to eat some, and our plates are empty, and you are not in your kitchen.' 'You are right,' I will answer. 'I am in my bed. I am warm and comfortable in my bed.'"

"Good night, Monsieur Pierre, and thank you."

Despite the late hour, and the weariness that made his head heavy, Heinrich lingered in the lounge. He looked out at the sea and down at the shore, but his mother was gone. Once more, he stretched out on the sofa and closed his eyes.

In the morning, he received directions from Monsieur Pierre and headed out to find Sarah Ashevak. In front of the Parks Canada office the teenage girl whom he'd spoken with on the previous day stood smoking a cigarette.

"Hello," she said, and she sounded neither pleased nor displeased to see him.

"Oolako."

Hearing his pronunciation, she grinned.

"Oola̱ko," she corrected.

"Oola̱ko."

"Oo."

"Oo."

"La."

"La."

"Ko."

"Ko."

"Oola̱ko."

"Oola̱ko?"

"Never mind, Mr. Deadman." She blew a ring of smoke. "You remember, I couldn't find you in the computer? I looked in the old records, the paper ones. You disappeared thirty years ago."

"I am in your records? You have my file?"

Relief traveled, small and trembling, down his spine and along his arms, and he half expected to see his arms start floating at his sides, such a powerful sensation of lightness was spreading through him.

"Your family came looking for you. One of them left you this letter. I was gonna bring it to you when I get off work. It was in your file."

She pulled an envelope from her back pocket and held it out. He snatched it from her and read—"For Heinrich Schlögel." His name was penned on the outside, in a hand unmistakably Inge's, the tiny vowels crushed between stiffly upright consonants. With utmost care, fighting the desire to tear at it, he unsealed the envelope.

"You don't look much older than me, Mr. Deadman," the girl murmured, shifting her gaze away from him and down the road, as if an unexpected sound had caught her attention.

He did not respond but started reading. The shaking of his hands made it hard for him to decipher his sister's words.

"You all right?" the girl asked.

He nodded.

"You sure you don't need any help? Some crackers? A cup of tea?"

She lingered for a moment, watching him. She would have preferred not to feel so nakedly curious about this qallunaaq who had stared at her computer screen the day before as if he'd never seen one; a qallunaaq whose name belonged to someone who'd disappeared out on the land decades ago.

He glanced up from the letter in his hands, but he did not respond to her offer of crackers and tea, and his eyes returned quickly to the words that he was holding. Over and over again, he kept reading them. She left him and went back into the parks office.

Heinrich, perched on the edge of a picnic table overlooking the wharfs and the fjord, began once more at the top of the page:

August 28, 1980

Dear Heinrich,

Since you are reading this you must be alive. I cannot stay here any longer. I am going to Toronto. It is my fault you came to this country. Mama and Papa have just gone back to Tettnang. They are devastated. They will want you to come to them straightaway. Perhaps, if you are in fact reading this, you ought to go straight home. I will send them my address so that you can write to me. I don't know where exactly I'll be living. I have met a woman here, in the weaving studio, who is being very generous. She came to learn from the weavers but has now returned to Toronto, and has told me that I should go there. She thinks that she may be able to help me. I do not want to go back to Germany. Tomorrow, when I arrive in Toronto, I will start looking for work. If I can give German lessons or do some translating, and not be thrown out of the country, I will stay and wait for you. I will let Mama and Papa know my address, once I have found an apartment and have a telephone number where I can be reached. I must choose to believe that soon you will be reading this letter. I hope we will speak again, my dearest brother. Be well.

Inge

He slipped the letter carefully back into its envelope, got up from the picnic table, started to lose his balance but caught himself. Through an effort of concentration he walked. He lifted one foot, placed it down solidly before lifting the other foot, and by this method he reached the door of the Parks Canada office. The door swung open without resistance. He stepped meticulously inside.

"Please. I must find a telephone number in Toronto. Can you help me?"

The girl was typing on the same small keyboard as the day before.

"Whose phone number do you want? What street do they live on?"

"Her name is Inge Schlögel. She's my sister. I don't know her address."

The girl's fingers knew where to go and darted from key to key while her eyes examined the screen that was not a TV screen. It was somehow receiving information from her typing fingers. He'd never been good at typing.

"54 Raglan Avenue. Your sister lives at 54 Raglan Avenue and her phone number is 416-654-7839."

He leaned forward and saw Inge's name written on the little screen, followed by her address and telephone number.

"Do you have a telephone I can use?"

"Not for long distance. Maybe at the hotel."

"Thank you."

He turned to go.

"You think, in Toronto they won't notice you're dead?" she asked, grinning.

He stared at her. For several seconds he stopped breathing.

"You're right, they probably won't notice," she continued. "There's lots they don't notice in Toronto, that's what my grandma says. You'll be okay, Deadman."

"Excuse me, I must go and telephone my sister."

"Computers. You haven't used computers much, eh?" she asked. "That's because you've been out on the land a long time. You have lots of catching up to do. That's what they used to tell me in school, lots of catching up."

"I must go to the hotel and call my sister."

The girl shrugged.

"Qarasaujaq," she remarked. "Something that works like a brain, that's the way we say 'computer' in Inuktitut. You want to call your sister from here? If you don't stay on the line too long, you can use this phone. I'm not meant to do this. But for you, Deadman, it's okay."

She lifted the receiver, held it out to him across the counter. She dialed.

His heart had become a small animal scurrying in circles. He would have liked to sit on the floor, to slide down slowly, the information counter supporting his back. But the telephone cord was not long enough to allow such a descent, and so he remained standing.

The ringing was cut off by a recorded announcement. A gently reprimanding female voice informed him, "The number you have dialed is no longer in service." The small animal inside his chest held still. While the woman repeated her message his fingers released the receiver, which was no longer of any use to him. The plastic object struck the counter and lay there. He could hear the woman inside the receiver urging him to take action: "Please check your number and try your call again."

The girl's thoughtful eyes observed him. She reached out, took hold of the receiver, and silenced the voice inside it. The useless object lay in its cradle.

"The number is no good," he said, and he tasted salt, his own, running down his cheeks and slipping into the corners of his mouth.

The girl slid a box of Kleenex across the counter.

"You'll find your sister. Come around here. I'll show you how to search for her."

He went behind the counter and stood next to the girl. She showed him a tiny dark arrow on the screen of her machine. Steering with a device that she called a "mouse"—a gliding hummock of plastic that fit under the palm of her hand—she guided the arrow in all directions. Then she took away her hand.

"You want to try? It's easy."

She attempted to teach him to right click and left click. With each click, the screen changed its contents. This fascinated and alarmed him. "Page." "Icon." "Scroll." "Cursor." "Google"—all of these words she taught him.

She told him to type "Inge Schlögel Toronto" and when he hesitated she typed it for him. They learned that his sister was a member of the League of Interpreters and Translators of Ontario, or had been in 2009. That was only a year ago. Why wasn't she a member anymore?

"She has no web site, no Facebook page, no address or telephone number. She doesn't really want to be found, your sister, does she?"

"She is not someone who spends time with other people. She is very private. She was very private, when I knew her, that's how she used to be."

"We'll track her down. She'll be happy to see you. If I had a brother like you . . . I dunno. What would I do with a brother like you, Deadman? We could call the League of Interpreters and Translators of Ontario?"

"Yes."

While she dialed, he went around to the correct side of the counter, the public side; then she passed him the receiver.

Heinrich learned—this time from a live voice that spoke to him from Toronto—that a woman named Inge Schlögel had indeed been a member until a year ago, when she'd failed to pay her dues.

"It's not uncommon," the voice explained. "Sadly, many allow their memberships to lapse. People no longer understand the importance of community and common action. Not to suggest that your sister undervalued our professional community, she could have had other reasons for not paying her dues. She might have left the country, she might have been going through a rough spell, it happens. Working as a freelancer means uncertainty. She should have let the league know, that's why we exist, we're here to help. I'm sorry not to be of more help. So many families get torn apart. I hope you find her. For some, the league used to be a family, a better one than the family they were born into. But that's all over now. Good luck with your search. Sorry not to be of more help. Have a great day."

Click. Dead air, unreceivable sound waves crackling, searching.

Heinrich set down the receiver, then lowered himself to the floor, his back against the information counter. He brought his knees up and rested his head on them. The girl came and crouched beside him.

"Sounds like she's still in Toronto, your sister. You'll find her but you'll have to go there. What are you going to do next? I could call my grandma and ask her to walk over and get you."

He raised his head from his knees and looked at her.

"Your grandmother?"

He could imagine giving in, letting this girl whom he hardly knew do all his thinking for him.

"Sarah Ashevak, my grandma, she says you're going to be staying with us. Weren't you on your way to her house?"

"Yes. Yes, I was."

"I'll call my grandma."

She saw his breathing become calmer. If he were a dog, she would have felt his nose. On the whole she preferred dogs to boys and men. She wanted to scratch this qallunaaq behind the ears, stroke the top of his head. Instead, she went back to the phone.

"I'll be okay," he said. "Don't bother your grandmother."

She stopped dialing.

"I'll go on my own."

"If you get lost, ask someone the way to Sarah Ashevak's."

"Will I see you later, at your grandma's?"

"Yup."

"What is your name? You know mine. But I haven't asked your name."

"Vicky."

"Thank you for your help, Vicky."

"You're welcome, Deadman."

She stood behind the information counter, restless, waiting perhaps for him to leave.

"Goodbye, Vicky."

She caught his eye but said nothing. He was like all qallunaat and said "goodbye" even when he was going to be seeing you again in a few hours. A qallunaaq, her grandmother said, is a person too busy talking, not seeing what is going on. A person who only sees himself, and has lots of breath to waste.

If my Schlögel archive were of value to anyone but me, would I have the courage to sell it? My financial worries are becoming acute. I have been spending far too liberally since my search for Heinrich began.[23]

---

23 After I left home, my parents acquired gambling debts of which I was unaware, debts that more than devoured their estate. Am I becoming as compulsive as my parents, and will I end by owing as much as they did? Soon we will all have to pay off our debts.

Last night, not for the first time, I dreamed of Heinrich.

He was on his way to Sarah Ashevak's house, and stopped in at the fish-processing plant. I watched him climb the steps, open the door, and go inside. So, I thought, he's as worried as I am about how to make ends meet. Straightaway, someone appeared and outfitted him with rubber boots, rubber gloves, and a large apron, which was also made of rubber. He was shown through the plant, a noisy place of metal surfaces, knives, and refrigerators.

Water gushed from taps and hoses; everything was neon bright and bustling. A smiling woman demonstrated what to do with a cold, stiff portion of fish. She showed Heinrich how to take it in his rubber-gloved hand, and how to wield his knife so as to cut away any excess bone that the filleting machine had missed. Every few minutes more arctic char and turbot, piled on plastic trays and carried by a conveyor belt, rolled toward Heinrich and the woman. She was deft at her job and Heinrich hoped he would soon become proficient and not disappoint her. The manager stepped forward, assigned Heinrich to a workstation, showed him where to hang his apron, where to store his boots and gloves, and told him to return the next morning. After thanking the manager and promising to arrive punctually, Heinrich went on his way, and I woke from my dream, smiling.

However, I did not smile for long. By the time I'd showered and dressed, the weight of my financial troubles pressed in on me with renewed intensity.

I do not want to be forced to sell what little I own. I've noted down my dream and dropped it into a file marked "Miscellaneous," cross-referenced "The necessity of earning a living." Who would buy my Schlögel archive? Who will take my research seriously? After all, here I am including in my archive a dream that I had last night of Heinrich, as if a dream of mine could constitute solid evidence of his experiences.

But am I not justified in including a dream? Who is to determine what constitutes valid evidence? For better or worse the archive at the moment belongs to me, and I am free to introduce any evidence that strikes me as valuable.

Sarah wore a flowered dress; her sewing glasses hung from her neck as she came shuffling toward Heinrich in her slippers. Just that afternoon she'd gone to her cousin's and had her hair curled, and she smiled at the young man on her doorstep, and felt pleased that her hair was looking its best. In the living room she sat her new guest down, her paying guest, with a cup of tea, and showed him her collection of knives. The ulu is a woman's knife, she explained. She had a dozen uluit of various sizes. Each consisted of a blade in the shape of a half-moon, with a short handle protruding from the center of the side not used for cutting. She removed her glasses, set them safely on her coffee table, and selected a medium-sized ulu. "This is how to hold it. This is how to sharpen it." She drew the blade back and forth, swiftly, more swiftly, without losing precision, across the iron braced between her clenched knees; she paused and threw Heinrich a mischievous look. "This is how a qallunaaq sharpens an ulu." The blade jumped in awkward spasms against the iron. She set aside her sharpening tool and uluit, slapped her thighs, and rocked with laughter. Her eyes began to water. Pulling a Kleenex from the pocket of her dress, she dried her eyes.

"Now I see you better."

She settled deeper into her sofa, wriggling her stiff toes inside her slippers.

"They hire you at the fish plant?"

"Yes."

"Good. Then you can pay me for your room."

Again, laughter rippled through her flesh.

"You want more tea? A cookie?"

The ticking of clocks surrounded Heinrich. Clocks occupied every available surface, their chorus making it impossible for him to know if he wanted more tea and a cookie or not. He counted them. At forty-five he stopped. A clock mimicking a hockey stick, one in the shape of a fire engine, a woman's fancy lace-up boot clock, a pale blue porcelain cat clock, another posing as an open Bible, as a potted flower, a postal box clock, a dog's head with eyes that rolled and a tongue that protruded on the hour, a pig clock missing an ear, a Niagara Falls clock, a ticking cowboy from Calgary. In every corner of the room, clocks were dicing and distributing time, some loudly, others softly.

"You like my clocks?" Sarah asked.

Heinrich nodded nervously. The thought crossed his mind that if he kept on nodding, soon he'd be nodding in time with the clocks. "How long have you been collecting them?" he asked.

"For a very long time. My friends, my family, they go somewhere and they bring me back a clock. They know Sarah loves clocks. You know how many I got?"

Heinrich shook his head.

"Fifty-seven. You want to see your room?"

"Yes, please."

"How long you'll stay here?"

"I don't know."

"That's okay. You tell me when you know."

Sarah heaved herself from the depths of the sofa and Heinrich stood as well. He stood in the overheated, ticking room, the thick pile of the wall-to-wall carpeting soft under his stocking feet. On the coffee table lay a catalog, a glossy photo of a living room on the cover. Outside, a cloud of dust drifted, raised by a passing pickup truck. The dust from the road hovered in the picture window, framed by pleated velour curtains. The heavy curtains reached down to the broadloom carpet. Heinrich, staring out into the suspended dust, wondered whose dream he was caught inside of. Perhaps, like the living room furniture, he'd been ordered from a catalog? Maybe Sarah had selected him to go with her sofa and coffee table?

He wondered if, whenever he sat in this living room, his long hike beside the Weasel River would play itself over and over inside his chest, like a story on a broken tape recorder. He heard his father repeating, "I've read about people like you in the paper. I've heard about people like you on TV." What did he, Heinrich, know for certain? At the edge of town the broad unpaved road ceased to exist, and footpaths spidered out across the bald land.

Day after day, the blade of Heinrich's knife sliced through the resistance of frozen fish flesh. The exhaustingly bright din of the processing plant and the numbing monotony of standing in one place became familiar. How many days elapsed? Many more than several, and Heinrich promised himself that soon he would buy a plane ticket, that somehow he'd obtain up-to-date papers, solid proof of a credible identity to present at the airport, and then he'd be off. But the more intensely he imagined his reunion with Inge the less attached their reunion became to any particular moment in time. Despite her letter tucked in the innermost pocket of his backpack, he started to wonder if he had a sister or if he'd invented her. In the remaining pages of his journal, every day he wrote the hour at which he got up and the hour at which he went to bed. These tiny entries framed the muteness invading him.

In the hotel lounge, where he often went during his off-work hours, to say a quick bonjour to Monsieur Pierre and to watch the ocean through the picture window, he became known as a shy but attentive listener. From the hotel's varied guests—the prospectors and their helicopter pilots, the literacy consultants, the specialists in psycho-social dynamics, the retired biologists, the civil servants on holiday, and the men dredging the harbor—he concealed his true circumstances. He was afraid of becoming an object of interest, a phenomenon—the German Who Slipped through a Hole in Time.

The carvers who came looking for tourists with money to spend on sculptures of dancing bears and reclining seals had already heard about Heinrich from Sarah, how he'd spent years out on the land before returning, and they did not try to sell him their carvings, not even the miniature kayaks and inuksuit that they silently slipped from their pockets onto the hotel coffee table.

Some of the women who cleaned the hotel rooms and served at mealtimes smiled at Heinrich with a shyness and reticence that he felt was similar to his own, and when he found the courage to ask them about their work or about the weather they answered him warmly.

"I've been to Montreal," one of the women told him. It was early in the morning and they'd crossed paths where the road widened above the harbor. A light rain was falling. She wore her hair pulled back in a ponytail and had a beauty mark on her left cheek. "I went for an operation. When I got better and could go outside, I was scared. I didn't walk around much because of the squirrels and the sound the trees made. The leaves moving so much. Everything scared me. I was young."

He would have liked to speak with her longer, but the rain was falling more heavily with every passing minute. The child riding in the hood of the woman's amautik continued to sleep, despite the drops of water landing with increasing frequency on its forehead and cheeks. The woman said that she would be late for work if she stayed, talking in the road, and with an amused smile she walked away.

The end of August arrived and it was dark by eight, the sun setting earlier every day, and the weather becoming rapidly cooler. "High of seven degrees today. You're lucky," teased Vicky.

Once or twice, in the privacy of Sarah's house, Heinrich pulled out his empty camera and looked through the lens. He had no film. He'd promised himself that he wouldn't take any more pictures. The day of his panic and despair behind the hotel, over a month ago, the day he'd intentionally ruined an entire roll of images, made it hard for him to trust himself with a camera. He might act as destructively again. He hesitated to spend money on a new roll of film. He shoved his camera deep into his pack, angered by the apparatus's mixture of power and impotence. Was it logical of him to hold his camera somehow responsible for the strange behavior of time and the alienating predicament in which he found himself? Always a moment came when he would reach down and yank his camera back to the surface. One afternoon, he went into the Northern Store and asked for a roll of film. To his relief and surprise they pulled an old roll out of a drawer and sold it to him.

Sarah's living room became his first subject. While shooting, he experienced a sensation of reciprocity. The scene he was composing was also composing him. This fleeting impression of connection with his surroundings relaxed him. Then the click of the shutter put an abrupt end to his delight, and once more his solitude overwhelmed him—he was a young man alone, clutching a device for capturing and removing moments from one flow of time to deposit them in another.[24]

Only in Vicky's company did he come close to feeling at ease for more than a matter of minutes.

At dinner, Heinrich offered to set the table but Sarah refused his help.

"That's Vicky's job. If she's not here, I do it."

They ate bannock, grilled char, and boiled broccoli, while on the large television screen that faced the kitchen table, a man with a handsome jaw drove through the dim labyrinth of an underground parking lot. Without turning his head, the man explained to the woman

---

24 My Schlögel archive includes ten photographs of Sarah Ashevak's living room. Naturally, I have my favorites—three in particular. Their eloquence moves me. Do they express Heinrich's uneasiness? I think so, yes, something about the composition. But I am no judge of photography. I do wish that he'd taken a shot of Sarah. Perhaps his shyness prevented him. Possibly Sarah expressed a desire not to be photographed. If such a shot does exist, I'd very much like to acquire it for the archive. But that would mean yet another temptation to spend money that I don't have. It may be best if such a shot does not exist.

seated next to him that he couldn't leave his wife, not yet. Somewhere an orchestra was playing, and the woman burst into tears.

"You like my bannock?"

"It is delicious."

Sarah smiled with pleasure.

"Good. I am happy you like my bannock. I make the best bannock in Pangnirtung. Everybody tells me my bannock is best. I don't know. If people tell me, sometime I believe them. Vicky, she should come home for dinner. I don't like it when she comes home late. We will save a plate of food for her. She'll warm it in the oven when she comes home. All the young people come home late, even now, when summer is finished. I don't like it. It's no good."

On the television screen, the woman's glistening eyes examined her lover's profile. Her eyes searched his jaw and nose for some clue to his true feelings. His heavy, competent hands guided the car around each grimy curve. As the luxurious vehicle approached the exit, she told him, "I'm pregnant," and he put his foot on the brake.

Sarah plugged in the kettle for tea and brought a plate of cookies to the table.

"You help Vicky bake?"

"Only the last batch," said Heinrich. "I took them out of the oven."

"Vicky asked you?"

"Yes. She didn't want to be late for work, and she had to take her cousin home first."

"I know. She called me. She said she hopes you won't burn the cookies."

"I am sorry. I am not good at baking, Sarah. When I smelled them I ran back down the hall."

Sarah grinned. "The burned ones I throw out. I tell Vicky it's her problem. She asks you to do her work, that's her problem. She is a good girl but she is late. I am tired. I am going to bed. No tea for Sarah. You want me to leave the TV on?"

"No, thank you."

"Don't lock the door when you go to bed. You lock the door, Vicky can't come in. Okay?"

"Okay."

Heinrich poured water into the teapot and took the pitcher of milk from the refrigerator. He put their dinner plates in the kitchen sink.

"You leave the dishes. That's Vicky's job. Only your room is your job. And the door, you don't forget. Don't lock the door."

"I won't lock it, I promise. Good night, Sarah."

He lay on the sofa, listening for the back door, and soon he fell asleep. In his sleep, a sudden curiosity made him turn his attention to the kitchen. Two sober gray eyes that belonged to a slender little girl with a wide mouth were watching him. It was Inge, and she was no more than four or five years old. While eyeing him carefully, she pressed her small self into the pillar of warmth that was Vicky's leg. Standing at the kitchen counter, Vicky was rolling out sugar dough.

"She's my cousin. I'm looking after her, we're making cookies."

No, thought Heinrich, she's not your cousin, I recognize that dress, it's the one that Inge was forced to wear on Sundays, until she hid it so that she wouldn't have to go to church anymore, and nobody said the word "Gypsy" but she knew she could get away with making her dress disappear because the circus was in town.

The story of his sister's dress rushed through him at such speed that he could hardly get the words out. Then he realized he wasn't speaking.

Vicky glanced at the clock above the stove, a clock in the shape of a sunflower. She was cutting the dough in a hurry, cutting it into increasingly sloppy discs.

"Shit, I am so in trouble. If I'm late for work again and Sarah finds out, she'll be real mad, she'll go crazy on me."

Vicky yanked the oven door open and slid in the two trays.

"Hey, Deadman, can you do me a favor, a super big favor? Can you take these out when they're done? Only leave them in for five more minutes and you gotta remember to turn the oven off."

"Yes, of course," he promised. He peeked through the window of the oven door. One of the cookies was so large that it occupied an entire tray.

"Eat as many cookies as you like. I gotta go, I gotta drop my cousin at her house and I was supposed to be at work fifteen minutes ago. Fuck."

Vicky rushed out of the kitchen to get her car keys and purse. Heinrich could hear her in the mudroom by the back door, urging Inge to hurry and pull on her shoes. She was speaking Inuktitut, explaining that they couldn't wait for the cookies to cool, that the qallunaaq was going to watch and make sure the last ones didn't burn. How is it that I can understand her? Heinrich wondered.

He stood absolutely still, the way he used to hold himself at home, in the upstairs hall in Tettnang, listening to two recorded voices coming from inside Inge's bedroom, a man's voice and a woman's, carefully, deliberately uttering incomprehensible Inuktitut words.

"Thanks, Deadman," Vicky called to him from the mudroom. "You've saved my life." And the back door slammed shut.

There was a bit of raw dough left in the mixing bowl. Heinrich scraped it out with his fingers, rolled it between his palms, then put it in his mouth. The little planet of buttery sweetness softened, coating his tongue.

He picked up his camera from the kitchen counter. It contained a photograph he regretted, a photograph of which he felt ashamed. He didn't remember taking the photograph but knew that it was of Inge, and that she hadn't wanted him to take it.

I'll give my camera to Vicky, he decided. That way, I won't be able to take any more pictures. It will be a great present. But perhaps she already has a camera.

He ran from the kitchen, along the hall to his bedroom, where he took the envelope that contained his money from its place in his dresser drawer. He needed something to count, a means of measuring. It reassured him to feel the dollars between his fingers. Their increasing number meant fewer days separating him from Inge. Soon he'd have enough to buy his plane ticket. From the kitchen came the smell of burning cookies.

He was running down the hall to the kitchen to save the cookies from being ruined when a cramp in his side woke him. He sat up and saw Vicky standing in the kitchen, a can of Coca-Cola in one hand and a glass in the other. How long ago had she let herself in the back door?

"Hello," he mumbled, as she came into the living room.

His hair was a mess, and the left side of his face pink from being slept on. He felt her eyes slide over him as she crossed the room. He'd go to his bedroom, so as not to be in her way. That was his immediate plan. But he made no move to leave the sofa.

"Did you come in long ago?" he asked.

"Nope. Not long."

Vicky, having set her drink on the coffee table, flopped down on the sofa beside him. She started talking and did not want to stop. A stream of words poured out of her.

"A while ago, when you weren't around, before you came back from out on the land, three guys I know were in a tent sniffing propane and a fourth guy, he came looking for them. He was smoking a cigarette and he blew them all up. They were hurt real bad. Today they came back from Iqaluit, from the hospital, and I went with my friends to see them. Two of them were in my class at school, until they dropped out. And one of them, he was burned real bad. He's got new skin on his face but it's all shiny and sort of puckered and weird. They don't look so good, but they're going to be okay. One of my friends had a bottle of vodka, and she said we should celebrate. The whole bottle got drunk up real fast, and things got crazy, but I didn't want to celebrate, and everyone was asking if anyone knew where we could get another bottle. But I wasn't in the mood, Deadman, I just wasn't into it." She hesitated. "You better not tell my grandma or my mom. Well, you won't tell my mom, 'cause she's in Iqaluit, but you better not tell my grandma. Heinrich Schlögel. That's what I should call you. That's your name, in the file that says you disappeared. Heinrich Schlögel, what happened to you?"

"I don't know, Vicky Pitsiulak. I don't know what happened to me."

"How do you know my last name?"

"I saw it written in here."

Heinrich got up from the sofa. From the kitchen he brought the book of recipes that he'd seen beside the sink when he was clearing the table after supper. *Cupcakes for Every Occasion.* He opened the book and showed Vicky her name: *Vicky Pitsiulak*, scrawled in pink marker.

"Did you burn my cookies, Deadman?" she asked.

"No. I ate them."

"All of them?"

"I ruined one tray, the bottom tray. I am sorry. I can make you cupcakes instead, Vicky. I am sorry."

"You shouldn't stay here, burning cookies, Deadman. You should go looking for your sister. I'm not gonna stay. There's a lot you don't know about what happens here. You should be thinking what you're going to do next. Next year, I'll be in Iqaluit, at college. My mom wants me to train to be a ranger like her, but I'm going to study office administration. I don't like going out on the land. If you're a ranger, they teach you to shoot. At first my mom wasn't too good at it, but she's got better. Now she's a good hunter. My cousin Jennie, she loves to hunt and my uncle taught her, and she goes with him and they bring us back country food. That makes my grandma happy. I like eating country food, but I don't hunt. Not me. That's not for me. The land scares me. My mom, she'd be working if her back didn't hurt all the time. When her back gets better she'll work as a ranger again, but the doctor says she's gotta lose some weight. My mom, she put on lots of weight when she left my dad. Last year a woman, a friend of my mom's, she asked her boyfriend to make some homebrew. It was Christmas and she wanted to celebrate. So he made some and they got drunk together, then he wanted to have sex with her and she didn't want to, so he took out his knife and he stabbed her in the thigh and he made her do it for three hours and the next day when my mom saw her friend, she couldn't recognize her, her friend was beat so bad. Her friend went to the police. People said she shouldn't have done that. It was her fault for asking him to make her homebrew and getting drunk with him. If she didn't want to have sex with him, why did she do that? My mom said he shouldn't have beat her, even if he was drunk. My mom said her friend was right to go to the police. My grandma wouldn't say anything. Usually my grandma always has something to say. My grandma went to her room and closed the door. So you see, Deadman, this is what sort of place you're in. Just so you know, and you don't get in trouble. But it's easier for me to get in trouble than you. Sometimes I want to get in big trouble. When I'm at college, in Iqaluit, I'll take classes in Inuktitut, 'cause my Inuktitut isn't too good. That's what my grandma says, she says my Inuktitut is like I'm five years old. After, I'll go to Ottawa, but only for a year and then I don't know, maybe to Yellowknife. The thing is, at college, in Ottawa, the Inuktitut is different from how we speak in Pang and Iqaluit, it's hard to say, so I might come back to Iqaluit or even to Pang, one day, but not for a boring job like what I do at the parks office. I'm beat. I'm going to bed, Deadman."

She got up from the sofa and started down the hallway but turned and came back.

"Have you got a grandma?" she asked.

While she waited for his answer, she flopped back down on the sofa and let herself sink again, into its soft depths.

"Yes, I have a grandma," he told her.

But it wasn't true. Thirty years had disappeared and he was pretty sure that he didn't have one anymore. Should he describe his grandmother as he remembered her? He wanted to tell Vicky something important, but couldn't think what.

"When I was little and couldn't fall asleep, my mother would trace the paths inside my ear with the tip of her finger," he told her.

"You're weird, Deadman. Do you know that? You are so weird."

259

One afternoon, drawing on courage that he did not know he possessed, Heinrich offered Vicky his camera.

Her response floats, jotted on a loose page:

You need your camera more than I do. And anyway, film costs too much, and I'd have to wait so long to see the pictures. Until I get my own camera, I can use my boyfriend's. You ever seen a digital camera? You want me to show you some of the pictures I took with his? Your camera's pretty cool, but you should keep it. Thanks for offering it to me, Heinrich Schlögel.

I found the loose page tucked in a book on caribou migration, a slender volume into which he wrote his name. I've filed it, her response, under the heading "Vicky," cross-referenced "Photography," cross-referenced "Unobtainable."

Yesterday afternoon, I pulled from my archive a snapshot of an Inuit girl wearing a caramel-colored T-shirt with green stripes. She is four or five years old. Her serious eyes assess the photographer cautiously while she presses her small self into the blurred legs of a teenage girl standing at a kitchen counter. The teenager is cutting pale dough into rounds. The teenager is missing her head. She exists only from the shoulders down. There are no names written on the back and no date given. If I am forced to sell my Schlögel archive, this photo I intend to keep.

Vicky Pitsiulak volunteered to teach Heinrich to navigate the Internet. She told him he should use the computer in the library, at the back of the visitors' center. It was free. It was for everyone. He should keep looking for his sister. Giving up was too easy. That's what Sarah always said. Didn't he want to find out everything that had happened in the world while he was out on the land? He might discover where his mother had gone. He could stumble on a video clip of her playing golf or shopping for groceries, that sort of thing happened online; you came upon people you were convinced you'd lost.

"I have to go to work," he told her. "They've given me extra hours."

"Tomorrow? Tomorrow I could show you."

"No."

"Why?"

"I'm not sure I want to go looking yet. I'm not sure I'm ready."

"You look ready to me, Deadman."

The polished surface of Sarah's coffee table, the little glass bowl filled with hard candies, the tidiness of her overheated, overstuffed living room inflicted upon Heinrich the same unease he'd felt as a child in the irreproachable living rooms of his aunts' houses in Tettnang. There he'd perched on the edges of chairs and sofas that refused to bestow comfort. He'd held his breath, surrounded by objects that demanded submission to unspoken rules of correct conduct. Sarah's rules were different, her living room less forbidding, the ticking of her fifty-seven clocks almost soothing, but he did not know her rules and could not guess what they might be, and there were moments when he wanted to plead with her to tell him how to behave.

"Lots of children in Iqaluit," said Sarah, "they don't speak Inuktitut too good. The young people make this TV teach them."

"Minguarsit," said the woman on the screen. "Minguarsit," the children repeated after her. She set down the paintbrush and held up a pair of scissors for everyone to see. "Anglerouyait."

"Anglerouyait," recited Heinrich.

"Good thing only I hear you," said Sarah, grinning. "You gonna be in school a long time."

"Anglerouyait," he tried again.

"Before, long time ago, I was a teacher," said Sarah. "Everyone always asking, 'Sarah, you can do this, we need you to do this.' I work lots of places, in the hotel, in the hospital. Now the hospital they moved to Iqaluit. They say, 'Now, you work in the school, Sarah. You speak good Inuktitut. We need you.' But I am tired. The young people they make this TV their school."

She reached down to the coffee table and pushed her bowl of candies toward her young qallunaat guest, the one who'd stayed out on the land too long and now couldn't find his way home. Her guest who liked Vicky, who maybe liked Vicky too much, and now he didn't want to find his way home. Her guest she might still have in her living room when the days became short, the sun gone before noon.

"Take one."

"No, thank you, Sarah."

She pushed the bowl closer to him.

"Take one. I am your teacher." Her smile became mischievous. "Anglerouyait."

"Anglerouyait."

"Bit better. You practice more, later you come show me your good work. Now, you take a candy."

Her pupil did as he was told and reached into the bowl. She leaned back into the softness of her sofa and admired her curtains. It was late afternoon and still there was light outside. Every day the darkness arrived a little faster. Inside, she could always have light, the blue light from the TV.

She remembered choosing her curtains from the Hudson's Bay catalog. After ordering them, she'd waited six months for the curtains to arrive. They'd traveled north in the hold of a sealift.

During her period of waiting, she had opened the catalog repeatedly, always to the page with the picture of her curtains, anticipating the ship's arrival, foreseeing how the sealift would glide into the harbor, how it would disgorge its contents into the fishing boats and other smaller vessels that rode out to meet it, while on shore more and more people gathered to watch as the crates were brought in and piled on the rocks and mud. Possibly her curtains would not resemble those in the catalog?

The risk of disappointment added to her excitement. Ordering from a catalog was like falling in love. You saw what you wanted but couldn't touch it, not yet. You waited. As soon as it became yours, you ran your hands up and down the length of it and sniffed and pinched it, and straightaway you knew if you'd loved wisely or foolishly.

From the catalog, she'd selected her coffee table, her dining room chairs, and her sofa. Most of what she'd ordered had turned out just as the glossy photographs had promised. What she'd bought had not disappointed her. People disappointed her. They said one thing and did something else. "You expect everyone to be as strong as you are," her daughter had told her once. "You want everyone to be obstinate like you, but people aren't all the same. You don't want your clocks to be all the same as each other, you want each one different, but you want everyone to be like you, and when they are, then you wish they were different."

Through her living room window, Sarah watched a woman she knew race by on a four-wheeler, raising a cloud of dust. Would my life be more easy, she wondered, if I knew less about everyone? That woman, Elisapee Aglukkaq, she was born feet first, she sings beautifully in church, but her bannock is not good like mine, it comes out dense and heavy.

Sarah knew that Elisapee's miscarriages outnumbered her living children, that a year ago her eldest son, who was an excellent hunter, had died when his snowmobile sank through thin ice; and now Elisapee raced by Sarah's window, on a four-wheeler, and all of Elisapee's life raced with her.

The four-wheeler disappeared down the road. Elisapee, the woman driving it, did not own beautiful curtains. If you married a man who drank, if you married a man who was not a good hunter, if you could not find work for yourself, if your husband lost confidence, if your mother became forgetful and could not remember to turn off the stove, if your sister had to go south to have her breast removed and needed someone to keep an eye on her children, these were all good reasons for wanting soft curtains that hung in deep folds and reached all the way to the floor; these were also reasons why you could not afford to order such curtains.

Sarah turned to the young qallunaaq seated beside her on her sofa.

"Good coffee. You want more?"

"No, thank you."

"You sure?"

"Yes. It is very good, but I don't want more."

"Okay."

She clicked up the volume on the television.

Heinrich Schlögel sat there, watching television with Sarah. He did not try calling Tettnang again. Why did he not make another attempt to communicate with his father? There are two obvious answers. He couldn't face the anguish of hearing once more, "You aren't my son," or he did not want to again startle his father, whose heart was possibly weak. Neither of these answers stops me from questioning the wisdom of his decision not to call. I feel he ought to have taken the risk. He could so easily have dialed that familiar number one more time.

But who am I to judge? I've recently learned that Heinrich's loneliness in Pangnirtung was even greater than I thought, and that one afternoon he contemplated going back out on the land to look for the exact place where "it" had happened. Vicky Pitsiulak found him in tears, on a path just outside of town. He described to her a large rock, split in two, and a lost snowmobiling glove. He couldn't decide, he said, in which precise location time had shifted. Through the split rock he'd followed a giant hare. But while staring at the snowmobiling glove, he'd felt his camera become a relic. As he dried his tears and asked Vicky for her advice, already the idea, fully articulated, of searching for the split rock or the lost snowmobiling glove (both of which he remembered with perfect clarity) began to frighten him; and when the idea of such a search stopped frightening him, it struck him as futile and absurd, and he dismissed the project.

It is from Vicky Pitsiulak that I've learned all this. I'd stopped hoping that she and I would ever speak. No one in Pangnirtung, despite or because of my determined efforts, during my brief visit in July 2011, was willing to put me in touch with her. And then about ten days ago Vicky stumbled on the picture of Heinrich that I, near the start of my search, posted on the Internet. She sent me an e-mail and suggested that we Skype. I hesitated. An irrational fear took hold of me. I'd imagined for so long speaking with her. I'd savored in advance her knowledge of Heinrich. I'd imagined her in detail. I'd read what Heinrich wrote about her, in his few journal entries that included more than a record of the hour at which he went to bed and the hour at which he got up. Yesterday, we spoke. Already her directness and acuity I greatly like. I am, she says, the only person she's come across who is attempting to discover what's become of Heinrich Schlögel.

Skype allows us to see each other while talking, at minimal cost and from a considerable distance. Yesterday evening, I watched her moving about her orderly, compact kitchen in Calgary, while she observed me in my study in Toronto. During our conversation, I learned a great deal about Heinrich Schlögel. Then she had a question for me. "What exactly happened to him in Toronto?" I jokingly offered to sell her my archive, but she assured me that I need it more than she does. Then she asked, "Aren't you going to tell me if Heinrich ever found his sister, or don't you know?"

"Later, when I'm not so tired," I promised. "Later I'll tell you everything I know."

"Yup," she said, "I believe you. You're gonna tell me everything."

And with a click of her mouse, she caused herself to vanish from my computer screen.

While Heinrich was in Pangnirtung, often he tried to recall the sound of Inge's voice but his ear remained empty of her exact intonations; these refused him. And yet, when he examined a towering slab of ice that had washed up on the shore or when he stood on a lip of frozen earth and stared straight down into the sea, it was Inge who caught her breath; it was her curiosity and awe that pulsed and gathered inside him, along with his own.

It was late September; by six in the evening the sun had set. A few more weeks and it would be dark by four in the afternoon. Temperatures were dropping rapidly; five degrees was an exceptionally warm day. Very soon, two degrees would be the best that Heinrich could hope for.

Increasingly, he hungered to grasp his own visibility. How, he wondered, did he appear to Sarah and to Vicky? In the hallway that led to the bedrooms, a framed black-and-white photograph hung on the wall. It showed a young woman caught off guard, radiant. She was glancing sideways, her smiling gaze drawn to something just outside the picture. The photographer's presence did not seem to disturb her. She wore an amautik, and from over her shoulder, a pinch-faced infant (of indeterminate sex) grimaced at whoever was holding the camera.

"Who is this woman, Sarah?"

"My mother."

"Your mother is beautiful."

"And me?"

"Maybe someone gave you a lemon to suck? Look at you! Or you don't like the photographer?"

"I don't remember."

269

"But your mother? You remember her?"

"Yup."

"Who took this picture?"

"I dunno. My children find it. In a museum, in Ottawa, someone from the museum asked them and they show it to me. I say, the woman is my mom, and they give it to me."[25]

"What was Pangnirtung like thirty years ago, Sarah? I maybe walked by you on the road, perhaps on my way to the parks office? I was preparing for my long hike. Maybe you saw me get in the fishing boat to go up the fjord? Are you sure you didn't see me?"

"I dunno."

"But you were here. What was Pangnirtung like? I passed through so fast. How was it different from now?"

---

25 Though the Library and Archives Canada possesses thousands of photographs of Inuit, dating from the late 1800s to the mid-twentieth century, very few of the Inuit in these images were identified at the time the photographs were taken. Nunavummiut (residents of Nunavut, Canada's largest, northernmost territory) have never had a chance to assist in identifying these people. Before digitization there was no inexpensive and easy means of transporting the photographs to Nunavut. This is the official reason no consistent effort was made sooner. The naming of these anonymous people has now become urgent. Today's Inuit elders are probably the last people able to identify the individuals, whose names may otherwise remain lost forever. The Naming Project began in 2001.

"Ask someone else. I don't know."

Without another word, Sarah walked down the hallway, went into her bedroom, and closed the door. A qallunaaq, she thought, as she rested on her bed, is someone who demands answers, but who doesn't want the answers that you give.

"Vicky?"

"Yup."

On the screen of my computer, Vicky, head bent in concentration, was applying tiny strokes of lavender nail polish to the toes of her left foot, her toes reaching away from each other.

"What's the likelihood I'll succeed in tracking down Heinrich Schlögel?"

"Not much."

"Why?"

"He doesn't want you to find him."

I waited for her to explain.

"He's never met you. He doesn't know anything about you."

"And you? Doesn't he want to find you?"

"He knows where I am. Maybe he doesn't have anything he wants to tell me right now."

She dipped her brush in the little bottle of silky color.

271

"I gotta go," she said, and went off-line. Darkness filled the screen of my computer.

The ticking of fifty-seven clocks. On her living room sofa, Sarah sat, listening to their chorus. Take away fifty from fifty-seven, what do you get? A seven-year-old girl, a girl who got sick and was taken south to the hospital, then put in a school. A man has fifty apple trees and he plants seven more, how many trees grow in his orchard? An apple is a fruit. It does not grow close to the ground. An apple is much bigger than a blueberry. Once a woman picked an apple because of a snake. She obeyed the snake and bit the apple and gave it to her man to eat and they both were punished for being naked.

At seven years old Sarah had never held a book in her hands.[26] She knew how to read, but not books. Sky

---

26 "My grandma, she was born in 1940, out on the land. It was April or May, sometime before the ice breakup. I could tell you the name of the place but it's not on your map. She didn't know, when they sent her south, she wasn't going to see her parents for three years. She was lucky, though. It could have been a lot longer. But her parents left the land and settled in Pang when she was ten. They had to, if they wanted to get her back. There was a day school in Pang. Lots of people didn't move, not until the dogs

and water, faces and the actions of people, the behavior of dogs, of seals, of fish, and of ravens—these she knew how to read. She knew how to read stories that do not hold still, stories that go away and sometimes come back, pretending to be a new story. In the hallway of the school, the school where she was sent to learn, a round, gold disc caught her eye and she walked over to it. She stood in front of the grandfather clock and the clock's steady ticking swallowed the voice behind her, a sharp voice telling her something she did not understand; she fixed her eyes on the gold disc and the ticking grew louder.

A man has twelve cows. If he sells half his cows, how many does he have left?

In the classroom they sat in rows. She asked, "What is a cow?" She asked, "Do people hunt cows?" She received no answers. She asked, "Why does the man want to sell his cows?" She asked these questions in Inuktitut because she did not know what to expect of English words, what they might turn into if she mixed them together. Sometimes

---

died, about ten years later, lots of them from disease, and since people couldn't hunt they were hungry, so they got moved to Pang. Also the RCMP shot dogs. They had lots of reasons. If you don't behave, I'll shoot your dog. Your dog wasn't chained up. We told you to keep it on a chain. I was born April 6, maybe the same day as my grandma, but I'm not much like her. I wouldn't mind being more like her."—Skype conversation with Vicky, June 18, 2013

English words were thrown at her; other times they drifted by, and some of them she caught and even savored. But she thought in Inuktitut. She did not invite her ideas and her questions; they arrived of their own accord, and they arrived in Inuktitut. She turned and spoke her thoughts aloud to the girl seated beside her.

The teacher scrubbed her mouth clean of Inuktitut. He told her, "If you behave badly, you will be punished—there's a nice simple equation even you can understand."

Her head filled with more questions. If the teacher could have seen inside her head, he would have scrubbed away all her thinking, scraped out the dirty Inuktitut words that were constantly forming new equations and more questions inside the safety of her skull. How many apples did the woman in the garden eat? Was it because the snake gave her the apple that she was punished for eating it, or were all apples bad? If apples were bad, why did a man with fifty apple trees plant seven more? When is a garden called an orchard? If the woman in the story was not allowed to eat an apple, why am I given an apple at lunch and what will happen to me if I eat it? Will I lose my clothes? If the story about the garden isn't a warning, why tell it to me in such a serious voice, in the sort of voice used to tell someone not to walk on the ice in that place where it is too thin?

Though she was hungry, and the apple was the first piece of fruit she had been given since her arrival at the school, Sarah refused to eat it. She received a lesson. She received it with open hands. She held out her palms and a wooden ruler bit her skin.

From that day on, when given a piece of apple, she pretended to eat, hiding bites of apple in her cheeks, to be spat out later, to be swallowed only as a last resort. And she hid her language under her tongue. When a word wanted to wriggle out, like a worm, she swallowed it quickly and clamped her lips shut. Words slithered back up her throat and into her mouth. She kept her teeth pressed tight together, so the wriggling words wouldn't show. When it was over she stood in the front hallway and stared at the golden disc. When she received a lesson for breaking a rule, she hid her throbbing hands in the slow and steady ticking of the tall clock.

Outside the school, she was not much safer than inside the school. Outside, trees grew, trees full of leaves that made an awful sound, the sound of something approaching, and of something trying to free itself.

Sarah sat, now, in the depths of her own sofa, which she'd chosen from the catalog, and she read the time on the clock nearest to her, a bright-red mounted policeman clock from Edmonton, and she wondered: What lessons is Vicky learning right this minute? What rules tell Vicky who she is? Does she know what rules she's following?

In the tiny library at the back of the visitors' center, Vicky grinned and gestured for Heinrich to sit down.

"Here, Deadman," she said, "you can go on the computer now. Nobody's using it, and the library doesn't shut for another two hours. Besides, I have the keys. Just go to Google and type in what you want. You remember how to find it?"

Heinrich promised her that he'd be fine.

He typed "1989" and clicked the mouse. He'd intended the last nine to be a zero, for 1980, the year he'd left home, but he'd never been good at typing. The words "1989 - Wikipedia, the free encyclopedia" appeared on the light-filled screen. He clicked on the line of words and landed on a set of four photographs. As he dragged the small black arrow over each image, labels sprang into existence—one per picture. The rubble became: "Iran-Iraq War." The seabirds coated in a black substance: "*Exxon Valdez* Spill." The two smiling men: "End of the Cold War." The group of women and men balancing on a wall became: "Fall of the Berlin Wall." Each label vanished as quickly as it had popped into existence. Heinrich wriggled the mouse frantically on the picture of figures crowding the top of a wall, and the same mocking caption resurfaced: "Fall of the Berlin Wall." Vicky'd warned him, "People post anything, all sorts of made-up shit."

What sort of encyclopedia was this? He double-clicked, causing the photo to grow. Some of the people were drinking straight from bottles, beer by the look of it. His eyes wandered down the screen and read: "In 1989, soldiers stood by as citizens gathered in increasing numbers . . . the gate formerly known as Checkpoint Charlie . . ."

Most of the women and men on the wall were standing, but a few had made themselves comfortable, legs dangling. They wore raincoats or leather jackets, and these were zipped or buttoned against the damp of the overcast evening. Heinrich clicked, found more text, and kept reading. There was no end of photos to examine.[27] Eventually, he pushed his chair back and went to find Vicky in the visitors' center.

"You don't look so good, Deadman. Did you find your mom or your sister?"

"No. The Berlin Wall."

"They tore that down ages ago. Before I was born. I read about it, though, and I've seen pictures. I think it all

---

27 When the CBC first showed footage of people crowded on top of the wall, I called my parents. "Is it a trap?" I asked. "Are they going to suddenly start shooting? What is really going on?" Divided Germany—it feels like an invention now, a blurred fantasy, as brief a fabrication as I, some mornings, feel that I am. Yesterday, quite by chance, I came upon a website about two Canadian artists traveling across North America tracking down large and small pieces of the Berlin Wall, bits that have landed this side of the Atlantic: http://www.freedomrocks.ca.

turned out okay. That's what I read. You're not so happy they got rid of it? You okay?"

He sat down on the floor, the way he had the day she'd given him Inge's letter, in the parks office.

"Can you help me get some fake ID, Vicky? Something they'll accept at the airport?"

"I can't get you a passport, but I know someone who makes good fake student IDs. You want to go to the University of Alberta or British Columbia? My friend, he'll need a photo of you. We can take one with my boyfriend's camera. Then you gotta choose which university. Don't look so worried, Deadman. My friend does good work. It'll look real. It'll get you to Toronto, no problem. I'll tell my friend why you want it, and he won't ask you to pay too much."

Heinrich became a hunter who had no wife. He was lying in bed, listening for the back door, for feet in the mudroom, when he fell asleep. Unlike all the other men, the men who had wives, he prepared his own meals and sewed his own clothes from the animal skins that he himself scraped clean and softened. One evening, upon returning from hunting, Heinrich found a fire lighted and the kettle boiling. The next day, a meal was cooking. Not only that, but a skin that he'd barely begun preparing had been scraped entirely clean and stretched out to dry. Heinrich felt very pleased and decided to return even earlier on the following day. Just as he arrived, he glimpsed a person wearing white fur boots slipping into the entrance of his house. It was a woman. He married her. In the winter, he took her to live with his parents and his extended family. This is not a good idea, Heinrich thought. I should not be taking my wife to live with my relatives. But he ignored his intuition.

He and his young wife lived peacefully until one afternoon she stepped close to one of his uncles, and the uncle asked, "What is that fox smell?" Everyone present advised this uncle not to be rude. But some days later, a cousin burst out laughing and exclaimed, just as Heinrich's wife walked past, "The air reeks of fox." Covering her face with her hands, Heinrich's young wife ran out the door, a thick, white tail protruding from under her parka. Heinrich pursued her. Crying out her name, he followed her far into the hills. When he could no longer make out her shape in the distance, her tracks showed him the way. At last, he came to a mound of stones with a round hole for an entrance. Stomping his foot above the entrance, to let her know that he'd caught up with her, he shouted, "I am cold! Let me come inside."

"Come in then," his wife answered.

"But the hole is too small."

"Breathe on it, and it will get bigger."

He breathed on the hole, slipped through it, and she lifted him onto her lap. She rocked him back and forth until he fell asleep. This was the song she sang to him: "Do not wake until the summer comes, do not wake until the flies buzz, and you hear the flowing sound of water and the fox barking in the hills."

For a very long time, Heinrich slept.

When he woke up, he went outside. It was summer, the flies were buzzing, and he looked around for someplace his spirit might inhabit. He entered a blade of grass and lived peacefully until a wind came. The continuous swaying exhausted him, so he left the blade of grass and slipped inside a raven. Ravens never go hungry. Inside the raven he felt content, until his feet grew chilly. It was time for a change. He left the raven and entered a caribou.

"I am hungry. What is there to eat?" he asked, and the other caribou showed Heinrich how to loosen moss from the ground, using his front hoofs. He ate so much moss that he became fat. Though he moved with the herd, from one place to the next, he was always falling behind.

"Look up at the stars, not down at the ground," the other caribou instructed him. "That way you won't trip so much."

From then on, he kept his eyes on the stars instead of the ground and was able to move more quickly. But a wolf spotted the herd and attacked, causing the herd to run into the sea. Heinrich saw his chance for another change and slid out of the caribou into a walrus. He was hungry and his stomach rumbled loudly. He dove to the bottom of the sea, but the clams lying in the sand refused to open their shells. He returned to the surface and complained: "The clams won't open for me."

"Swim to the bottom and call out 'yok, yok, yok,'" the other walruses advised him.

He did as he was told, and the clams opened their shells and were eaten by Heinrich and the other walruses. After feasting, he and the walruses lay on the rocks in the sun, resting. But when the others slid back into the sea he did not go with them. He wanted a change and pondered what to become next. A seal swam past. He entered the seal. For many days and weeks his spirit lived well inside the seal. He enjoyed his new existence but curiosity drew him close to the shore and he spotted a camp. One of the women in this camp had no children. Heinrich waited and watched for her husband. When her husband crouched down, right by the water, Heinrich poked up his head for air and the man grabbed his harpoon. Heinrich laughed when the harpoon struck. He was dragged along the ground and into the camp. When the woman's relatives began cutting him into pieces, he left the seal and entered the husband's mittens, which the husband removed and threw to his wife. The mittens landed in her lap. Heinrich slipped inside the woman and after some days and weeks she gave birth to him. His human life began again, and he woke with a start.

Heinrich climbed out of bed. In the hallway he looked about. Light was leaking from under Vicky's bedroom door. He went into the kitchen, plugged in the kettle, took a mug and a tea bag from the cupboard, and sat down to wait for the water to boil. As steam rose from the kettle's spout he yanked the plug from the wall. I could become steam, he thought. I could forget entirely who I am if I stay here much longer. I must leave.

Crackling static leaked from the high-frequency radio on the sideboard. Sarah heaved herself up from the sofa's soft depths, crossed the room, snatched up the handset, and spoke loudly. The radio continued its voluble, indiscriminate capturing of sound waves, and every few seconds released a string of clear words to which Sarah responded.

Heinrich took a candy from the bowl on the coffee table, unwrapped it, and popped it in his mouth.

"My sister," said Sarah, her radio conversation over. "She's on her boat, fishing. She says my brother, he can't go out this morning. Before, he can tell from the wind and the clouds how it's gonna be. Now, he can't tell so easy. The weather, it behaves different."

"And you, Sarah?"

She raised her eyebrows, inquiringly.

"Do you get out on the land, sometimes?"

"Sure, I go. My brother, he takes me in the summer. Last year he put a big window in my camp. The sea is outside my window. Beautiful, more beautiful than here, better. I go there and I am very happy. But you know what?"

She grinned at him.

"What, Sarah? I don't feel like guessing."

"No more window at my camp. A bear broke my window." She burst out laughing. "No more window."

"Can you still go out? Is it fixed?"

"Oh, yeah. My brother puts big boards over the hole."

Heinrich got up from the sofa.

"You don't want a candy? You don't want to sit down? You take a candy, if you want."

"No, thank you. I've had one already."

"You going somewhere?"

"Yes, Sarah. I am going out. I won't be late."

"Deadman, I've got something for you," said Vicky, setting down a bag of groceries on the kitchen counter. She opened the fridge and put away a carton of milk, then she reached in the pocket of her sweatshirt.

Heinrich stared at the plastic card that she dropped on the counter for him to admire. A snapshot of himself, the words "University of Alberta," the institution's coat of arms and motto, his student number, every detail convincing. Date of birth: March 3, 1990.

"My friend, he did a crazy good job."

Heinrich picked up the student ID.

"Thank you, Vicky."

He set the ID down again and pulled his wallet from his pocket.

"How much do I owe your friend?"

"He doesn't want you to pay. You don't owe him anything. It's a good thing Sarah can't hear you. We have this word, inuuqatigiitsiarniq. I'd tell you how to say it in English, but I don't think it exists in English, not the same."

"Maybe it exists in German?"

"It's looking after each other, no matter what. If someone really needs something, doesn't matter who they are, you gotta help. If you don't, nobody's gonna survive. It's not like you get to choose."

Heinrich slipped his new identity card into his wallet. He was searching in his mind for the right German words. "Sich um jemanden kuemmern" meant looking after someone. But he knew that what she meant was different. What she meant smelled like the steam that pours out when you cut open a seal; it came from a particular reasoning, it was a word that belonged to a place where the floor of a house mustn't touch the ground or the heat leaking out will melt the permafrost and the house will start to sink.

If "sich um jemanden kuemmern" had a smell, it was of potatoes cooking. He could see his mother's hand, she was wiping the windowsill clean of dust, using an old tea towel that had become a rag. Embroidered on the towel were the words "Fuenf sind geladen, zehn sind gekommen, giess Wasser zur Suppe, heiss alle willkommen." "Five were invited, ten came, add water to the soup, and welcome all." Words embroidered a long time ago, used now for dusting windowsills and legs of chairs.

"Please, thank your friend for me."

"What if you don't find your sister?"

"I don't know."

"I'm going to leave soon, too."

"You'll be in Iqaluit, with your mom?"

"Not with my mom. I'll get a room at the college, and my mom might come back here to be with my grandma. It depends if my mom can get a job, here, in Pang. If she moves back here and goes hunting, then Sarah can eat more country food and have skins to sew, and she'll be happier."

"And you?"

"I sew pretty good, but not as good as Sarah."

"I meant, and you in Iqaluit. You won't be lonely?"

"My boyfriend, he's coming with me. It won't be until next fall. I say it's soon 'cause I want it to be soon. Anyway, this time, I'm not getting pregnant. I don't want to do that again. When I had the miscarriage, last year, I had to quit some of my classes. I couldn't concentrate. I had to work real hard to catch up. In the spring, I'm gonna graduate. Now I'm older, I gotta be more serious. Sarah doesn't know my boyfriend's gonna come and live with me."

"I won't say anything. I'll leave soon and look for my sister, I promise."

"Your sister will be old. Are you scared?"

"Yes."

On his way to the hotel, to say goodbye to Monsieur Pierre, Heinrich crossed paths with Johnny Ugalook, the printmaker who worked best with a radio playing and who, even when not working but walking along a road in the freezing dark as he was doing now, held his small radio pressed to his ear.

Heinrich's ears, as he walked along, were filled with a rushing sound that he could not explain. It was early October, little lakes were freezing over and smaller streams acquiring a skin of ice. The noise in his ears made no sense. It was very particular—not unlike that of a brook or small stream, yet different. Hearing it, immediately he pictured the blue ropes of twisting meltwater that he'd seen carving brilliant troughs into the ice of the Turner Glacier.

Seduced by the color of the glistening flow, months ago or decades ago, he'd knelt on the glacier's gritty surface, ignoring the intense cold piercing his knees. The sun burning the nape of his neck, he'd stared into the racing water. For an indefinite period of time he'd remained kneeling.

When he'd stood, it was not to admire Mount Asgard, or the view of the mountains and valley, but to follow, in a state of ecstasy, first one gorgeous, liquid vein, then another, as these led him across the vast frozen surface.

He'd felt no fear, wandering across the glacier, surrounded by its beauty and magnitude. Now, however, as he walked along the frozen road uneasiness grew in him, his ears filled by a relentless rushing. He nodded to Johnny Ugalook, and the sound in his ears intensified. He stepped off the road into the light snow between the houses. Even the act of plugging his ears with his mittened thumbs did not reduce the rushing. He fixed his gaze on the vinyl siding of the nearest house, but doing so did not free his inner eye from a vision of frenetic blue veins carving channels into a broad body of ice.

All the way to the hotel, the sound in his ears persisted. He climbed the steps; the door was locked and he banged on it. He peered through the glass, and a large figure in a white apron came hurrying slowly toward him.

What did Heinrich and Monsieur Pierre speak of on the day of their last encounter?

"Ah, mon ami. It's good to see you."

"Monsieur Pierre, in less than a week I am leaving Pang. I am going to Toronto to find my sister."

287

"Viens. I have a recette for you."

And Heinrich followed Monsieur Pierre up the four steps at the back of the lobby. Together they walked in silence past the freezer, up three more steps into the lounge, with its picture windows looking out on the sea, and down the hall and into the gleaming kitchen. Monsieur Pierre handed Heinrich a paper with a grease stain descending from its upper-left corner, then busied himself slicing onions. Heinrich thanked Monsieur Pierre for his precious crêpe recipe, tucked the paper in his pocket, and left.[28]

"Are you going to take her a present?" Vicky asked, biting into a slab of bannock. "When my mom goes someplace, she brings me back a present, and gets my grandma a clock. For my grandma, she always brings a clock. For

---

28 I don't know which silence is worse, the one that spreads from a severed telephone connection or the silence that slides into place the moment a computer screen goes blank. Again, last night, I spoke with Vicky on Skype, and again I annoyed her with my hunger for information about Heinrich Schlögel. Abruptly she went off-line. I climbed into bed but couldn't sleep. I got out of bed and poked about my Schlögel archive, not knowing what I hoped to find. I pulled out a folded slip of paper. The grease stain that spread down from its upper corner pleased me.

me, last time, she chose a T-shirt that said, 'Whitehorse,' and had a picture of a guy panning for gold. You could get your sister a Pang hat or one of the scarves they weave at the craft co-op. Or from my aunt you could buy directly. She's working on a pair of green felt mittens. They have a head of a seal that she's embroidering on each of them. Her embroidery's the best, except for Sarah's. My grand-ma's mittens are super gorgeous."

"Thanks, Vicky. To take my sister a present is a good idea. I would like to give my sister an ulu."

"What would she do with an ulu? I guess she could put it on a shelf and say, 'My brother brought me this knife from up North. He got lost for a long time but found his way back.'"

"Couldn't she chop vegetables and meat with it?"

"Yup, she could do that."

"I like the Pang hats and your aunt's mittens are beau-tiful. I've seen them at the co-op. But I haven't seen my sister in a long time. I don't want to choose something for her to wear."

"My cousin, he has three ulus almost ready. I could call and ask if he's finished making them. It would be a lot cheaper than if you buy one from the co-op."

"Yes, please."

While in Pangnirtung, Heinrich Schlögel did not record the frequency with which the rushing sound in his ears occurred. At least, I can find no written evidence that he made any attempt to document its patterns. I assume that he hoped it would just go away. Did the intensity of the sound fluctuate with the local weather? Was it more persistent in the evening or morning? Did it subside or grow in strength when he was in the presence of others? I have asked Vicky. But even to her he did not mention that his ears were troubling him.

"Except, one time. Yup, he did. And I thought it was a joke."

In her bright, compact, far-off kitchen, which I look into when we have our conversations, Vicky paused, then added in a tone so low that I barely caught her words, "Oh, shit, I had no idea he was really hearing things. I thought he was teasing me."

Heinrich chose the largest of the three uluit. In the corner of the room, a battery-powered wheelchair stood beside the TV, and on the sloping sofa sat Vicky's cousin. He was a heavy man. His smooth face had the closed expression of someone unavailable, of someone accustomed to the company of his own thoughts—or that is how Heinrich understood him to be, and he thanked the maker of the ulu for the ulu, and the maker of the ulu nodded.

A bulky worktable, with a jigsaw and an array of smaller tools, occupied the center of the plywood floor. These tools were full of intent and purpose. Much handled and well cared for, the hammers, the files, and the pliers spoke one language, and the raw poverty of the room, with its few pieces of battered furniture, its sink full of dishes, its old stove and peeling countertop, spoke another language. From the middle of a glossy poster pinned to the dull green wall, a benevolent Christ smiled upon the scene.

A skinny girl wearing sweatpants appeared from a back room. Heinrich had seen her with her child in the Northern Store and also in the visitors' center. He'd seen her standing in the road with the other young mothers, talking and laughing, and he'd walked past them, shyly. Now, she glanced at the ulu that he was buying from her father.

"I made the handle," she remarked as she pulled on her winter jacket.

He touched the wood and wanted to respond but couldn't think what to say.

"It's very nice," he managed, and smiled, but she was opening the door to leave.

Questions were buzzing like flies in his mind. How old is your baby? When Vicky's with you, does she miss her lost baby, the one she miscarried? Do you like hunting? How did your father lose the use of his legs? Did his snowmobile flip over, or was it from illness? Do you regret having had to quit school? But she was gone, her boots thumping down the outside stairs, and the room became swollen with silences.

Each silence, Heinrich imagined, held an answer to a question, but perhaps not to any of his questions. He listened as hard as he could, but felt uncertain how to separate one silence from another, so instead he fixed his gaze on the tools laid out on the workbench; he stared at the metal shavings swept into a small heap on the floor, and he observed the pieces of wood waiting to become the handles of uluit, and he avoided looking at the craftsman, whose home he'd entered and who he supposed was suffering because of his ruined legs, though perhaps the craftsman wasn't suffering, or not in the ways that Heinrich guessed?

Heinrich heard more flies buzzing. Then the rushing in his ears returned, drowning the buzzing of the flies. He glanced over at Vicky.

"You ready?" asked Vicky, taking the car keys from the pocket of her jacket. "I gotta get back. I promised Sarah, I'm gonna take her to the Northern Store, then over to her sister's place."

They left. With the ulu for Inge in a paper bag, they drove away. Vicky pressed on the gas pedal and the tires of the car raised fine clouds of dry snow.

"Do you hear water flowing?"

"Nope. Not me, Deadman."

Over the next few days, in his journal, in addition to noting the time he got up and the time he went to bed, Heinrich jotted down new words in Inuktitut. Memorizing distracted him from the rushing in his ears. He wished he'd made the effort sooner and that he'd acquired a larger vocabulary. Sewing, he wondered. How do you say "sewing"?

The soft whirring of the sewing machine stopped as Heinrich stepped into the back room, where Sarah sat working.

"Sarah."

"You like getting in the way?" she asked, turning to eye him with amused irritation.

"How do you say 'sewing' in Inuktitut?"

"Mirsuk. Saara mirsutuq pualuuniq. Saara mirstuviniq pualuuniq."

"Pualuuniq?"

Rather than answer, she applied her foot to the sewing machine's pedal, causing the motor to whir. It wasn't loud enough to overwhelm the rushing inside his head. Heinrich watched the needle fly up and down.

"Sarah."

She raised her eyebrows.

"Do you hear the sound of ice melting?"

"Winter is coming, not spring."

"So you don't hear it? I am scared, Sarah."

Again, she pressed down with her foot and the needle shot up and down faster and faster, the machine humming urgently.

"I came to tell you, my flight is at ten tomorrow morning, Sarah."

"I know that. You already tell me. You are a good boy, but you talk too much, and sometime you forget and don't take your boots off when you come in from outside. Why you tell me again that your plane goes tomorrow? You want me to say to you: 'Don't leave tomorrow'?"

"No, Sarah. I know that I have to leave."

She laughed.

"You think water is running when no water is running. But you hear good. The cold is not like before. My brother, he shoots a seal and it went under the water, hard to pull into his boat. The skinny seals do not float good in the warm water. You want me to tell you? Be scared, don't be scared? Men come here and shoot sled dogs. Some men come and not shoot the dogs. Anyway, dogs are dead now. They get very sick. Not enough food and bad sickness. Do men kill dogs? I don't see, I don't hear nothing, but the dogs are gone. I hear men walk on the moon. I don't see them walk. Do they walk on the moon? Men talk lots. You decide what you better believe. Good idea, sometime, to be scared. Sometime, scared not a good idea."

"I will miss you, Sarah."

"You think so?"

"Yes."

"Maybe you miss me. You find out."

He stood where he was. He waited.

"I got work to do. Why you standing there? You want me to give you work?"

His legs took him outside and made him walk. He followed the icy road down to the harbor, where he picked his way along the shore, a portion of his thoughts calculating the safety of his footing, and the rest of his ideas disappearing into the darkness and the smell of the sea.

He was standing at the airport. There were passengers coming and going through the glass doors, and people waiting for family to arrive, and other people stepping outside to have a smoke in the cold wind. Sarah Ashevak presented him with a pair of blue felt mittens.

"I thought I wasn't gonna finish. You watch, and not let me sew," said Sarah, frowning.

"Thank you, they are beautiful, Sarah."

"You put them on. I see if they fit you okay."

He slipped the mittens on and they fit perfectly. They were the most beautiful mittens he'd ever seen.

"They are wonderful, Sarah."

Sarah grinned with pleasure.

He looked anxiously about the terminal to say goodbye to Vicky. Without saying goodbye to Vicky, he couldn't leave. There were passengers sipping coffee from plastic cups, and passengers wandering to and from the washrooms. There were people hanging around who weren't passengers but who perhaps wished to become passengers one day. A call had come from the airport in the early morning to say that due to a fast-approaching storm, Heinrich's flight would leave early. Vicky had driven at top speed, which she'd greatly enjoyed but Sarah had not enjoyed. Now he couldn't find Vicky. There were people eagerly watching for the arrival of the next plane, and people opening their luggage to readjust the contents. Vicky threw her arms around him from behind.

"Did I scare you, Deadman?"

He nodded.

"Are you going to forget me?"

He shook his head.

"Send me an e-mail, when you find your sister?"

He nodded, still not daring to speak, too much emotion caught in his throat.

"Goodbye, Deadman."

"Goodbye, Vicky Pitsiulak."

In his journal he wrote:

> Today, I walked out onto the runway, clutching the most beautiful mittens I've ever owned. The plane rose in the air. Pangnirtung shrank below, and the sea widened.
>
> In Iqaluit I changed planes for Ottawa without difficulty. Now I am hanging above the clouds, through which I will soon drop, to land in Toronto.

"Did I tell it well, Vicky Pitsiulak? Is that how Heinrich left Pangnirtung?"

"You told it pretty good."

Owing to a technical difficulty, when I spoke with Vicky Pitsiulak this morning I could not see her, though she could see me. The video function on my computer had never failed before. It was in this context of inequality that our conversation took place.

"And Toronto?" she urged.

"I've told you all of it, I've already described Toronto and everything that happened there to Heinrich. Telling you took me close to an hour and left me exhausted."

"There was a bit missing. You kept hesitating. Tell it to me again."

"If you want to know more, the Schlögel archive is for sale."

"I don't want your archive, I want you to tell it, the whole story."

"An archive is a story."

"I'd have to search and piece it together. I'm not in the mood for that."

"Are you sure that you're the Vicky Pitsiulak that Heinrich Schlögel knew in Pangnirtung?"

"Yup."

"She liked to decide things for herself. She didn't ask other people to do her thinking for her."

"She liked stories too."

"All right, I'll tell you again what happened to him in Toronto."

"You should see your face."

"What about my face?"

"You look so self-important."

But she didn't go off-line; she lingered, invisible, listening, wanting to know something that I couldn't tell her. Or maybe this time, I would succeed in telling it better.

To meet the expectations of someone who matters deeply to me, how unfamiliar that would feel.

When I returned to Munich nearly three years ago to empty and sell my parents' apartment, to pay off their gambling debts, I found a box full of snapshots in the hall closet. The snapshots were of my childhood.

Until my parents passed away I'd remained unaware that their love of card games had mutated into a destructive compulsion. I lived on another continent. Had I lived close by, still their gambling might have consumed them.

I laid out several of the snapshots on my parents' dining room table. It was the first piece of furniture they'd purchased as a married couple, an oval table, sleek, modern, with no sharp angles.

Staring into the photos, I searched for what portion of reality each one contained. How differently might my parents' last years have played out if I'd returned more often to visit them? Quickly, I dismissed this question as childish. Only children see themselves as central to every event. I put away the photos and poured myself a small glass of schnapps.

Now, arranging these same snapshots on my desk in Toronto, I feel tempted to fire off an e-mail to Vicky suggesting that we Skype. My search for Heinrich Schlögel is not over.

PART FIVE

Toronto

1

Inge

Young men and women were perched on countertops, on chairs and sofas and the backs of sofas. There was talk of a bargain plane ticket, the cleverest way to avoid crowds at the Parthenon, how to board the Maid of the Mist at Niagara Falls without paying for the boat ride, and how to skip the queue at the Lenin Mausoleum in Moscow. Heinrich stood and listened, trying to decide whether to take off his backpack.

At high volume, a nervous girl and a bald man with a glittering earring were comparing regrettable eating experiences. Then eating was forgotten, overtaken by cramped Nepalese bus rides along the edges of cliffs, and by a mugging at knifepoint in Capetown; a young man, muscular and blond, recommended cures for mouth sores; the kettle boiled, cups appeared, socks were removed, books left in a chair, emotions typed into iPhones, necks massaged, dance moves practiced, songs hummed, advice texted, abbreviations sent skipping across the world. Heinrich slid his backpack off his shoulders and lowered it to the floor.

In the days that followed, companionable conversation nearly always greeted Heinrich when he stepped into the common room of the Canadian Adventure Youth Hostel, and he looked about unsuccessfully for a quiet corner. The furniture, utilitarian, a bit battered, was neither dirty nor uncomfortable. Sunlight fell through two tall windows well into the late afternoon. Not one voice spoke in the rhythms of Inuktitut.

The absence of Inuktitut felt abrupt and sweeping to Heinrich. A linguistic wind had lifted away Sarah and Vicky, as well as others who'd become more familiar and important to him than he'd realized. This sudden auditory erasure unnerved him. He tried to recall as many faces and voices from Pang as possible. All around him, English was being caressed, truncated, perforated, or yanked on. But Vicky's English was not present.

His own English three Germans immediately recognized, and he succumbed to their eager interrogation: How long had he been traveling? Where had he visited? Where did he plan to go next? With each German word that crossed his lips, he wondered if he sounded like someone who'd been traveling abroad for a few months or for thirty years. When he told them that he'd briefly visited the Arctic and was now headed home, they nodded, and did not look surprised. Perhaps, he thought, I will be able to conceal indefinitely the truth of what has happened to me.

A slender young man with a ring through his eyebrow announced that he'd lost a bishop from a portable chess set. A female voice, in response, asked who had left the pack of condoms beside the sink. An arm covered in tattoos handed Heinrich a cup of tea. The arm belonged to a tiny woman, one of the dancers. She advised him that when the computer provided in the corner of the common room was being monopolized by "you'll-soon-find-out-who," the best option was to try the nearest public library, which was at College and Spadina.

The sound of rushing water returned. Heinrich glanced at his watch. Five o'clock.

"Water noise in my ears, 5:00 PM. October 12, 2010," he jotted in his notebook. Tracking the evolution of the disturbance in his ears felt less daunting than searching for Inge. Yet he wanted more than anything to find her.

The doors of the Lillian H. Smith Library were guarded by two winged and imposing griffins cast in bronze. One had the head of a lion, the other the head of an eagle. Both sat back on their haunches, claws exposed, necks arched, fierce eyes staring down. Heinrich passed between them, entered the library, and continued the online search for Inge that he'd begun in Pangnirtung.

He discovered nothing new. As before, Inge's old address surfaced. And when he clicked on the link that read "League of Interpreters and Translators of Ontario," the warning "lapsed membership" appeared.

He typed "Helene Schlögel." Several women smiled at him from the screen but none of them was his Helene Schlögel. He resented these women for stealing his mother's name. He busied himself retrieving decades of world events that he'd missed.

Next to him, a florid man, humming loudly, began rocking back and forth in his chair. Two computers over, a woman wearing a headset shouted, "Fucking right. Dead on. You know dick all," addressing her disdain to the face on the screen in front of her. To the left of the reference desk stood the "Push-Up King." "Anytime you want, I'm ready to show you," he told the librarian.

Even on wet, cold days, Heinrich moved from one library to the next in his restlessness. He walked, tracing a zigzag route through the core of the city. Inge, he reasoned, was likely using the public libraries also, but which ones? If earning her living gobbled much of her time, for her the criteria of convenience would dominate. But perhaps she was out of work and wandering the city, as he was?

The friendliness of the staff, the carpet pattern, a certain study table near a window, the height of the ceiling, the number of computers made available to the public—these details determined which libraries Heinrich visited most often. Whenever possible he sat in a central spot, where Inge, were she to stop by to return her books and borrow new ones, couldn't help but notice him.

54 Raglan Avenue, Inge's old address, proved to be a three-story brick apartment building, located on a side street lined with parked cars and aged, ailing maple trees, many of them missing limbs. As Heinrich stood looking at the building, wind moved through the branches above his head, bringing down more leaves. Strewn at his feet, the leaves disconcerted him. He had not anticipated their beauty.

In Pangnirtung when he'd imagined trees, he'd pictured them obstructing his view of the sea and the land. In Pangnirtung, he'd most often conjured images of trees because he was thinking of his father, remembering how, together, they'd strolled through an orchard in bloom or they'd entered a well-tended woods that smelled coniferous. When he opened the door of the fish-processing plant, and stepped inside, and sliced with his knife, cutting away any bits of fish bone missed by the filleting machine, often his father appeared beside him, unfolded his knife with the walnut handle, and joined him in his work. Of his father's frequent presence Heinrich spoke to no one, not even to Vicky. To no one did he admit the degree of his longing.

Now, the leaves lying on the sidewalk at his feet made him want to weep and call out his father's name. Instead he walked quickly away from number 54.

The second time Heinrich approached 54 Raglan Avenue, he resolved to press the buzzer marked "Superintendent," but he did not do so.

A third time he approached, and, now, he pressed the buzzer. A white-haired woman opened the door, a glass of wine in one hand, cell phone in the other. She wore a shimmering, oyster-gray jogging suit and her flamboyant earrings matched the red laces of her running shoes. Heinrich tried to imagine Helene with white hair and dressed in a jogging suit, a miniature phone in her hand,

and he wanted to kick someone, or to swing his fist. The person he wanted to kick was his father, for refusing to give him any information about his mother.

"Please," he asked the woman in front of him (the superintendent?), "my sister used to live here, and I am trying to locate her. I wonder if you might help me. Her name is Inge Schlögel. I can show you proof of who I am."

"Inge Schlögel?"

"Yes. I am her brother, Heinrich."

He extracted his wallet from his back pocket.

"I don't need to see your ID. Don't bother taking it out. I don't know where your sister's moved to, because she didn't leave no forwarding address. I told her, someone'll want to get in touch with you. I asked her more than once, but she didn't listen. Not that your sister wasn't a good tenant. Quiet's something I like in a tenant. But her, she was more than quiet. Aloof, that's the word I'm looking for. Your sister was a bit aloof, not the easiest. You don't mind me saying so?"

"No, I don't mind."

"Listen, honey, I hope you find her. You got a number where I can reach you, just in case?"

Heinrich tore a page from his notebook, copied out his name and the hostel's phone number. The woman in the oyster-colored jogging suit took it from him.

"If I hear from your sister, I'll let you know."

Heinrich discovered the city's network of alleys and it pleased him. The bottoms of narrow gardens, laundry flapping against a chilly sky, unruly shrubbery, slits in fences, a garage door thrown open, another closed to conceal a motorcycle, a lawn mower, or something more private.

The rhythmic whine of a saw caught his attention, the noise escaping from a garage a few meters away. Heinrich approached. The door was open. He looked in. White plastic garden chairs lay toppled on the floor. At a workbench, a broad-shouldered man with a dark ponytail was sawing through the leg of a garden chair, which he'd clamped in place.

"Hello," said Heinrich.

The man stopped sawing and glanced up. His expression was neither inviting nor hostile. Heinrich stepped closer. On the floor behind the workbench, a large skeleton was taking shape; the curved white plastic of several dismembered chairs had transformed into immense ribs. Knobby bits, taken from the same sawed-up furniture, were becoming colossal vertebrae.

"What animal is it?"

"Whale," answered the man.

"When it's all put together, how many meters do you think it will be?"

"I dunno. Can't exactly say, not yet. Close to four meters, maybe."

"What do you plan to do with it?"

"Get it out of this garage," the man answered with a grin.

"Thank you for letting me look."

"You live around here?"

"No. I am only a visitor. I'm looking for my sister."

"You lost track of her?"

"Yes."

"What's her name?"

"Inge. Inge Schlögel. You may know her?"

"Nope. Afraid not."

"Have you made other skeletons besides this one?"

"Nope. This is my first."

"Best of luck with the whale."

"Good luck finding your sister."

Heinrich continued down the alley, avoiding the potholes and broken glass. Soon a light rain began to fall and he pulled up the hood of his jacket. All afternoon he walked under the delicate rain that continued to fall.

On a Tuesday, at the intersection of two congested streets, each bursting with vehicles, Inge shot past on her bicycle, then came to an abrupt stop. A parked car was blocking her way. Her hair, streaked with gray, hung longer than he remembered, but her alert posture, the tension in her slender torso, gave her away. He ran up to her and she turned. Her eyes and mouth were wrong, her entire face a mistake.

"I'm sorry. I thought you were someone else."

Though the woman smiled and did not appear to mind being mistaken for someone else, Heinrich walked off as quickly as he could. He headed south down a street called Bathurst, unsure where he was going but eager to lose himself in the noise of the traffic.

During the course of the next week, Inge stood waiting on the northbound subway platform of the Yonge line, she was buying a loaf of bread as Heinrich stepped into the Harbord Bakery, the lights dimmed in the Bloor Cinema and she slipped into the row of seats in front of him, on Dundas Street across from a large public park, she drove up in a small beige car, a German shepherd on the seat next to her; and always, the moment he hurried forward or leaned closer to greet her, she changed into a stranger. It became clear to him that he might never find Inge, and the pain of this realization intensified his determination to locate her.

Will I find Heinrich Schlögel? I do not think so. But I must keep searching. I have no choice. "Nope," says Vicky. "You've got a choice. You could stop." I could have chosen to visit my parents more often; my parents could have resisted when their card-playing took over, not gambled away everything save the dining room table. Time is short. Time runs out. If I do meet Heinrich, I'll ask him about choice, about how to choose what to ask of others, and what to ask of myself—I said this to Vicky, yesterday, and she slapped her thigh and laughed at me. "You think he'll hear you? His ears are full of rushing water."

Whenever a telephone rang or yelped, shivered or sang, instinct made Heinrich turn. In Pangnirtung there had been no tiny phones that you could slip into your pocket. Now, all around him, people dove their hands into their purses or jackets. He imagined people shouting and laughing into tiny telephones while hurrying along a Munich sidewalk, or while strolling in the tranquility of the Englischer Garten, and these images struck him as so absurd that he laughed aloud. Not one person turned, curious to know the reason for his laughter.

In the confines of streetcars and buses, voices announced to invisible, intended listeners, as well as to anyone nearby, the sudden blindness of an uncle, a boss with a

sexual hunger, the loss of a dog, the spread of evil, the pur-
chase of real estate, the crumpling of a marriage. Heinrich
took out his journal and noted the return of the rushing
sound in his ears.

For over a week he'd been free of it. Now the racing
imposed, as before. His mind filled with images of water
twisting in ropes of luminous blue that carved channels
in a body of ice. He wrote down the hour, then he shut
his notebook, as if doing so might put a quick end to
the rushing and delay its return. But when the rushing
of water did cease, he caught himself eagerly, perversely,
anticipating its resurgence. Nothing in his surroundings
felt as real. Across screens on subway platforms slid snip-
pets of world news—terrorist attacks, company merg-
ers, floods, infestations, and droughts. Cars were being
wrapped in tissue paper for Christmas, and tiny pills
promised libido.

Heinrich returned to the alley where he'd heard the
sawing. The same garage door stood open. He stepped
inside but the man with the ponytail was nowhere to be
seen. Stacked on the floor, more neatly than Heinrich expected, lay the white, sawed-off arms and legs, the seats
and backs, of plastic garden chairs.

He looked up and caught his breath. It hung from the
rafters—the completed skeleton of a whale, immense, in-
tricate, and graceful. He walked beneath it, marveling at
its elegance and its huge fluidity. He stepped through the

beautiful shadows it cast on the garage floor and stared up through its pattern of curves and joints.

A smaller door at the back of the garage swung open and the tall, ponytailed man, the whale-maker, walked in, visibly preoccupied. He spotted Heinrich, and his expression changed to one of pleasure.

"Good to see you."

"It is amazing, your whale."

"Now I have to find somewhere to put it."

"Could you sell it? To an art gallery, maybe?"

The man laughed, then indicated the thermos in his hand.

"You want coffee?"

"Yes, thank you."

"I was thinking of leaving it in a park, but it wouldn't last long with people climbing on it and kicking it in the ribs. Trouble is, it takes up too much room. I can't work on anything new, not until I get it out of here. You any closer to finding your sister?"

"I am starting to think I won't find her."

"Why's that?"

"I've been looking every day, and every day I see women everywhere but not her. And my money. I am running out. I don't have a work permit."

"They'd hire you to wash dishes in the restaurant where I work. Pay's pretty shitty but regular. Or I know a guy who moves stuff. He has a truck. He can sometimes use help."

"Thank you. If you have the names and the numbers so I can call?"

"Sure."

"I'm Heinrich."

"Andy."

"The whale. It is magnificent."

"Glad you like it."

"You have spent a lot of time looking at whales?"

"Some. Your sister in trouble?"

"I don't think so. No, I am the trouble, the problem."

"I know that feeling."

Andy fished a stub of pencil from his shirt pocket.

"You got a piece of paper?"

He wrote two names and some phone numbers into the notebook that Heinrich handed him.

"When you call the restaurant, ask for George. Tell him you're a friend of mine. I'm the cook. He owns the joint. If that doesn't work, try Boris, the guy with the truck. I've given you his number too."

"Thanks."

Andy rummaged in his toolbox. He located the drill bit that he'd come looking for. Bending, so as not to knock his head, he left through the small door at the back of the garage.

Heinrich's new life began, a life of dishwashing at the Argos Grill; and his old life of searching for Inge continued also, and every day the rushing of water in his ears surged and subsided with no discernable pattern or verifiable meaning.

"George is a crocodile," commented Heinrich, between sips of coffee. Above his head hung the whale's skeleton, while on the garage floor a new project was under way. In the corner stood a black leather sofa missing most of its skin. Andy had hauled out a sewing machine. Shoulders hunched, foot on the pedal, needle racing, he was stitching together the final panel of a black leather teepee.

"Have you got tent poles?"

"Yup."

"George sits behind the counter and looks like he's sleeping, but he is not. He grabs his victim—usually a waitress but sometimes a waiter—and drags this person to the bottom of the river to soften in the mud, to make this person easier to digest."

The whirring of the sewing machine stopped. Andy looked over at Heinrich and grinned.

"George can be a real shit."

The whir of the machine resumed.

317

On a Sunday afternoon, at the Toronto Reference Library, Heinrich glanced up and there she was, rising inside a glass elevator, soundlessly, to the next floor. She wore a turquoise raincoat, and a voluminous book bag hung from her shoulder. Heinrich took the stairs two at a time. She was being whisked upward faster than he could climb. On the fourth floor, she stepped lightly out of the elevator and walked off into the stacks. Heinrich, arriving several minutes later, raced between the bookshelves. He made his way frantically along the rows, and emerged just in time to see the elevator carrying her down, the silent glass tube dropping her from floor to floor.

At each level the tube paused to let people on and people off. Passengers crowded into its transparent confines. A large man, whose paisley necktie threatened to cut off his breathing, was pressed up against her—the woman in the turquoise raincoat.

She was perhaps not Inge after all. She kept her head bent, looking down through the glass, as the long study tables, the plants, computer terminals, and people wandering in the atrium raced up from below to greet her.

Bounding down the stairs, Heinrich reached the ground floor. At the security counter, the guard was asking the woman in the turquoise raincoat to open her capacious shoulder bag. She complied, and the guard fished, languid, indifferent, removing several books, subjecting each to his inspection. Heinrich joined the line.

A toad-shaped man clutching a swollen briefcase preceded him, also a stern, gray-haired woman who resembled a stork. Stork woman raised an unlit cigarette to her lips, as if in a meaningful gesture. No matter the direction in which Heinrich leaned, he could not get a clear view of her—the woman in the turquoise raincoat.

"These ones are all marked out on my card," a female voice assured the guard, a voice so familiar that Heinrich felt the blood drain from his head. So as not to lose his balance, he fixed his eyes on the floor and concentrated on the air entering and leaving his lungs. Several immeasurable seconds later, feeling less faint, he looked up and there she was.

Her chin was Inge's chin and her nose also belonged to his sister. The profile was hers. She wore glasses. If only he could see her mouth better, and her eyes better. She was, of course, older, her cheekbone more pronounced, her neck vulnerable in a way that he couldn't define. Already the guard was nodding her through. The toad-man unlatched his bursting briefcase for inspection.

"Please," Heinrich heard himself cry out. "My sister. That woman, just going out the door, I must catch up with her. I'm sorry. Please." His right hand trembled as he unzipped his day pack while he pushed forward with his shoulder, shoving both the unexpectedly forgiving stork-woman and the indignant toad-man out of his way. The guard serenely nodded him through and Heinrich ran for the exit. He burst onto the sidewalk and stared in all directions. She was walking briskly south, her back held very straight, her steps small but vigorous. He dodged between pedestrians. A finite expanse of cool autumn air separated him from her elbow.

"Inge."

Her name broke free of him, sprang from his mouth. The woman turned, startled. Her eyes filling with confusion, she stared at him. He did not dare move or speak another word.

The woman's arms hung at her sides. She examined him with her eyes, counting on her eyes, it seemed, to tell her something more, something that might set her mind at rest. Her glasses had simple black rectangular frames. Other pedestrians, preoccupied, hurried around Heinrich and the staring woman. The wind blew a thick strand of graying hair across the woman's face and she lifted her hand. With her fingers she pulled the tip of the strand from the corner of her mouth.

"Inge?"

Was it her? He could no longer be sure. Should he trust himself? Was his intense longing, or perhaps some malfunctioning of his mind, misleading him into believing that this person planted on the sidewalk was Inge?

The woman's hand tucked the intrusive strand of hair behind her ear. It was an oddly boneless and pale hand.

Heinrich remembered that these were two qualities that Inge'd always disliked about her hands and feet: their pallor and their fleshy lack of visible structure. "My fat feet and hands," she used to complain, though the rest of her, however smooth and pale, could never have been construed as fat—on the contrary.

Heinrich wanted to reach with the tips of his fingers and explore the softness of this woman's cheek. Only around her eyes had her skin noticeably aged.

"Yes?"

The voice was indisputably Inge's. A single word in the form of a question, "Yes?" He waited to hear what she would say and to see what she would do next.

"I'm sorry to be staring at you in this way. But you remind me of my brother. Forgive me." Her words tumbled with a nervous quickness.

"Inge."

"I feel we've met before." She paused and swallowed, clearing her throat. "But I'm afraid I can't pinpoint where?"

The worry in her eyes was intensifying, the set of her mouth expressed unease. He thought he saw her fingers curl in on themselves but she slipped her hands into her pockets and he lost sight of her fingers.

"We met the day I was born. You were two years old." He continued in German, the words flowing easily. "When you were seven, you went out in the fields and collected dead birds. We met in Tettnang."

Her hands flew to her face, covered it, then the fingers of her right hand spread apart and her terrified eye peered at him. Her book bag started to slip from her shoulder but immediately she lowered her hands, reached over and stopped its progress. She wrapped her arms around her rib cage, holding herself.

"When you were fifteen," Heinrich pressed on, "you started studying languages."

Slowly she began to sway, rocking back and forth on her feet, from toe to heel, from heel to toe.

"Two years later, you found a kit for learning Inuktitut, and sometime after that you came down the hall and knocked on my bedroom door and gave me the diary of Samuel Hearne and told me to read it."

"Stop."

He said nothing more. He held perfectly still.

They went into the nearest coffee shop and sat down at a small table. How did they get from the sidewalk into the café? Who led, who followed? Did they walk quickly or slowly? Later, neither of them could remember. They sat across from each other. She wrapped her hands around a cup filled with hot coffee. On the middle finger of her left hand she wore a large opal ring. She began twisting this ring and continued doing so, which he found unsettling to watch. The fine creases in her skin, those fanning out from the corners of her eyes, fascinated him. Her actual eyes, the iris and the pupil, had not changed, nor had their message, one of hunger and insistence, a look that invited precision, that demanded logic prevail. It was a look Heinrich remembered perfectly. And yet it was the way she cradled her cup, lifting it to her wide mouth, then drinking in a series of urgent sips, that most deeply convinced him of who she was. Inge, my sister. My sister, Inge, he repeated to himself, while they sat in silence.

At last, she spoke, and Heinrich felt grateful, his own mouth parched and wordless.

"Where have you been?" she asked.

He drank some water and told her.

He described his hike, which had felt timeless but could not have lasted more than twelve days, as he'd brought with him only twelve days' worth of provisions. All that he'd witnessed, how their grandfather had appeared from behind a rock, the scene between their parents, how he'd encountered Hearne and argued with him, all of this he told her, and that he no longer knew if any of it was true. He paused, waiting for her to respond. He asked if she believed his story.

"What choice do I have? Here you are, and you're barely any older than when I last saw you."

Her response ought to have pleased him, but it didn't. Underneath, she was no more satisfied than he was with what he'd conveyed. A crucial element was missing: the essential detail that might make sense of what had happened to him. His explanation could not make her any happier than it made him; she, the smart one. But instead of challenging him she smiled. It was a gentle smile. Part true happiness, part pretend, he decided. He shook his head. This was not what he wanted.

Heinrich and Inge, reunited in a small café. They contemplated each other. In a state of suspended disbelief, they examined one another.

"I nearly didn't go to the library today, I almost didn't find you," he told her.

"I feel ancient, sitting opposite you. You look so young. Your body isn't about to fall apart the way mine is."

"No, it's not, you look wonderful."

She had no real answers to offer him—he knew this now. She understood no better than he did. Yet he'd counted on her for an explanation.

"Why don't you ask me where I really was?"

"Fine. Where were you really, Heinrich, while I was living here all these years?"

"I don't know."

She sat where she was, her face unreadable, and twisted the ring on her finger.

"I . . ." she started.

He waited.

"When you disappeared," she said.

She stared down at the hard surface of the table, perhaps trying to make sense of all that had occurred, perhaps going over and over a set of feelings or images in her
mind. Under the table, her leg began to shake. It shook
until she stopped it with her hand. Then she looked up
at him.

She spoke of her work. She earned her living as a translator, freelance for the most part, English into German.
It could be invigorating, challenging, though much of it
she found exacting in a tedious way. Washing-machine
manuals, instructions for software. Once she'd been asked
to translate industrial performance reviews of prosthetic
limbs. He smiled as she spoke. My months, her thirty
years, he thought, and a vast unimpeded sadness spread inside him. He wanted to weep but pushed the feeling down.

She went on telling him about her work. There was
rarely a shortage, not often a break, and the worst was
when her clients needed their text ready by the following day. She was talking more than he remembered ever
hearing her talk, talking as if talking might save her from
drowning or perhaps stop him from disappearing again.
Listening to her voice intensified the ache inside him, and
listening to her voice softened the ache. His ache acquired
the rhythms of her speech.

"But I do like it," she said. "Once I find the right words, when they fall into place, neatly, when I know that I am good at it."

She didn't dare turn down a job. She lived alone.

Suddenly, he wondered about the friend she'd mentioned in her letter to him, the woman she'd met in Pangnirtung, who'd told her to come to Toronto. Inge's letter, folded small, was tucked in his wallet. He reached for his wallet, then hesitated.

"Not even a cat?" he asked.

She smiled. "A few plants. No cat."

Heinrich pulled her letter from his wallet.

"This is how I knew to come to Toronto."

She stared at the paper, which he held between his finger and thumb.

"Didn't you make friends, in Pangnirtung, with a woman, studying weaving?" he asked.

He reminded himself how long ago that was for her, how long ago it was for everyone but him, and again he wanted to cry, and a sob formed in his chest, but he realized there was no point in crying, and he pushed the feeling farther down. It did not occur to him that he was lucky to have been given an extra thirty years; this thought did not cross his mind. He felt only his loneliness, and the chafing weight of inexplicability that had wrapped itself around him—the impossibility of his presence.

"Yes, she was my friend. We met when I came to Pangnirtung to look for you. She was there to study weaving. She was adventurous, like you. We did become friends. But once I arrived here, in Toronto, it was different. She had lots of friends and wanted to introduce me. I couldn't say much. I've never been good at conversation. I'm not like you. I stopped being able to speak, even with her. I wrote to her. I sent her a letter, telling her what I wanted to say. I sent her so many letters, and I knew I wasn't behaving the way other people would, that they'd just go out for coffee, sit like this, the way you and I are now, but I couldn't. She'd call. She never answered my letters. She'd say into the phone, 'Let's have coffee. We live in the same city.' But what would I have said, once she was sitting across from me? I stopped answering my phone."

Heinrich let go of the letter, her letter to him, and it lay on the small table between them. She took it. Reading it made her frown.

"Is there something wrong?" he asked.

She returned the letter to him.

"Karl is not well. I've been meaning to go and see him. I had planned to be there, in Tettnang, now, this month, but so much work came along, jobs that I couldn't afford to turn down. Or maybe I just didn't want to go." She paused. "Isn't it amazing?" she told him. "You wouldn't have found me, if I'd gone. And we wouldn't be here together." Her mouth curved in a sudden smile, as if finding each other outweighed everything else.

"Yes, it's amazing," said Heinrich, and, reaching across, he placed his hand on hers. She waited several seconds before withdrawing her hand and slipping it under the table.

"I really should go to see him much more often," she said. Her hands reappeared and she began twisting her ring.

"I spoke with him."

He told this woman, this woman who was Inge, his sister, of his futile conversation with their father, Karl; how he'd sat in the lobby of the Pangnirtung hotel, talking hopelessly into a pay phone.

"Yes," she said. "He told me that someone had called pretending to be you."

"Cruelly pretending? Did he tell you that the person who called him was cruel?"

"No."

"Troubled? Soft in the head?"

"Yes."

"And him, how is he unwell?"

"He has Parkinson's disease."

Heinrich lifted his teaspoon but couldn't think what to do with it and set it down again.

"I upset him."

She gave him a sharp look.

"It's not because you upset him, Heinrich. There's no point indulging in feelings of guilt. A distressing telephone call doesn't cause Parkinson's disease."

"No? You think he brushed off, so easily, such a weird and nasty prank? Some stranger who'd found out so much about him? Didn't he worry that perhaps he was wrong? Didn't he wonder if maybe he'd hung up on his son?"

"Yes, it kept troubling him, of course it did. That's not why he's ill."

"And Mama?"

Inge twisted the large opal ring on her finger. Around and around it went, rotating on her pale, seemingly boneless finger.

"Mama left."

"Where to?"

"After you disappeared, and we all searched and waited and finally decided—well, they decided, or half decided, that you were probably dead, Mama learned of a farm in Northern Scotland, a sort of international commune for people who talk to plants. She wrote to them and signed up for a week, then stayed on. She worked on the farm. I think she was quite happy. I got the impression she felt freer there than she'd ever felt with Karl."

"She felt freer, was happy, but isn't anymore?"

"She died last year."

He looked away. The effort of not sobbing caused a tightening in his chest.

"I'm sorry, Heinrich. I should have told you right away."

Now tears did run into his mouth, and some continued on their path, slipping over his chin.

"You could go there, Heinrich, to Findhorn. You could visit her friends, and see the place. You could see where she lived. I have some photos of her that she sent. I'll show them to you."

Inge paused. She watched her brother dry his face. He used the sleeve of his shirt. She went on explaining as best she could.

"I never went to see her. Mama kept urging me to come and visit. She said how good the sea air would be for me, that she wanted to offer me a holiday by the sea, that she worried when she thought of how hard I was working; and did I really not mind being alone all the time? She convinced herself it was for my sake that she was inviting me. You know what she was like. She told herself that all her motives were pure, her desires selfless. If she'd just had the honesty to admit that it was as much about her needs as mine, that she wanted my approval, that she needed me to admire the wonderful refuge she'd discovered, I might have gone. I did want to see her. And, I suppose, I wanted her approval too. But mostly I wanted her to be direct, to stop denying what she was really asking me to give her. But in any case, I doubt that I could have lasted more than a day in that kind of place. All those people, discovering their spiritual connection with the earth, and feeling good about themselves, and imagining that their pure, superior thoughts might have the power to save the world—it would have driven me crazy, I'd have thrown myself in the sea. But I do think she was happy."

Inge gestured for the waiter.

"Can I have a glass of water, please?"

"Perhaps I will go there," Heinrich blurted out.

But I am too late, he thought. Mama is gone. I am always too slow, and arrive too late. I don't even have a passport. Inge is free to paint any picture of Mama that she likes. I can do nothing to stop her.

"You should go. That's where Helene was happiest and felt understood. Besides, they'd love you there, if you told them about your hike in the Arctic, about slipping through a hole in time."

"You don't believe me, do you?"

"Please, Heinrich."

Her leg was once more shaking. He raised his voice without wanting to.

"If I didn't slip through a hole in time, then what happened to me? If I'm not really your brother, then what are you doing sitting here talking to me? You're going on about Mama, and how much she loved you or didn't love you, and how honest she was or wasn't, as if nothing strange has happened, as if I'm not suddenly thirty years younger than you."

She covered her face with her hands. Now her shoulders were shaking, as well as her leg.

"Inge. I am sorry."

She lowered her hands and stared at him angrily.

"What do you want me to do?" she asked.

He couldn't answer and directed his gaze at the traffic passing outside the café.

In a voice quivering with fury, she told him, "You've always wanted me to know everything."

"I should leave."

"Please, Heinrich."

Now she gave him a desperate look, and to stop her hands from trembling she tucked them under her thighs.

"Inge."

"I can't stand this."

She released her hands, and gestured for the waiter to bring the bill. They both stood up, pushing back their chairs, the legs scraping the floor. She paid for both their coffees.

"I have money," he told her.

They emerged from the café onto the sidewalk.

"I should have asked you right away," she said. "Do you need some money?"

"I'm all right, thanks. I've got a job, washing dishes in a restaurant."

"And a place to stay?"

He nodded.

"Where?"

"A youth hostel."

"Is it okay?"

"It's noisy, cheap, friendly."

"I'd ask you to stay with me, but my place . . ."

He interrupted her, "Shall we walk? Will you walk with me a bit?"

They went west along Bloor Street. At University Avenue, a red light stopped them.

"I'll write out my address and phone number for you," she said.

Her book bag was slipping from her shoulder. She caught hold of it, and fished for a notebook, and tore out a page, then searched for a pen. When she'd given him the paper with all her information on it, they continued to walk. He told her about the sound of rushing water that was invading his hearing. She made him promise to see a doctor. He asked if she'd help him to call Karl. They might speak with their father, together.

"Yes," she promised. "Of course."

Several streets later, she looked at her watch and announced, "I have to go. I'm sorry. I have an appointment. I'm really sorry. It's for work. Will you call me tomorrow?"

"Yes."

"Or I'll call you?"

"Yes. Yes, Inge."

He held her tightly. Her smooth pale cheek pressed against his. He released her. He had no choice. He stood on the corner and watched his sister, the woman in the turquoise raincoat, walk away.

2

We Are All Erratics

Under a surprisingly cloudless November sky, Heinrich headed south down University Avenue and found himself surrounded by hospitals. Princess Margaret, Mount Sinai—he read the signs, debating which doors he should go through to ask to have his ears checked. On the opposite side of the broad avenue stood two more hospitals—Toronto General and the Hospital for Sick Children. Six lanes of traffic surged—cars, bicycles, and taxis competing. A finger of manicured grass, of low flower beds and tall trees, separated the southbound lanes from the lanes pouring north.

Inside his ears, liquids rushed, gurgling and tumbling. In his mind's eye luminous blue ropes of water were carving deep paths in a vast body of ice. At Elm Street a red light told him to stop. While he waited to cross, something caused him to glance over his shoulder. A few meters behind, on the sidewalk, stood a fox and a stag. The fox was lean, with a healthy coat, an auburn plume of a tail, and a nervous energy. It was sniffing the air. The stag, broad-chested, full-grown, observed its surroundings without moving a muscle. Its antlers were immense. I mustn't stare, thought Heinrich. The light changed and he continued to walk south, as if he had not seen the two animals. This felt like the most respectful course of action. To pointedly acknowledge their presence might make them panic and run into the traffic.

He passed a building marked "Rehabilitation Sciences," and without having to look he knew that the fox and the stag were following close behind; he could feel their eyes watching him. At Dundas Street, another red light. He allowed himself to glance over his shoulder. There they were, also waiting for the light to change: two wild animals on the sidewalk of a broad avenue in bright daylight, strangely serene. Both seemed indifferent to the noise of the traffic. Both ignored the pedestrians who passed, several of whom turned to stare. As soon as the light changed, Heinrich crossed Dundas, and the fox and the stag crossed with him.

The noise of racing water was growing in volume inside Heinrich's ears. He would have changed direction, gone back toward the row of hospitals, but how could he enter a hospital accompanied by two wild animals?

Perhaps he was mistaken and they were not accompanying him but simply headed for the lake at the south end of the city or for some green refuge that they knew of—a park, or a grassy strip beneath a highway?

The fox trotted and the stag walked, unperturbed, past the facade of the US Consulate General. They passed in front of the imposing Canada Life Building. A young woman hurried toward Heinrich. She was pointing at the fox and the stag and saying something that he could not make out, her words drowned by the rushing in his ears. As he came parallel with the Boer War memorial he slowed his pace. A bronze woman, flanked by two soldiers, was pointing her raised arm in the direction of empire and victory. He and his two animal companions started across Queen Street.

There were now numerous pedestrians staring, and many, having taken out their cell phones, were snapping pictures. Heinrich reached the south side of Queen Street, and, in a panic, darted down a set of stairs, away from the cameras and attention.

The stairs descended into Osgoode subway station. Will the animals follow me down these steps? Heinrich wondered. If they do, I'll have to lead them out of here, back up to the street, and continue walking. The fox may try coming down. But the stag won't. Heinrich waited. Neither animal descended. He wondered what was happening to them. If I climb back up to the street, will they

337

still be there? By now, someone will have called the police or the fire department. He listened for the wail of sirens, but could hear only rushing water. I can't help them, he told himself. But he knew this wasn't true, and in a matter of seconds he was dashing back up the stairs, taking the steps two at a time.

He emerged onto the sidewalk. The fox and stag were waiting for him, a growing throng of curious people surrounding them. The twisting, high-pitched notes of an approaching siren cut through the roaring in Heinrich's ears. He held himself still, and the fox and the stag held equally still. The eyes of the two animals met his, but he could not read their thoughts.

The Search for
Heinrich Schlögel

On November 24, 2010, the Canadian national newspaper, the *Globe and Mail*, published a photograph showing a young man walking down University Avenue, possibly being followed by a fox and a full-grown stag.

The young man has a long, loose stride, and his attention is fixed on some point farther ahead, outside the frame. It is impossible to say if he is aware or not of the two wild animals advancing with apparent calm along the broad sidewalk a short distance behind him.

The article accompanying the picture offers little information. It does not name the young man. It states: "At approximately two in the afternoon of November 23, pedestrians were astonished to see a fox and a stag proceeding down University Avenue, as if part of a larger, invisible parade." Though quite a few people captured the event on their cell phones, nobody, according to the article, could say where the animals had come from.

The young man was observed dashing down the stairs into the Osgoode subway station. At the top of these stairs, the two wild animals stopped. They stood for quite some time, maybe waiting for the young man to resurface from underground. What connection existed between the young man and the two animals? This question, when put to the public, prompted a variety of responses. Several witnesses declared that the animals, quite obviously, were hoping to be reunited with the young man. Other observers pronounced unequivocally that the young man who descended into the subway did so without having noticed the animals, and that he had no intention of returning.

The article states that in front of the city hall the police used a Taser to stun the stag and the fox, which had by then broken free of the growing throng and headed east along Queen Street, the stag leaping and the fox running. Staff from the city's health department, the article reassures, worked alongside the police to safely remove the two Tasered animals from the scene. "Both will later be released in a suitable location outside the metropolitan area," the article promises.

In the week following its original publication in the *Globe and Mail*, the photo of the young man, the fox, and the stag was reproduced in several more newspapers, including the *National Post*, the *Toronto Star*, and the *Toronto Sun*.

In each publication, a new and slightly different article attempts to shed light on the photograph. All of the articles agree that on the night of November 23, 2010, a German visitor, possibly the young man in the photograph, entered the emergency department of the Toronto General Hospital and asked what it would cost him to have his ears examined. The young German told the triage nurse that he'd been hearing, off and on, for close to a month, the sound of rushing water. His auditory disturbance, he said, had recently grown to a roar and gave no indication of subsiding.

The nurse informed the young man of the fee. He had difficulty hearing her, and asked her to write the number down, which she did. He agreed to pay. He gave his name, Heinrich Schlögel, and showed her his student ID, the only identification he had with him. She slid a form across the counter for him to complete. While he was filling out the form, the nurse glanced at the television screen suspended in the waiting area. A map of weather patterns vanished and was replaced by an image of a fox and a full-grown stag. The two animals appeared to be freely following a young man down University Avenue. The German looked up from the form he was filling out, saw the nurse's questioning expression, and traced her gaze to the screen behind his shoulder. Without another word, the young man hurried out of the receiving area, abandoning on the counter the half-filled-out form.

"He had a lovely smile and a gentle voice," the triage nurse is quoted as having commented. "I'm quite sure it was him."

Each article concludes with an appeal to "any member of the public possessing information concerning Heinrich Schlögel and his possible whereabouts" to contact the Toronto Police.

Acknowledgements

Heinrich Schlögel is immeasurably indebted for his existence to Iris Häussler, Greg Sharp, Guy Ewing, Conor Goddard, Madeleine Thien, and Karl-Heinz Raach. I thank Joanne Schwartz, Annie Beer, Dominic Denis, Sophie Perceval, Glenda Goodgoll, Susan Glickman, Marianne Apostolides, Carolyn Black, and Mary Ellen Thomas for reading with care. Special thanks to Markus Wilcke for his wise ears, and to Anne Egger for sending me to Hannah Tautuajuk, and to Corinne Hart for sending me to Markus Wilcke.

Particular thanks to those with whom I hiked to the Turner Glacier and back: Mr. Slap Chop and Officer Wheeler (of Blackfeather), Weather King, the Finisher, Little Miss Sunshine, Blista Sista, Valery Huff (human book of plant knowledge!), and Dr. Freeze.

My warmest thanks to Hannah Tautuajuk, her daughter, and her granddaughter for their hospitality during my stay in Pangnirtung, and to Louis Robillard for his cuisine and humor.

Thanks to the Core Sample writing group for encouragement, insights, and camaraderie. Thanks to Boris Steipe for his engagement in the early stages.

This novel has benefitted from the devotion and skill of two extraordinary editors, Meg Storey (of Tin House) and Beth Follett (of Pedlar Press).

Much thanks to my loyal and discerning literary agent, Samantha Haywood, for placing me in such excellent hands.

I thank the Pirurvik Centre for permission to quote from their Inuktitut language-learning dialogues and grammar lessons from their Tusaalanga website.

The artworks that the character Andy creates in his garage are fictional replicas of works by Brian Jungen.

I first encountered the tale of the fox wife many years ago. Vastly differing versions of the fox wife tale exist. The same is true of the Sedna tales, one of which I came upon, as well as the aliok tale, in *Stones, Bones and Stitches: Storytelling through Inuit Art* by Shelley Falconer, Tundra Books, 2007.

None of the quotations about animals come from *Brehms Tierleben*, and all are attributed to fictitious titles. All animal information taken from Internet sites has been reworded. I do thank, however, Mole Direct, for permission to quote verbatim from their site.

Thanks to the Krishnamurti Foundation of America for permission to combine sentences from several texts by Krishnamurti, resulting in the passage read by Helene Schlögel in her garden.

Thanks to Basil Hiley and David Peat for permission to quote from the work of David Bohm and David Peat, as follows: "This order is primarily concerned not with the outward side of development, and evolution in a sequence of successions, but with a deeper and more inward order out of which the manifest form of things can emerge creatively." David Bohm and F. David Peat, *Science, Order, and Creativity*, Bantam Books, 1987, p.151.

Rebecca Comay's fascinating *Mourning Sickness: Hegel and the French Revolution* introduced me to Schiller's *Letters on the Aesthetic Education of Man*.

Sara Tilley's lovely novel *Skin Room* (Pedlar, 2008) inspired a moment recalled by Jeremy.

My thanks to the Toronto Storytelling Festival for unforgettable tales and tellers.

My immense thanks, always, to Mary Jane Baillie, Donald Baillie, Emma Lightstone, Jonno Lightstone, and Christina Baillie.

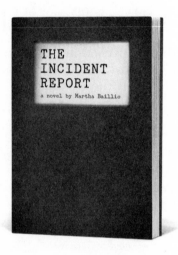